Wise Woman

Appalachian Journey
Book 4

CC Tillery

Spring Creek Press

First Edition

ISBN: 0-9894641-4-8
ISBN-13: 978-0-9894641-4-7

Published by:
Spring Creek Press

Cover © 2015 Kimberly Maxwell

Since this is the last book in our Appalachian Journey Series, we would like to dedicate it to our readers whose generosity, kindness and support have inspired us since the first book was published. You've stood behind us for four years, encouraging us to continue writing Great-aunt Bessie's and Great-uncle Fletcher's story. If it weren't for all of you, there probably would have only been the one book, and we are truly grateful to each and every one of you and so glad we had the chance to meet you, whether it be in person or on the Internet. We feel so blessed to have the best readers in the world.

Also, as with all the other books in the series, this is for our dad Raymond Earl "John" Tillery, whose story we've included in this final book. We can never thank you enough, Daddy, for all the stories and anecdotes, the laughter and good times, the love and care you show us. Thanks for being such a wonderful father. We love you very, very much.

And to Great-aunt Bessie and Great-uncle Fletch, who gave Daddy the foundation to become the man he is. We are forever grateful for that and hope we've done justice to the incredible lives they lived on their beloved mountain.

Chapter One

Summer 1924

If things get any better around here, I may have to hire someone to help me enjoy it.

You wouldn't think three little words could make much of a difference in the span of a lifetime, especially one as long as mine proved to be, but that was all it took to alter the course of my life in a way I never imagined possible. When I said, "We'll take him," to my sister Jack during a visit to Knoxville in the summer of 1924, I had no idea the changes that lay ahead nor the impact my nephew John would have on me.

I spent most of the trip home replaying that horrific scene with Jack in my mind, hoping I'd made the right choice bringing John home with us. I had assured Papa before we left that he could trust me to love and care for John. Then on the trip home when Preacher Justice asked me how I felt about the whole thing, I told him I considered it a blessing from God, that He had given me a child of my heart. I meant it, but the truth was, even with my reassuring words to both of them, I was a little apprehensive. Despite my gift of foresight from my Cherokee ancestors, there was just no way of knowing all that might happen in the future. I could only do my best and hope I would not, to borrow a phrase from one of my favorite poems by Robert Frost, tell this story with "a sigh, somewhere ages and ages hence". Though I was sure in my heart I would look back and say it made all the difference in my life, I could only pray John would say the same thing.

If I was happy to leave Knoxville behind, I was downright thrilled to see the mountains looming in front of us. Though I'd enjoyed seeing my family again, the city hadn't suited me at all. I felt like I couldn't find enough air to breathe with all the noise and people and spent a good deal of the time I was there yearning for home.

We stopped for a quick lunch on the banks of the French Broad River, just as we did on the trip over. When we got back into Preacher Justice's Model T, I climbed into the backseat with my husband, John nestled between us. As we drove through Hot Springs, I started telling him about growing up there. He must have asked a hundred questions about Papa and I answered as best I could until eventually the restlessness of the night before caught up with him and he dozed off. He slept until the tires left the paved road in Old Fort and we started the bumpy ride up Stone Mountain. I took his little hand in mine and pointed out the few houses we could see, telling him who lived there. I hoped it would give him a budding sense of familiarity with his new home.

When we passed the road that led to our farm, I squeezed his hand and gestured to the left. "Your new home is less than a mile down that road, John. You'll have your own room with your own bed and 400 acres to run. Do you like animals?"

He shrugged. "I guess."

"Well, we have a dog, numerous barn cats, a horse, two cows, a lot of chickens, a couple of mules and some pigs."

He knuckled his eyes and yawned.

I smiled. "Oh, I know you're tired and probably hungry too, and we'll be home soon enough, but first we're going to go to our church. Preacher Justice is the reverend and he's spent this entire trip home planning his sermon for tonight. After that, we'll go home and get us some supper." I patted his hand. "It won't be long now."

When we arrived at the church, I seated John on the

piano bench and after a quick conference with Preacher Justice chose the music for the hymns he suggested for the sermon, adding a couple more I thought John might like. Sitting down beside him, I played softly as we waited for the congregation.

Fletcher, as deacon, stood at the door and greeted people as they straggled in, often pointing to John and smiling as he explained who he was. John, meanwhile, snuggled closer to my side until he was almost sitting in my lap.

After I finished a hymn, I looked down at him. "There's nothing to be afraid of, John. They're only people, just like you and me and your Uncle Fletch."

"Yes, ma'am," he muttered.

I could tell he didn't believe me so I shuffled through my music until I found one of my favorite hymns, *His Eye is on the Sparrow,* because of its message that Jesus is always watching over us and will keep us from harm. While I played, I sang the words in a quiet voice to John, "Why should I feel discouraged, why should the shadows come, Why should my heart be lonely, and long for heav'n and home, When Jesus is my portion, my constant friend is He, His eye is on the sparrow, and I know He watches me."

John watched my hands and I felt him relax a bit as I hoped he would.

After I finished the hymn, Preacher Justice, who had been standing at the pulpit scribbling furiously on a piece of paper, looked up and cleared his throat to get the attention of the congregation. I switched to the Doxology as I wondered which version of our much-loved reverend would show up that night. He could, I knew, speak softly and encouragingly to his parishioners, urging them with his tone to do as he bade them. Or he could, as Fletcher termed it, be a fire-and-brimstone preacher, yelling and threatening the congregation with eternal hell and damnation.

Though the latter was very effective, I hoped for John's sake Preacher Justice would go with the former.

Thankfully, that night he was a combination of both, raising his voice only when he felt he needed to emphasize a certain passage of his sermon. He preached, just as he said he would, about building a fence around Hell to keep the evil from our midst. It was a heartfelt sermon and I think his earnestness only made it that much more meaningful to his congregation. I know it did to me.

After church, Fletcher took John by the hand and led him to the door where he introduced him to everyone as they went out. John stayed close to Fletch the whole time, not saying much but greeting everyone with a polite handshake or shy smile. All except Thelma Hall's younger brother Hoover, who whispered something in John's ear and pulled him outside. I found out later he wanted to show John the frog he'd caught earlier that day which he kept stuffed in his pocket during church. Fletcher watched them go out, then smiled and turned to me with a nod. I relaxed and finished tidying up my music. When I went outside later, after speaking to several friends, I saw John actually laughing at something Hoover was telling him and, of course, my heart turned over in a way that had become familiar and somehow comforting to me.

It was only a matter of a few minutes before we climbed back into Preacher Justice's automobile and made the return trip down the mountain to our farm. Excitement raced through me when our little house finally came into view. I wondered what John would think of his new home, saying a quick prayer that he would like it and be happy there. I wanted so much for this child; happiness, security, acceptance; but most of all, I wanted him to know he was loved deeply and would always have a home with us.

While Fletcher lingered outside with Preacher Justice for a few minutes talking about church matters, I took John by the hand and led him inside to the spare room where he would be sleeping.

"This is your room, John." I set the small sack containing his clothes on the bed, vowing to myself we would get him more clothes soon. "Why don't you put your things away in the dresser and then you can come out to the kitchen with me while I look for something quick to put together for supper. Are you hungry?"

"I reckon."

"Well, we'll eat soon. It won't be much but it'll be enough to tide us over until breakfast. You put those things away and then come on out to the kitchen or you can stay in here for a while if you want. I'll call you when supper's ready. All right?"

He nodded. I reached out and cupped his chin in my hand, nudging it up so his eyes met mine. "I hope you'll be happy here with us, John. I know you're scared right now but promise me one thing. Give it some time before you make up your mind. Can you do that?"

He tilted his head to the side and my heart turned over. He looked so much like Papa and I desperately wanted him to be happy.

"Yes, ma'am."

There was that dreaded word, the one I had so hated hearing from my sister Loney's mouth on the day our little brother Green died, knowing that would more or less signal the end of my childhood. But this time I didn't want to hear it for an entirely different reason. I figured as long as John called me "ma'am" at every turn, it was because he was scared and unsure of what was going to happen to him. When he finally dropped that formal address, it would mean he had relaxed enough to trust me. I knew I would live for that time in the days to come and prayed it came soon.

I left John there to go out to the kitchen to see what I could rustle up for supper, but first I opened the back door and whistled for Fritz. He bounded through the door, never one to pass up a chance to come in the kitchen where there was always the possibility of food being dropped on the floor. I scratched between his ears then pointed to the door of the spare room. "Go on into John's room, Fritz, and keep him company while he unpacks his things."

Fritz looked at the door then back at me. "Go on, now. He's a good boy and could use a friend right about now."

After a quick shake of his rangy body, Fritz ambled toward the door. "Good boy," I whispered.

I turned my attention to food. There wasn't enough time to kill the fatted calf as a welcome for John but I suspected I could come up with something good enough to satisfy him. Maybe some of the sausage I had canned last fall along with green beans and corn from last year's garden. I thought I had another jar or two of peaches. And I could quickly put together a batch of biscuits to eat with some of the wild strawberry jam I'd canned a couple of weeks ago.

Not a fatted calf, to be sure, but wholesome and tasty, and I doubted John would be disappointed.

I smiled when I noticed John standing in the doorway, his hand resting on Fritz's neck. I walked over to him, wanting to put him at ease. "I suppose I should introduce you two. Mr. John Tillery, meet Mr. Fritz Elliott, the second. Fritz helps your Uncle Fletch out around the farm. Shake John's hand, Fritz." I grinned as Fritz politely lifted his right paw and John shook it. "He's a fine handyman, a fair to middlin' hunter," I grinned at John, "when he wants to be, and a world class napper. Why, if they had a dog nap competition in those Olympic games they're putting on over there in Paris, France, I bet Fritz would walk away with one of those gold medals hanging around his neck."

It pleased me to see John's lips stretch into a boyish grin. Giving Fritz a quick scratch between his ears, I finished the introduction. "Fritz, this is John. He's going to be staying with us for awhile." I put my hand on his shoulder and squeezed. "A good long while, we hope." Dropping my hand, I smiled. "Are you hungry, John, or thirsty? Supper'll be ready in a bit, as soon as those biscuits are done. Why don't you go on out back and tell your uncle to wash up? And you can use the privy while you're out there, if you need."

He blushed as he nodded.

"Take Fritz with you. He has a mighty strong craving for my sausage and won't leave me alone until he gets some."

His hand buried in the fur on Fritz's neck, as if clutching a well-worn and dependable baby blanket, John walked slowly out the door. I watched him go, saying another silent prayer for God to guide my hand when it came to this child. I didn't think my heart would need any help as I already felt a deep love for him.

While I longed to see my nephew run and play and, most

of all, laugh like he had at the church with Hoover, I knew it would take time. I would need to be patient and give him room when what I really wanted to do was grab him up and hold him tight. But that wouldn't do. I had learned with my students that the ones who are the most reserved don't do well with someone who hovers over them, constantly prodding and poking, no matter how well-intentioned the attention might be. No, the reticent ones do best when you stand back and, while not exactly leaving them alone, give them ample space and time to make up their own minds. Plus, I knew from experience, young boys would always respond to silliness and I didn't mind being silly for such a worthy cause as this one.

When I stepped out on the back porch a few minutes later to ring the dinner bell, John and Fritz and Bose Dalton's dog Charlie were chasing fireflies around the yard while Fletch and Bose talked over by the barn.

I tugged on the bell. When the men turned to look at me, I waved to them, calling out, "Join us for supper, Bose?"

He took off his hat and grinned at me. "No thank you, Miss Bessie, I've had mine already."

"Coffee then?"

He shook his head. "I've got to be going." He pointed to the sky. "Looks to be a good night for Charlie and me to tree some coons."

"Well, you're welcome any time. Supper's ready, Fletch. You and John best wash up before you come in."

"Will do, Bess." Fletcher turned to shake hands with Bose as I stepped back inside.

Later, after we'd finished supper, we settled into the parlor where I started questioning John about the family, thinking it might help him to feel more at home. My plan backfired when John only gave me one-syllable answers to my queries. I looked at Fletch and nodded, and he began reading Ecclesiastes 3 from his Bible, the verse about everything having a season. John sat at his feet and appeared to be listening raptly, his eyes growing heavier with every word.

I watched him, stared at him, really, wondering if he had

any qualms about sleeping in a strange bed in a house he was unfamiliar with and with people he didn't really know.

I was so wrapped up in my musings, Fletcher's voice was only a quiet humming in my ears when I heard the ghost slaves. It had been a good long time since I'd heard them, and though it always thrilled me, it also worried me a bit. Most times, hearing them didn't portend any upcoming calamity but there were times when it did.

I rose, walked to the window, and leaned out into the night air as I had the first time I heard them. Just like that time, the moon was a sliver in the dark sky, the crickets, katydids, and the frogs down by the creek seemed to be having a contest to see who could sing the loudest, and the lovely scent of cedar mixed with pine rode a slight breeze.

Behind me, Fletch stopped reading. "What is it, Bess? Are the ghosts back?"

I turned and saw John was wide awake, sitting up straight, his hand clenched in the ruff of Fritz's neck. Fletch had closed the Bible, using his finger to hold his place, and watched me with a slight smile curving his lips.

I hesitated, wondering whether I should say anything in front of the boy. Ghosts, after all, were not a subject conducive to sleep for most people, young children especially.

My husband had no such qualms. "Your aunt's hearing ghosts again, John," he said as if it was the most natural thing in the world for a person to hear spirits.

In the months to come, I would learn to appreciate Fletcher's openness and candor with John but at that moment I still hesitated, wondering how hearing there were ghosts around would affect a young child.

"What are they singing tonight, Bess?"

John's eyes widened a bit more and I shook my head at Fletcher. He only continued to stare at me and I thought maybe he was right. "*Swing Low, Sweet Chariot,*" I murmured.

"That seems to be their favorite. I still wish I could hear them." He placed the Bible on the table beside him then leaned down to ruffle John's hair. "Did you hear them,

John?"

John's wide eyes lifted to Fletch but he didn't say anything, only shook his head.

Fletch winked. "Don't worry, son, they won't hurt you. It's only your aunt they show themselves to."

"I can't see them, Fletcher, you know that." I looked down at John. "You're not afraid are you, John? They won't hurt … they can't hurt you," I said emphatically. "You know that, don't you?"

His hand tightened in Fritz's fur, causing the dog to give an involuntary yelp. Fletch leaned down and loosened John's grip then pulled him up into his lap. "There's nothing to be scared of, John. Just some haints that visit us sometimes. Or more accurately, visit your Aunt Bessie. I've never heard them, she's never seen them, and the most they do is sing a song or two. Ain't that right, Bess?"

I walked over and sat back down. "That's right, John. Nothing to be afraid of." I smiled at him "But you already knew that, didn't you?"

"Yes, ma'am. Grandpapa John always says ghosts and monsters aren't real, they're only made-up stuff."

But he didn't sound as if he believed it.

"My great-grandmother, Elisi, she'd be your great-great-grandmother, once told me a story about ghosts. It's about a little Cherokee boy. Would you like to hear it?"

"I guess."

"All right. First you should know that your great-great grandmother and your great-grandmother were full-blooded Cherokee, which makes you, um, let's see, one-sixteenth Cherokee. Did you know that?'

"No, ma'am. Grandpapa John never told me that."

I wanted to sigh. His mother should have told him but I guess it wasn't important enough to Jack to teach her child about our family. "Well, you are. Do you know what a Cherokee is?"

He shook his head.

"They're a tribe of Indians who have lived in these mountains almost since the beginning of time. They have a long, proud heritage, and since they've been around so long, they have a lot of stories, everything from how the world was formed to how the stars came to be in the sky to why a possum has a skinny tail with no fur.

"The story I'm going to tell you is about a young Cherokee boy who lived a long time ago, far back in the mountains, close to the Tennessee border near the Cheoah River. One day, someone in the boy's family died and his papa told him they'd have to go sit up." At his questioning expression, I said, "They believed that someone, usually a relative, must sit up with the person who died. So the young boy and his family began the long walk to the relative's home. It was early evening when they started, still light enough to see but with dark coming on fast. They had to cross the river, jumping from rock to rock, and then they started up a hill. By that time it was so dark, all the boy could see were the mountain laurel bushes lining the trail.

"As it continued to grow darker, the boy grabbed onto his mother's skirt because he was afraid of the dark. Mostly his fear came from sitting out on the porch at night and listening to the old people tell stories, and a great many of those tales were ghost stories.

"So, the family continued climbing up a hill with the boy still clutching his mama's skirt when he heard a sound." I whistled softly several times. "The boy was frightened and asked his papa what it was.

"His papa said, 'Oh, don't you worry about that, everything's all right.' The boy tried to be brave but he was getting more and more scared, and after a few minutes, he closed his eyes. That didn't help either because he could still hear the noise." I whistled softly a few more times. "With his eyes closed, it sounded a lot like someone breathing, and it kept getting nearer and nearer.

"The boy moved as close to his mother as he could and said to his papa, 'It's getting closer, what is it?' And his papa said, 'Everything's going to be all right. Don't get scared. If you don't get scared, everything will be just fine, you'll see.' But the boy was so frightened he started shaking and moved up to walk between his papa and mama. A few more minutes passed and the whistling sound continued. The boy grew more and more afraid but he kept walking until finally his papa stopped and said, 'All right, everybody stop. Get back up on the side of the trail and let that thing go through in front of us.'

"The family moved off the path and waited. As they stood there, the boy looked out in the darkness, listening to the whistling noise which sounded like breathing to him, and he saw something that looked like a sheer white cloth, like a clinging curtain, with shoulders but no head.

"The boy closed his eyes tight just as his papa said, 'All right. You've scared my children enough. Go on by us, step ahead of us. I don't care about you. You're not going to hurt my children and I'm not going to hurt you. Just go on by, we made room for you to go by.'

"The breathing turned into a sound like the ghost was chomping on leaves on the other side of the trail. The boy didn't dare open his eyes, he just stood there and shivered. Then his papa said again, 'Go on by and leave us alone. We're not afraid of you.' The chomping sound stopped and the boy opened his eyes and saw the sheer cloth climbing up the mountain laurel bushes and then, just like that, it went through the bushes and vanished. And his papa said, 'There now, he's gone, he's left us alone so don't worry about him anymore. Don't ever get scared and everything will be all right.'

"And the boy felt much better about being in the dark after that. Not that he didn't still get scared sometimes, but when he did, he always remembered his father's words, 'If you're not afraid, a ghost can't hurt you. The only way a ghost can hurt you is if you get scared and panic, you might run over a cliff or fall and hurt yourself. But if you're not afraid and stand your ground, a ghost can't hurt you.'"

I wasn't entirely sure if my story would work, but when I looked over and saw John snuggled into Fletcher's chest, his eyes drooping, I decided it might have been the right choice after all.

·

Chapter Two

Summer 1924

As safe as a tick on a hound dog with a stiff neck.

JOHN

I don't remember much about my trip with Aunt Bessie and Uncle Fletcher to their home on Stone Mountain other than an overwhelming sense of trepidation and loss. My mind was a jumbled mess, thinking about the things Mama had said and wondering if she really meant them combined with a great fear for what lay ahead. What if Aunt Bessie and Uncle Fletch didn't like me? Would they abandon me too? I sensed their concern for me but at the age of six was not comforted by this. Before I left, Grandpapa took me aside and explained he wanted me to stay with him, but due to his poor health, he could no longer look after me and it would be best I go with them, that they would take care of me and love me. I could only take him at his word. Although Aunt Bessie told me I had met them before, that was when I was an infant and, of course, I didn't remember. They were strangers to me when they came to Aunt Loney's house and I didn't have much of a chance to get to know them the short time they visited. I didn't understand why I couldn't continue to live with Mama and Grandpapa at Aunt Loney's house, even though

Grandpapa wasn't well. At six, I figured I could take care of myself as well as anybody. Although I wasn't told, I sensed Aunt Loney's son Gene, who resented my presence in that home, had helped motivate the reason for my leaving.

Aunt Bessie showed me the road leading to their farm but we didn't stop there. Instead, Reverend Justice drove us to the Stone Mountain Baptist Church where we made it just in time for Sunday evening service. I sat by my aunt while she played the piano, so tired I could barely keep my eyes open. Afterward, Uncle Fletcher introduced me to the congregants as they left and I met a new friend, a boy named Hoover Hall who showed me his frog.

Night had fallen by the time Reverend Justice drove us back to their home place on Stone Mountain. It was so dark– almost pitch black–I could barely make out the cabin in front of me. Their dog seemed happy to see Aunt Bessie and Uncle Fletch and sniffed me while wagging his tail. I had always wanted a dog and as I scratched behind his ears hoped he would be a companion, someone to run and play with. Although I couldn't see much, sounds were all around us, croaks and whirs and chirps, and from far away a forlorn "who" which I learned later came from an owl residing in the barn.

While Uncle Fletcher talked to the reverend, Aunt Bessie took me inside their cabin and showed me my room. Although it was small, it looked like a king's chamber to me as I had never had my own room let alone bed. I had my meager belongings tied in a sack, which Aunt Bessie placed on the bed before turning to me with a smile. She told me to go ahead and unpack my things then if I wanted I could join her in the kitchen while she fixed us a bite to eat. I figured I'd stay in my room until dinner, but soon after, the door opened and their dog came into the room. I knelt down beside him and hugged him and told him I wanted to be his friend. I think he understood, and when he went to the door, I followed him into the kitchen.

Aunt Bessie introduced me to their dog whose name was Fritz and told me to go ahead and wash up and use the privy if I needed. Fritz and I stepped outside, where my uncle was talking to a man I heard him call Bose. The man's dog came over and started playing with Fritz, and before long, we were chasing fireflies around the yard until Aunt Bessie called us for dinner.

I didn't eat much that night, too worried about what lay ahead for me and not yet comfortable around my aunt and uncle. After dinner, we sat in front of the fireplace where Aunt Bessie told me Uncle Fletch always read from his Bible before bedtime. I answered what questions I could put to me by my aunt about my family back in Knoxville but reckon I wasn't too forthcoming so Uncle Fletcher began reading from his Bible. Aunt Bessie seemed distracted and Uncle Fletcher said she heard ghosts sometimes. That scared me a little bit but she told me a Cherokee story about ghosts which helped alleviate some of my fear.

Before long, Aunt Bessie said it was time for bed. She tucked me in, saying, "I know you must be awful fearful about all that's happened to you, but you're safe here and we'll take care of you and love you as if you were our own son."

Although I was tired, it took a long time to go to sleep that night, my mind filled with doubts about what lay ahead for me. The sounds outside my window were strange and ominous. I was used to the noises humans made, their voices and laughter, scratchy music from the phonograph Mama sometimes played until Grandpapa yelled at her to turn it off, car horns blaring and tires whooshing down the street, and not the strange chorus that serenaded me outside the cabin. I heard a panting noise in the room and sat up, fearful one of the forest creatures or one of the ghosts Aunt Bessie heard had gotten inside. Fritz placed two paws on the bed and cocked his head at me, whining softly. When I patted the bed beside me, he jumped up and lay down next to me. I fell asleep, my arm around his small body, forging a friendship that lasted his life.

The next morning when I got up, I found Aunt Bessie and Uncle Fletcher in the kitchen. Aunt Bessie eyed Fritz standing beside me but didn't say anything although I suspected she knew he had kept me company during the night. She showed me where to sit at the table and served up what I thought to be a fine breakfast, fried eggs, sausage, biscuits with gravy, and milk my uncle told me was fresh. I wasn't sure what he meant but didn't question this, too anxious to eat. I ate more than I meant to, but this seemed to please Aunt Bessie. After breakfast, she told us she had to get to school to get her classroom organized and cleaned so she could shut the school down for the summer. She smiled at me. "I teach school, John. I'll be teaching you too."

Uncle Fletcher watched her gather her things together, saying, "You going to take young John with you?"

She turned and looked at me. "I reckon he can stay with you for a bit, Fletch. I'll be busy putting everything away and there's not much for him to do there. He can help out around here, don't you think?"

"I reckon I can find a thing or two to keep him occupied," Uncle Fletcher replied, picking up his hat and dusting it off on his leg.

With a smile, Aunt Bessie kissed our cheeks and hurried out the door.

Uncle Fletcher turned to me. "I got some plowing to do today, John. You want to go with me?"

I shrugged, not really knowing what that meant.

"Well, come along then." He led the way outside, saying, "First I'll introduce you to the animals in the barn. They play an important part on this farm."

As we walked along, Fritz by my side, I got my first real look at where my aunt and uncle lived. Everything was so green, the mountains around us covered with heavy brush and trees that looked like they went clear up to heaven. The grass at our feet was lush and soft, and I liked the way it felt against my bare feet, feathery and cool as the dew. The sky above was a bright, clear blue with patches of fluffy clouds drifting lazily along that looked so soft, I wondered, if I had the ability to fly, would I be able to lay on them. I had never seen so much open space in my life and for the first time felt part of something a lot bigger than me. I heard the gurgle of the creek that ran through the property and liked that sound.

I told myself maybe it was God's way of letting me know things would be all right and took comfort in that thought.

We walked by a chicken coop where hens darted here and there, pecking at the ground. A rooster strolled around, his head lifted high as if he were king of the world. A bad smell assaulted my nose and I caught sight of several large, fat pigs rolling around in the mud inside a pen close to the barn.

Uncle Fletcher opened the large wooden door and I peeked inside the dim interior, curious what sort of animals could be so important to my uncle. I followed along behind him, stepping back when he opened what looked like a half door to what he called a stall. A large horse with big, dark eyes stared at me. It made a snorting sound and I jumped. I must have startled Fritz because he yelped and took off outside.

Uncle Fletcher tried to hide the grin playing around his mouth but I caught it. "Never mind old Fritz, he's about as jumpy as a long-tailed cat in a room full of rocking chairs." He reached out and patted the side of the animal's head. "You ever seen a horse before, John?"

I nodded, staring at this creature, thinking how beautiful it was. "I've never touched one, though."

"We call her Pet. Bessie rides her to school from time to time if she don't feel like walking." He led the horse outside its stall. I studied it, never having seen a horse up close. Its legs were long and looked too thin to hold its weight. I noticed its feet were rounded and it had no toes. I reached my hand out and the horse put her nose in my palm and breathed. I smiled with pleasure. I swear, that was the softest thing I'd ever touched. Even though the animal towered over me, I felt no sense of panic or fright. I leaned closer to the horse and breathed in an odor I had never smelled before but which was oddly comforting. "I like the way she smells."

"I do too, John. Ain't much smells better than a horse." Uncle Fletcher ran his hand up beneath the long hair cascading off the horse's neck which I later learned was a mane. "She's a good old gal." With a final pat, he sent the horse off down the aisle toward a fenced-in pasture behind the barn. I watched Pet's long tail flick back and forth as she walked and hoped we would be friends.

"Come meet our two cows," Uncle Fletcher said, leading me to two more stalls. I stared in amazement at two animals almost as big as the horse but that didn't look anything like her and weren't near as pretty. Their heads were blocky and their ears shorter, their bodies not as sleek and muscular. "This is Ginger and this is Bell." Uncle Fletcher unlocked the half door to each stall. The animals were shaped the same but had different fur, one with brown and white spots, the other almost black. They stared at me with their large, doe-like eyes and seemed friendly enough. They didn't smell as good as the horse though. "These are Bessie's milk cows. That fresh milk you drank this morning came from these two." Uncle Fletch grinned at my look of wonderment. "You didn't know milk came from cows?"

I shook my head.

"I reckon afore too long, Bessie will be teaching you how to milk them. Maybe you can help her out of the morning, you think so?"

"I sure can." I wondered how in the world you got milk from these furry creatures then figured I'd surely learn soon enough.

I watched as Uncle Fletcher led the cows, the bells around their necks clanging softly, to the same pasture the horse had gone into.

"I got a couple more to introduce you to." He opened more stalls and I stepped back as two creatures moved into the aisle. Although they resembled the horse, there were differences. Their ears were larger and their faces more narrow, their bodies smaller. They were both so dark brown they looked almost black.

"They ain't horses too, are they?" I asked.

"Nope. These are the mules, Amos and Jack. I use them for plowing." One of the mules threw back his head and made the awfulest ruckus. I tried not to show my fear but moved behind the door just so it wouldn't step on me. Uncle Fletcher smiled. "Don't worry none, John. He ain't mad, just anxious to get to work. Settle down now, old feller," he said, pulling a jingling leather contraption off a nail on the wall and fitting it around the mule's head. After he had both mules hooked together, he stood behind them, holding what he called reins, and softly tapped them with it. The mules moved out of the barn and into the barnyard. I walked beside my uncle as we made our way across the yard. Fritz joined us, touching noses with the mules.

"Are they friends?"

Uncle Fletcher nodded. "Fritz makes it a point to be friends with all living beings." He studied the dog for a moment. "I think, John, God was having a good day when he made dogs. Ain't nothing breathing that tops a good one. Bessie thinks they're God's angels and I reckon she just might be onto something there. Why, between you and me, most days, I'd rather be around the animals than humans. Animals have purer souls, seems to me." He led the mules to a large piece of land across the creek he said he used for the garden and stopped them beside a machine I had never seen before. It was made of wood with two large sloping handles behind a curved piece of metal. "This here's a plow," he said, hooking the mules to the contraption.

I stepped closer to inspect it, curious what you could do with such a big apparatus like this. "What's it do?"

"Why, it plows up the dirt so I can plant seeds for our garden." He studied me. "You ain't never plowed before?"

"No, sir, I don't reckon I have."

"Well, I bet afore the day's over, you'll be plowing instead of me."

I don't know why but that made me feel good.

After the mules were hooked to the plow, Uncle Fletcher lightly snapped the reins and they moved over the ground. I watched in wonderment as the hard earth turned over from grassy mounds to a dark, crumbly dirt. Barefoot, I followed along behind, loving the way that fresh soil felt on my feet, soft and warm as it sifted between my toes.

My uncle hadn't plowed long before I spied baby animals in one of the rows and ran over to them. They were funny looking, furry gray things with big ears and twitching noses and little white tails that looked like cotton balls. Uncle Fletcher had turned the mules and was coming back when he spied me studying them. He came over to have a look. "Them's baby rabbits," he said, taking his hat off and wiping his forehead with a handkerchief he pulled from his pants pocket.

I reached down and touched one. It felt soft and fuzzy. "Can I have them?"

He shook his head. "I reckon we best let them stay where they are. Their mama's probably off somewhere wrestling up a meal for her babies. She's gonna be missing 'em afore too long and'll be looking for them. But don't you worry none, she'll take good care of 'em 'til they're big enough to take care of themselves."

I nodded, wishing my mama had felt the same for me.

He stared at my feet, which were as brown as the dirt beneath them. "You don't reckon you ought to put some shoes on?"

I shook my head. "I like to go barefoot and the dirt feels good on my feet, almost as good as the grass."

Uncle Fletcher nodded as if he understood. "I felt the same way when I was a young'un. Why, I didn't put on a pair of shoes 'til I was 12 or 13. Helped my pa cut a cord of wood and he bought me a pair of them brogan shoes to thank me. I didn't have any socks so wore 'em without. Wasn't long before I decided shoes weren't comfortable at all and was back to going barefoot again. My pa kept asking me why I wouldn't wear the shoes. I didn't want to tell him 'cause they hurt too much so would just answer I didn't want to get 'em dirty." He winked at me and ruffled my hair before going back to the plow.

I watched this tall, muscular man with a gentle kindness to him, unlike my grandfather's gruff affection, and decided I wanted to be like him. I wondered why Grandpapa didn't like my Uncle Fletcher, who appeared to love my Aunt Bessie and provide well for her. With a shrug, telling myself it wasn't any of my business anyhow, I fell in behind the plow.

When the sun was directly overhead, my uncle unhitched the mules from the plow and we made our way back to the barn. I was beginning to tire by that time, so he picked me up and put me on the back of Jack, the smallest mule. "Just hang on to his mane and you'll do fine," he said when he saw how scared I was. "Don't worry about Jack. He's a gentle soul and he knows you're up there. He'll take care of you."

I held on tight at first but quickly grew used to the gentle sway of the mule beneath me. I liked the way it felt straddling his broad back, my hands clutching his scratchy mane, which felt like pieces of twine, the way my body moved, almost like in a rocking chair.

When we reached the barn, Uncle Fletcher helped me off Jack then put the mules in the pasture. "It's time for lunch and I reckon they're as hungry as I am. What about you, John? You think you could eat a bite or two?"

I nodded. I hadn't done anything but follow along behind the plow but found I had a powerful appetite. "Sure could," I told him.

In the kitchen, I watched as he found the lunch Aunt Bessie had set aside for us that morning. I tore into a ham biscuit, finishing before my uncle had eaten half of his. He held it out to me. "I reckon I'm not as hungry as I thought, John. You want the rest of mine?"

"If you're sure you don't want it."

"Nope, you go on and finish it off. I reckon I'll eat some of that apple pie your aunt made. Although she don't think so, she's an awful good cook. It's a wonder I'm not as big around as I am tall, eating all her good food."

I laughed at that image.

He waited until I ate all the biscuit, then cut a big piece of pie and put it on my plate. "Go on and finish that off, now, or Bessie will think you don't like her pie and we can't have that else she might get the notion to quit cooking altogether."

"Yes, sir." The pie was delicious and it didn't take me long to clean my plate. I sat back, feeling content.

Uncle Fletcher scooted his chair away from the table and stood. "I reckon I'm going back to plowing, John. If you want, you can stay here, maybe take a little nap. I expect you didn't get much sleep last night in a house you ain't used to.

Later, you might want to explore the house and barn, maybe read the Bible if you feel up to it. I know Bessie will have you read to her when she gets home to see how far along you are. But if you want to come with me, why, you're more than welcome to."

"If you don't mind, I'd like to explore the barn," I told him. "I saw a big gray cat in there this morning I'd like to make friends with."

"You do that and I'll see you when I'm finished."

I watched him fetch the mules then head out to the garden. Fritz darted off after my uncle but then stopped and looked at me. I guess he decided he preferred to stay with me because he turned back and joined me as I walked inside the barn. I liked the cool dimness of the interior, the smell of horses and other animals mingling together. Fritz stayed with me for awhile but must have gotten bored or hot, and soon found a cool spot near the door and curled up for a nap. I found a mama cat and her kittens and played with them for a bit until I could barely keep my eyes open. I crawled up on a bale of hay and fell asleep, sunlight drifting onto my body through the slats of the barn, making me warm and cozy. When I woke, one of the kittens had decided to nap with me and was curled up against my neck. I reached up and stroked his fur, liking the vibration I felt from his body to mine. After awhile, I got up and walked outside to check on my Uncle Fletcher. He was still plowing away, so I decided to explore around the barn and house.

Mid-afternoon, I saw my Aunt Bessie crossing the creek onto their property and ran to greet her. Fritz joined me, barking with joy. She smiled at me when I drew near, reaching down to pet Fritz, squirming with joy to see her. "Hello, John. Have you had a good day with your Uncle Fletcher?"

"I sure have." I fell into step beside her and began to tell her about watching Uncle Fletcher plow and the way the earth felt against my bare feet, all the animals I had met, and the kitten that slept with me.

She listened to every word I said and it felt good having someone to talk to. At Aunt Loney's, Mama was always running around, getting ready to go somewhere, and never took the time to take note of what I said. Aunt Loney focused on her children and tended to treat me as more of a nuisance than person. Her son Gene only talked to me when he was being mean and bullying. His sister Bessie was sweet and nice to me but older and with friends of her own. The only one who spent any time with me was Grandpapa but he was old and couldn't hear very well. I wasn't used to actually having a conversation with an adult and it thrilled me.

I reckon I talked all the way to the house and inside, following Aunt Bessie into the kitchen as she put down her basket and took off her bonnet. She was easy to talk to and I couldn't stop chattering until I'd told her every little thing that had happened to me that day. When I wound down, she asked me if I'd eaten lunch and gotten in a nap. After I assured her I had, she sat me down at the kitchen table and pulled out the Bible, then asked me to read to her. I was only six and a miserable reader and stumbled over most of the words. Aunt Bessie told me not to worry, she'd teach me how to read good and proper. I have to admit I didn't believe her when she assured me I'd grow up loving to read.

Uncle Fletcher came in, wiping perspiration off his forehead with the back of his shirt sleeve. He spied the Bible on the table. "That's the way my mama taught me to read," he said, gesturing at the Bible. "And I reckon if I could learn that way, you can too, John. Don't let those big words stop you, son. It won't take long to get the hang of it and you'll take off like old Fritz did this morning when that horse snorted."

I laughed at the memory of Fritz balking out of the barn. Uncle Fletcher ruffled my hair then bent down to give my Aunt Bessie a kiss on the cheek.

"We'll start your lessons tomorrow, John," Aunt Bessie said, rising to her feet. "For now, I reckon I best get supper started for my two men. Y'all must be awful hungry after all that hard work."

Uncle Fletcher looked at me and smiled. For the first time in my life, I felt part of a family. It was the best feeling in the world to me.

Chapter Three

Summer 1924

He's so confused he doesn't know whether to scratch his watch or wind his backside.

On a hot, cloudless Saturday in late August, I took to the porch with my latest harvest of snap beans, a ball of twine, and a pair of scissors. I had blanched the beans that morning and set them on a towel to dry in preparation for stringing them into leather britches. Setting those on the table beside my rocking chair, I went back inside to get my lunch, a cold glass of buttermilk with last night's leftover cornbread crumbled in it and a bowl of last year's canned peaches with fresh cream.

Sitting down in my rocking chair, I checked to make sure no one was around and raised my skirt up over my knees, trying to catch a breeze. It was almost too hot to eat but I spooned up my first bite of tangy buttermilk and crumbly cornbread anyway.

I swanee to my soul, the heat that summer was enough to sap the get-up-and-go from even the most energetic of creatures. Why, even my chickens, who normally spent the better part of the day pecking around their pen, had taken to napping in the chicken coop of an afternoon. The creek was running low but still running, thank the Lord, and the air had taken on that scent it gets in a long, hot summer, dried leaves mixed with brittle pine needles and the musk of plants wilting in the sun's brutal rays.

Fletch and John had been gone since early that morning on their weekly trip to Old Fort to pick up some essentials and sell some tanning bark they had gathered and dried to the Union Tanning Company. They also had a few raccoon pelts to sell. I didn't envy them walking all that way in this heat but knew Fletch enjoyed his weekly walk into town. Most usually, someone would come along and offer to give him a lift in their wagon.

Since it was so hot, I had asked John if he wanted to stay home with me but he had turned into his Uncle Fletcher's shadow and insisted he wanted to go with him, saying the heat didn't really bother him much. I suppose young boys handle it better than most people, and knew that if he got too hot, Fletcher would find a shady spot or perhaps even a place in the creek where they could cool off.

In an effort to keep cool myself, my thoughts turned to fall and what the upcoming school year would bring. I still hadn't decided whether to take John with me or to leave him home and teach him in the afternoons and evenings. I knew he wanted to stay home with Fletch but he needed to be in school if for no other reason than the interaction with the other children would be good for him. But I worried about how my students would react to having him in the class with them. Would they pick on him and call him the teacher's pet? Or worse, if the news got out about how he came to be living with us, would they ridicule him because his mother didn't want him?

I didn't think they would but there just wasn't any way I could know for sure so I had put off making a final decision. Still, I would have to commit myself one way or the other soon as the first day of school was rapidly approaching.

Finishing my peaches and cream, I had just threaded my needle and turned my attention to stringing the leather britches when Doc Widby rode his horse over the bridge and hailed me.

I quickly shoved my skirt down over my knees then

waved to him, wondering what in the world had brought him here.

"Hot enough for you, Bess?" he called out as he tipped his hat and urged his skittish horse over the wooden planks of the bridge.

"Sure is, Doc. Why, it's hot enough to charm ol' Satan himself out of Hades."

He chuckled. "Yep. I sure do wish he'd go back and beat on his wife for a while. Can't see anything dimming that cussed sun." He glanced up at the cloudless sky. "But could be if we got a good ol' thunder-boomer with the sunshine, it would cool things off.

I laughed. "What we need is a good ol' frog strangler with lots of lightning and thunder and winds gusting hard enough to bend the trees to the ground. That'd do the trick."

He wiped his sweaty brow before dismounting and tying his horse's reins to the porch railing. "Mind if I sit with you a while, Bess?"

Doc Widby was a solemn man but today he looked downright grim, like he did when we decided to open the temporary hospital back during the Spanish flu pandemic. The hair on the back of my neck stood straight up and the skin on my arms suddenly felt cold and clammy. I took a deep breath. "Of course not, Doc. Come on up. Can I get you a cold glass of water or some buttermilk?"

He shook his head. "Not just yet. Might have some in a bit but I'm fine for right now. I took a drink at the creek down yonder when I stopped to let my horse cool off for a minute."

I only nodded, waiting. Knowing Doc, he'd get right to whatever had brought him here, and judging by the sudden knots my stomach had tied itself into, it wouldn't be anything good.

Doc settled into the rocking chair beside me and pushed his hat back on his head. He looked straight ahead as he said, "Bob and Maisie Bartlett sent one of their young'uns, the middle boy I think it was, into town this morning to ask if I could come out to their place and take a look at their oldest son, Bob Jr. I've been out there all day."

The coldness spread to my chest and my heart sank. I

knew the Bartlett family. Their children, including Bob Jr., had all been, and in some cases still were, in my classes. "What's the matter with Bob Jr.?"

Taking his hat off and perching it on his knee, he scratched his head. "Well, that's the thing, Bess. I don't rightly know. I was hopin' you might could help me with that."

I strung another bean and told myself to remain calm. It couldn't be Spanish flu. There hadn't been a case of that reported for years—that I had heard of anyway. "All right, I'll do my best. What are his symptoms?"

He scratched his head some more before answering, "Well, now, the boy seems healthy enough just to look at him but he don't move and he keeps his eyes closed no matter how much Maisie tries to coax him into opening them. His temperature is a mite high but not high enough to cause his body to shut down. His pulse is normal but he doesn't respond to any poking or prodding. All he does is lay there. If he wasn't breathing and I couldn't hear his heart beating, I'd pronounce him dead."

"Did he fall or hit his head recently?"

"Thought of that, but there's not a bump or cut on him to indicate that. Maisie and Bob say he just shut down right in the middle of eating his supper t'other night."

"How long ago was that?"

"Coupla days, Thursday evening. Maisie said they bowed their heads to say grace and Bob Jr. didn't lift his when they said amen. He just sat there slumped down in his chair with his eyes closed as if he'd fallen asleep." He hesitated then went on. "He was in the war, you know. Enlisted back in April of '17, as soon as America declared war on Germany. Went through training up north somewhere and then was sent overseas." He shook his head. "There's no telling what he got into over there with all those killin' machines and the poison gases they used in battle. Anyway, he served his time, managed to survive a few of the bigger battles, and came back home when they released him in 1919 with hardly a nick or scratch on him."

"Did the army doctors examine him before they released him?"

"I don't know." He blew out a frustrated breath. "I tell you, Bess, this is a pure-D puzzle. You ever heard of anything like it?"

I shook my head. "Does he eat ... by himself, I mean?"

"No. Maisie said she's been able to get him to drink some broth and tea but nothing more solid than that. But I have a feeling it's more self-defense on his part to keep from getting strangled, nothing more than the natural instinct to automatically swallow when someone pours something down your throat."

I thought for a minute, going over the possibilities in my head. What in the world could have caused a perfectly healthy young man to, what was it Doc had said? To shut down that way? "He's running a low-grade fever?" I had seen people with a high fever get to a point where their body was just worn out and it put them in a kind of trance-like state.

"Yep, checked it six times," his lips curved a bit, "both ends. And Maisie says he hasn't been sick a'tall since he come home from the war."

"Do you reckon it could be a form of shell shock, Doc?"

"I've seen shell shock, Bess, and it sure wasn't anything like this. 'Course, it manifests itself in a lot of different ways. Could be this is a way I ain't seen before."

I nodded. "Maisie's sure he hasn't been sick since he got home? Not even a cold or a headache?"

"She said he did complain about a sore throat about a week ago and that his forehead and cheeks felt hot to the touch but not overly so. She fixed him some wild cherry tea and had him gargle with what she called heal-all. That one was a mystery to me but she showed me the plant. The wife grows it but she calls it self-heal or wild sage.

I nodded. "Your wife knows her plants and apparently Maisie Bartlett does too. Did it bring down the fever?"

"She said it did, said after a day or two he was completely better. No fever and no sore throat. She also said Bob Jr. was healthy as a horse most of the time and he certainly looked healthy when I examined him except for the fact he won't wake up." He scratched his head again.

"Anyway, the reason I'm here is to see if you have any experience with an illness of this nature, and if you do, what should we do about it? How do you treat it?"

I shook my head. "I don't have any idea what it is, Doc. Outside of people in comas, I've never heard of an illness like this. Have you checked your medical journals to see if there's any condition similar to this that's been reported in the past?"

"Nope, been at the Bartletts' house all day but that's the first thing I'm going to do when I get back home. Before that, though, I'm going to go on over the mountain and talk with the town doctor in Black Mountain. Ol' Doc Trenton's even older than I am and he's seen a lot of things in his time. Could be he can solve this mystery for us. Stopped by here since your place is on my way to talk to you in case you knew of something and could save me a trip, not to mention the eye strain I know I'll get from looking in those journals. Why do they have to print those danged things so small?"

He waved that away then his hand went to his head again. Before he had a chance to start scratching, I reached out and gently batted it away. "You're going to wear a rut in your scalp if you don't stop that. Scratch something else for a change."

He smiled. "You're right, Bess. Can't seem to help it. This case has got my mind so twisted it'll probably stay that way for the rest of my life." Settling his hat on his head and slapping his hands on his thighs, he stood up. "I'll head on over to Black Mountain and talk to Trenton. If he can't help me, I'll head back home and see if I can find anything in my journals. I appreciate you listening to me and would appreciate it more if you put your mind to figuring out what this mystery sickness is, or mayhap you could find a treatment in all those Cherokee remedies your great-granny taught you."

I set the beans on the table beside my chair and stood up too. "I'll do that, Doc, and pray one of us finds something. I hate to think of a healthy young man imprisoned in his own body like that."

"So do I, and to make matters worse, he's been courting

one of the young ladies over in Crooked Creek. Maisie said they hadn't gotten around to talking marriage but she thought it wasn't far off until they did."

I sighed. "Then that gives us even more incentive to solve this mystery. If I think of anything, I'll send a message to you or I'll come into town to give you the news directly."

"You know, I'm beginning to think it might be better all around if I got myself one of those new-fangled telephones."

I laughed. "What for? No one on the mountain has one to call you or to receive your calls if you call them. When will you be going back to see Bob Jr?"

"I told Bob and Maisie I'd get back over there tomorrow afternoon after church." He sighed then mounted his horse. "I figure I'll be checking in on him at least once a day if I can until he gets better, the good Lord willin' he does get better. I can stop by to check and see if you've thought of anything tomorrow before I go. It's not too far out of my way."

I nodded. "Why don't you drive your wagon and we can both go to the Bartletts' place? I know Maisie and Bob and taught their children in school so it's only polite I call on them. I won't poke my nose in or interfere with your work. I'd just like to visit them and see if there's anything I can do."

"Hell ... sorry, Bess. I came here to ask for your help. Poke your nose in all you want and maybe together we can get that boy back to spoonin' with his young lady."

I smiled as I held up one hand, middle and index fingers tightly crossed. "Good luck, Doc. And be careful."

He held up his own hand, his fingers mirroring mine. "You too, Bess. See you tomorrow after church," he called over his shoulder as he crossed the bridge.

I sat down and went back to stringing my leather britches while my mind searched for an answer to this puzzling illness. To my way of thinking, if we didn't have a clue what it was or what was causing it, the only thing we could do was try various herbal medicines to treat Bob Jr.'s symptoms. Maybe we'd get lucky and one of them would cure him or at least make him better.

I mentally went through my two jelly safes in the kitchen where I stored the majority of my plants and herbs, considering the ones I knew to be mild stimulants. Ginseng root, castor oil, and rose hips were the first I would try. Perhaps my spring tonic of ginseng, sassafras and Indian root would work. If it didn't, I could try some rose hip tea. And if that didn't work, there were others readily available on the mountain, supplejack or rattan vine and hawthorn berries.

I discarded the ones known for their calming effect, oat straw, fennel, wild cherry, and passion flower. But then I thought what if this sickness was brought on by nerves or anxiety? Wouldn't a sedative be an advantage in that case? I would discuss that with Doc Widby when I saw him tomorrow.

My mind went round and round, considering different techniques, teas, tinctures, tonics and even balms that could be rubbed on and absorbed by the skin. How much and how often to administer the decided-upon dose? Whether or not I should give Bob Jr. a combination of herbs instead of just one at a time.

I finished stringing the beans, took them to the kitchen to hang up so they would dry then went back to the porch to ruminate some more. I was still sitting there muttering to myself when Fletch and John came over the bridge. Fletcher pulled a small sled behind him, piled high with lumber and groceries, with John, perched on top of the lumber, grinning and waving madly in my direction. As I waved back, my heart lifted.

My men were home and I looked forward to hearing about John's day and maybe getting in one more quick lesson before bedtime.

The next day, I got a ride home from church with Thorney and Vera Dalton, squeezing in with their young'uns in the back of their wagon. As usual, Fletcher decided to walk and, of course, John wanted to be with him. They planned to go by the old Elliott homestead to visit with family and would most likely stay to eat Sunday dinner there.

I had just finished packing a basket with fried chicken, a couple dozen biscuits made fresh that morning, several jars of corn and some fresh butternut squash from my garden to take to the Bartletts when Doc Widby arrived.

I hooked my medicine bag over one arm—I had packed it with all the herbs and plants I wanted to try on Bob Jr. plus several pint jars of my spring tonic the night before—and grabbed the basket of food. Then I hurried out the front door. Doc automatically started to climb down from the wagon but I called to him to stay where he was, I could get up myself. After handing him the basket and my medicine bag, which he stowed under the seat, I clambered up to sit beside him on the bench seat.

He looked as if he hadn't slept at all. His clothes were wrinkled and he had bags under his swollen, bloodshot eyes and a gloomy expression on his face, telling me he had bad news.

Rather than a greeting, I said, "What is it? Did you find out something in Black Mountain?"

"Yep, I did, and I wish to hell … sorry, Bessie … I'd never gone."

Doc's penchant for apologizing every time he forgot and uttered the mildest curse word in the presence of a woman usually drew a smile from me but not this time. When he didn't say any more, a chill skittered up my spine despite the day's heat. Though sure I didn't want to hear the rest, I had to ask. "Well, Doc, what is it, or maybe I should just say, how bad is it?"

He shifted and then sighed. "Doc Trenton over in Black Mountain had a case remarkably similar to Bob Jr.'s last year. Only this was a middle-aged woman, married with four young'uns. Everything else is the same though, the same symptoms, the sudden onset of the illness, even complaints of a sore throat and a fever a few days before it happened."

"Did she get better?" His expression was enough to answer that question and I braced myself for the news that the disease had killed her even as he shook his head. What he said could, in some ways, be considered worse than death.

"No, she's still alive but her family shipped her off to Asheville to a sanitarium and she's still there today. The doctors there haven't been able to help her and have just about given up hope. But Trenton says they've seen a couple cases of the same thing and most of the doctors there think it stems from the Spanish flu."

"But I don't remember Bob Jr. having the Spanish flu. He didn't come to us if he … oh, wait, could he have had it while he was overseas?"

He shook his head. "Don't have any idea. We'll ask Bob and Maisie today. Don't see how that knowledge will help us since I don't think it has anything to do with the Spanish flu, but I guess it could."

He looked so hang-dog that I found myself wanting to hug him. Instead, I patted his arm. "You'll figure it out, Doc. The Cherokee believe the Creator put a plant on this earth that's capable of curing each and every disease known to man. I think that's true, and between us, we'll figure out what's wrong with Bob Jr. I know we will."

He did smile but it faded rather quickly as he rubbed his eyes. "Sorry, Bess. Didn't sleep too good last night. Too much on my mind. I tossed and turned until the wife got up and made me a glass of warm milk with honey. The little sleep I did get after that didn't help. Trenton went to Asheville about a month ago to check on his patient. Said he talked to the doctors some more while he was there and what they told him isn't good."

I bowed my head and said a quick prayer. Doc's tone was bleak enough to tell me we both would need a little help from above on this one.

"What did they say?"

"There's an Austrian doctor, a neurologist and psychiatrist, name of, wait, let me get this right, Con-stan-tin von E-co-no-mo." He enunciated each syllable like one of my students slowly sounding out an unfamiliar word in their primer. "He published a paper back in April 1917 about something he calls the Sleepy Sickness. Fancy name for it is encephalitis lethargica which means something like a brain illness that makes you sleepy. That Austrian doctor's seen enough cases to draw some conclusions about the disease but he hasn't discovered what causes it or how to cure it."

"Is it fatal?"

He shrugged his shoulders. "In some cases it is but not always. Some of the patients actually recover completely but the doctors have no idea why. Others recover to a certain degree but remain invalids, unable to care for themselves, and most of them end up in an institution for the mentally ill. The ones who aren't completely incapacitated can function but they suffer from a lot of other severe problems, both mental and physical. Almost half of the patients, about 40%, die from the disease."

"And nobody can figure out what's causing it or how to cure it?"

"Nope. They haven't had any success with that, not yet anyway."

I thought about that for a minute, turning it over in my brain until Doc went on. "I'm hoping maybe you can come up with something, mayhap a plant that doesn't grow over there in Europe, something that's native to our country or even to our mountain. Do you know of anything like that, some herb or wildflower, a tree or, hell … excuse me, Bessie … a toadstool that your great-grandmother or her people used?"

"Not right offhand, Doc. Like you, I didn't get much sleep last night. My mind wouldn't let go of this puzzle. Didn't do any good but I give you my solemn promise I'm going to try my best to solve this."

"Yes, that's the way I feel too. I'm going to try to get my hands on a copy of that paper and anything else that's been written on this thing but I'm afraid we're on our own for right now."

"Well, then, I say we try some of Elisi's Cherokee herbal medicine and see if we can't at least get Bob Jr. to respond. Who knows, we may just make history."

That seemed to buck Doc up a bit. He smiled, though it was a sad one. "I'm too old to be gallivanting around trying to make history. I just want to get this boy to the point that he can function again and hopefully well enough that he can marry his girl."

I patted his hand. "All we can do is our best and maybe we'll get lucky with the first treatment or maybe we won't but we won't let that stop us. I have some ideas and some of my spring tonic in my basket that we can start with. If that doesn't work, we'll move on to something else. And we'll keep trying until we either run out of things to try or Bob Jr. gets better and marries his girl."

He sighed again. "There's more, Bessie. More and worse."

"What is it?"

"Doc Trenton's retiring and he's sold his practice to a young man from up north somewhere, Philadelphia, I think. This young whippersnapper came in while Doc and I were talking and Trenton told him about Bob Jr."

"That's not so bad. The way I see it, the more doctors we have working on this the better the chance we can find a cure for it."

He shook his head. "This young doctor, name's Richard Denby, he's a firm believer in eugenics." He turned and looked at me. "You know what that is?"

I didn't and shook my head even as another chill raced up my spine. "What is it?"

Doc slapped the reins over the horses' backs. "It's been around since way back in the 1800s, 1880 or so. It's a way of filtering out the feeble-minded, insane, drunkards, criminals and any other people who don't quite live up to society's high notions of the type of person they want to associate with. First I ever heard of it was back around the turn of the century, 'round 1907 or thereabouts. Nothing much was done about it back then but recently it's been getting a lot of notice and more and more states are passing eugenics laws."

"But what exactly is it?"

"Racial cleansing," was all he said but it was enough to send that chill through my entire body and bring back memories of Druanna, the Melungeon girl I'd found hiding in our barn up in Hot Springs. She'd been falsely accused of stealing, and knowing she didn't stand a chance with the law because of her heritage, she ran away, making it all the way to Hot Springs from Virginia before severe stomach pain forced her to stop. I'd found her hiding in our barn loft, and when I suggested she should go back, she told me she couldn't because of the "one-drop rule" up in Virginia. Not exactly a law but a way the people had of discriminating against anyone who was different from them, especially Melungeons. Elisi had tried to help me save her but in the end she'd died when a doctor who was nothing but a drunkard attempted to remove her appendix—with Papa's approval.

It had been the beginning of one of the darkest periods in my life.

"I guess you know what that means, all right," Doc said.

I nodded.

"Well, Denby's a proponent of it and he firmly believes that we need it here in the mountains more than anywhere else in the country. Went on about how inbreeding was ruining the mountain people and the government would soon step in and fix that." He shook his head again. "Damn ... sorry, Bessie ... stupid program if you ask me. Involuntarily sterilizing a man or woman just because they're different from us and might possibly corrupt the human race. What kind of person thinks like that?"

"Inbreeding? Why in the Sam hill would he think that? It sounds to me like he's made up his mind about all of us before he's even met us."

"Yep, I told him the people up here don't all have six toes but he couldn't be bothered to listen to me."

I couldn't hold in the laugh. "Six toes? Do you even know anybody who has six toes?"

He grinned at me. "Only six-toed creature I've ever come across is that cat belonging to Nettie Ledbetter and she swears by all that's holy it's normal for the breed." He scoffed. "I tell you the truth, Bessie, it's people like Denby they should be talking about sterilizing. Those men, and some women too, who believe they're better than everybody else and anyone who doesn't live up to their expectations needs to be kicked off the earth. Why, I've heard some of those eugenics programs even include euthanasia in their plans."

"Euthanasia? You mean killing other people just

because they're different or society thinks they're lacking in some way?"

"Yep, that's exactly what I mean."

I shook my head. "Elisi always said human beings can't be happy without having someone to torment, the Indians, the Negros, and when I was young, the Melungeons. Why, even my mama used to threaten us with a Melungeon boogie-man. Said he'd come and take us away if we didn't behave." I huffed out a breath. "Maybe Elisi was right. I haven't seen much evidence of it since I moved here to the mountain with Fletch but I guess it's still around out there in the world."

"Your granny was a smart woman, if you ask me. Virginia just passed the Racial Integrity Act back in March so they could document the race of every person in the state and keep anyone who isn't pure white from marrying and producing children. A bunch of other states already have a eugenics law or are thinking seriously about enacting one. Wouldn't surprise me a bit to see it pass here in North Carolina soon especially with Furnifold Simmons and all his cohorts behind it."

Furnifold Simmons. Now there was a name to send multiple chills up my spine. Fletch and I had met one of Mr. Simmons' associates, a fellow by the name of Orson Belle, and we hadn't liked him a bit. In fact, Fletcher had to threaten him with violence to get him to leave our land, but he'd come back and brought pain and heartbreak with him.

"Here's the turnoff to the Bartlett place. I bet Maisie will be glad to see you with me, Bess. This has been hard on her."

I patted his arm. "I imagine it has." I sighed as I saw Maisie and Bob step out onto their front porch. "She looks as if she hasn't slept in a coon's age."

"Well, she probably hasn't. Not since last Thursday night, anyway," Doc said as he waved to them.

Neither of them waved back though Maisie's expression lightened a bit when she saw me. I vowed to myself right then and there I would do whatever I could to see it lighten even more before we left.

I hopped out of the wagon almost before Doc braked to a stop, ran up the porch steps, and hugged Maisie hard. She started crying and I held her for a good long while before she pulled back, wiped her eyes with her apron, then said, "Thank heavens, you're here, Bessie. I just don't know what to do."

I nodded to Bob. "Doc and I are going to do our best to make Bob Jr. better, Maisie. I can't promise we'll cure him but I like to think I've got a few tricks up my sleeve and Doc here's been burning the midnight oil gathering information on this illness." I took her arm and led her into the house. "Now then, why don't you go splash some cold water on your face while Doc and I have a look at Bob Jr.?" I turned and smiled at Bob Sr. "I'd be much obliged if you'd get the picnic basket out from under the seat of the wagon, Bob, and take it into the kitchen for me. I'll be in soon and put dinner on the table for y'all." Turning back to Maisie, I said, "Sure is quiet in here today. Are the children all down for a nap?"

"No, I sent them out to the barn to play. I didn't want them disturbing Bob Jr."

"I don't think the happy sound of his brothers and sisters playing will disturb Bob Jr. Could be a little normalcy and happiness will help him get better."

"Well, I reckon it's worth a try. Come on back and you can take a look at my boy, Bessie. You too, Doc."

Doc nodded. "I'll get Bessie's bag out of the wagon and then I'll be in. He still in the back bedroom?"

"Oh, no. We took your advice and moved him to the pantry off the kitchen so he'd be where we could get to him quick if we needed to. It's a tight squeeze with the bed in there, but you were right, it's more convenient for me since I spend most of my time in the kitchen. It's also close to our bedroom and if we leave the doors open at night we can hear him if he calls out. God willin' he will call out one day."

I took her hand. "He will, Maisie. But for now, take comfort in the fact that you're doing your best."

She pulled a hankie out of her sleeve and dabbed at her eyes. "That's my boy in there, Bessie. What else can we do but our best to handle this?"

"I have faith God is watching over Bob Jr., Maisie. And he'll take care of you and Bob Sr. too. For now, let's take a look at your boy."

They'd managed to place a small dresser in the room which I later found out contained towels and rags, plus some material Maisie had cut large enough to use as diapers for Bob Jr. Bob Sr. had also cut a tarp to put under the sheets on the bed in case of accidents. It seemed they'd come to terms with this mysterious illness and were more than ready to take care of their son for as long as this lasted.

It pained me to see Bob Jr. lying there in that small bed motionless and quiet. He'd always been such a vibrant boy, never still, frequently into some mischief or other, smiling and laughing constantly.

Bob Sr. came in the room with Doc following behind, carrying my medical bag. He set it on the dresser and joined me at the bedside, reaching out to place his hand on Bob Jr.'s forehead, checking for fever.

"Cool as a cucumber. Have you been checking it once an hour like I said, Maisie?"

She nodded and dabbed at her eyes again before answering. "More like ten times an hour. No fever as far as I can tell."

Doc moved his hand to her shoulder. "How are you holding up, Maisie? You're looking a bit peaked."

"Oh, I'm fine. A little tired maybe but I'm, I'm," she covered her face with the hankie and sobbed once before continuing, "I'm fine, Doc. I'm not the one to worry about right now."

"I know, but with an illness like this where constant care is needed, I always feel better if I check on the people who are tending to the patient."

I opened my medical bag and took out the jars of my spring tonic, lining them up on the small table, save one which I shook vigorously before holding it out to Maisie. "Can you get him to drink this, Maisie? It's a tonic of ginseng, sassafras and Indian root. Fletcher says it tastes awful." I smiled. "Don't tell him but we can add some honey and maybe some wild mint to hide the taste if Bob Jr. won't take it."

Maisie took the jar and opened it. "Can you sit him up for me, Bob?"

While Bob Sr. held his son up, Maisie carefully put the jar to Bob Jr.'s mouth, crooning to him like Fletch sometimes did with his horses and mules, encouraging them to do his bidding. It amazed me when Bob Jr. swallowed instinctively and continued until he'd finished the whole jar of tonic without spilling a single drop. Maisie's eyes ran with tears the entire time. When the jar was empty, she put it on the table and hugged her son tight, still crying as she whispered praise to him.

It made me think of Mama burping my brother Thee so gently on the day Green was taken from us in a flash flood, and I found my own eyes filling with tears. I blinked them back and instructed Maisie on how often to administer the tonic when Bob Jr. had been lowered back to the bed.

I wished fervently I could do more and said as much to Maisie. She hugged me almost as tight as she'd hugged Bob Jr. "All we can do is our best, Bessie. God bless you for trying."

As we were leaving, I remembered my conversation with Doc about the Spanish flu. I had just stepped off the porch but turned around, nearly colliding with Doc who was right behind me. "Maisie," I said, before she could close the door.

She lifted her eyebrows in an inquiring way.

"Doc and I were wondering if Bob Jr. had the Spanish flu while he was overseas. Did he ever mention that?"

She shook her head no then turned to her husband. "He never wrote about having it, didn't mention it when he got home neither. Did he say anything to you, Bob?"

Bob Sr. scratched his chin as he thought. "No, don't recall him ever mentioning the Spanish flu. Surely he would have if he'd suffered from it. Wouldn't you think, Maisie?"

"Surely so, Bob." She turned back to me. "I reckon if he'd had it, we'd have known, Bessie. His letters would have stopped for a time, don't you think? Or a military doctor would have written us to let us know our boy was sick."

"I'm sure they would have, Maisie," I said. "We were just

looking for a connection but apparently that isn't it. Well, Doc will be back tomorrow and I'll make the trip over in a few days to check how he's doing."

Doc and I tried many different medicines and herbs on Bob Jr., but it was quite a long time before he finally woke up. I still don't know if it was the last mixture of herbs we tried—a tincture of ginseng and wild ginger root—or a combination of all the treatments we'd given him before that did the trick. It could even have been simply God's will and I don't suppose it really matters. He was one of the lucky ones as he was able to function fully and wasn't any the worse for wear except he was thinner and weaker than he had been before. I suspect if Maisie hadn't diligently exercised his arms and legs each day, helping to ward off muscular atrophy, Bob would have been in much worse shape. Of course, he didn't walk as well as he did before the sickness and most times used a wheelchair to get around, but all in all, he seemed fairly fit. His girl, unfortunately, grew tired of waiting for him and married someone else just a week before he woke up.

Sadly, the woman in Black Mountain spent the rest of her short life in the sanitarium, dying only a few years after Doc Widby and I first consulted over Bob Jr.'s case.

Unknown to us, the mystery disease, encephalitis lethargica, would eventually be termed an epidemic, though it wasn't spoken of much. In fact, it would come to be known as the Forgotten Epidemic in time. But when I knew it in the 1920s, no one talked about it and not even the newspapers or Nettie's precious radio reported on it. Not like they did with the Spanish flu or small pox or even typhoid.

.

Chapter Four

Early Fall 1924

I bought it for a song and you can sing it yourself.

Fall began creeping its way onto the mountain, making small promises of better weather by teasing us with sporadic cool mornings and gracing us with crisp blue skies. Fletcher and John were busy with harvesting the garden Fletch and I had planted back in late spring and early summer and I spent each day with my classroom, longing for the cooler days to come but dreading the snow to follow, wallowing in the cool respite between.

It was at that time that Fletcher's Aunt Charlotte, or Lottie, as the family called her, came to stay. Over 90 and still in fairly good health, Lottie had taken to traveling around, visiting all her relatives. She was a strange old woman who always wore a red flannel petticoat, no matter how hot it was, with a bundle of money tucked inside which every night, without fail, she would sit down and count. John seemed intrigued by her obsession with her money and each day asked what she was saving it for, to which Lottie would answer, "Why, for my old age, child, and I'm going to give it to whoever I'm living with when I die." Her answer always tickled John, who would turn away with a snicker. When I would ask her for the petticoat so that I could wash it, she'd always say, "Why, Bess, I think you're trying to give me that pneumoney so you can get your hands on my money when I die." I got the same answer when I tried to get her to agree to a bath.

Lottie didn't stay long, leaving in a snit when Fletch decided to cut a door from the dining room into a small bedroom he had built for John to sleep in while Lottie was with us. When she told him he couldn't put a door in the house because that was a sure sign someone would die, Fletch laughed that off and continued cutting the hole in the wall. She packed her bags and left the very next day, the relative she chose to stay with winning the lottery, so to speak, when Aunt Lottie died a few days later. John asked me at her funeral how much money she had and I told him $30 or $40. With widened eyes, he said, "Think of all you can do with that much money, Aunt Bessie." I didn't have the heart to tell him it wouldn't go far.

Late one Saturday afternoon shortly after Lottie's funeral, I sat on the porch snapping green beans, watching Fletcher go about his evening chores with John following closely behind and Fritz trailing behind John. I smiled, thinking how blessed I was to have these men in my family, including the dog. Jingling harnesses at the road drew my attention and I glanced that way. I rose to my feet as I watched a trio of men on horses cross the bridge to our farm. John and Fletch stepped out of the barn, noticed the strangers, and began walking toward them. I waited on the porch, curious who these men were and what their purpose might be. The man in the lead reined his horse to a halt near the porch, tipped his hat at me, and climbed down from the saddle. The other two stopped a few feet behind but remained on their horses, looking around at the mountain behind us. Although I didn't know them very well, I recognized them from Old Fort.

The man on the ground spied Fletcher coming toward him and waited. "Good day to you, sir," he said when Fletcher drew near.

"Evening to you." Fletcher held out his hand. "Name's Fletcher Elliott. That's my wife Bessie up on the porch there and this here's our nephew John." I smiled as John held out his hand and gave the man one quick, firm shake before taking a step back and placing his hand on Fritz's neck.

"Name's J.T. Fesperman," the man said. He gestured toward the two men behind him. "You may know Mr. Whitmire and Mr. Lavender from Old Fort."

The men gave Fletcher a curt nod.

Fletcher nodded. "I do. How you gentlemen doing this fine afternoon?"

Both replied in the affirmative and as was traditional on the mountain inquired after Fletcher's health and that of his family.

Amenities finished, Mr. Fesperman looked at me. "Mrs. Elliott."

I smiled. "Mr. Fesperman, nice to meet you. Hello to you, Mr. Whitmire and Mr.Lavender."

"Ma'am," they both said, with nods and smiles.

Mr. Fesperman looked around, saying, "Lovely place you have here, Mr. Elliott."

I studied him as he stared off in the distance, noting from his speech he was not a mountaineer. He was tall and angular, wearing a suit that looked store-bought. Wireless eye glasses perched on his thin nose and his black hair was fine and wispy. The two men behind him, although not wearing suits, dressed more formally than men on the mountain usually did, and I suspected whatever business Mr. Fesperman had, it must have meaning.

"I reckon it'll do us," Fletcher agreed. My husband, not one to stand around and chew the fat, got down to business. "There anything I can do for you, Mr. Fesperman?"

He turned his attention back to Fletcher, a smile playing around his lips. "I reckon you might. I'm the State Secretary for Boys Work and I've come from Charlotte to look for a camp site for the State Young Man's Christian Association, better known as the YMCA. Sheriff Nanny told me your family owns a big portion of Round Mountain and might be inclined to lease acreage to the YMCA. Said you'd be a good person to show me around, that is, if you think your family might be interested in such a lease."

"We got land all over this mountain," Fletcher said. "Any particular part you're interested in?"

Mr. Fesperman nodded. "Sheriff Nanny says there's a beautiful parcel on top of the mountain, even has a lake on it."

"There is. Belongs to my Aunt Mintie Jane. It passed to her when her husband Marcus died back in '02." He studied Mr. Fesperman for a long moment. "This the first place you're inspecting?"

"No, sir. We've spent the whole day looking at half a dozen sites in this area. Was about to give up till we ran into Sheriff Nanny. You reckon it'd be a good place to set up a campsite for the YMCA?"

Fletcher rubbed his chin. "It's a right pretty place. Got some flat land and a bit of an incline but it ain't too bad. I suspect it might do."

Mr. Fesperman nodded, his eyes alight with interest. "Do you think I might take a look at it? No use talking to your aunt if it doesn't meet our expectations."

Fletcher nodded. "I reckon I can take you up there. When do you want to go?"

Mr. Fesperman glanced at the sky, I imagine noting the position of the sun to gauge the hour. "Looks like there's some daylight left. If you have the time, would it be possible to take a look at it now?"

Fletcher glanced at me before saying, "If you want, I can take you on up there. Unless my sweet wife needs me for anything." He gave me a questioning look.

I smiled my thanks. "I'm fine, Fletch, you go on ahead." I looked at John. "You want to stay here with me, John?" I asked, knowing the answer before he even opened his mouth.

He shook his head. "I reckon I'll go on up with Uncle Fletch," he hesitated, "unless you need me here, Aunt Bessie?"

Bless that child, he was such a sweet boy. "You go on with your uncle, he may need your help." I sat back down and picked up my bowl of green beans. I watched as Fletch saddled Pet, then climbed on, pulling John up behind him.

With a wave, he led the men off our property and onto the road. After barking a goodbye in my direction, Fritz raced after them. I petted our barn cat, who liked to sit on the porch with me. "Looks like it's just you and me, sweet girl." I went back to my chore, relishing the first nip of cool weather which would settle over the mountain until the sun rose tomorrow to chase it away.

Chapter Five

Early Fall 1924

Go whole hog.

JOHN

I was excited to go with Uncle Fletcher and the men to the top of Round Mountain. I'd been to Aunt Mintie Jane's old home place several times before and it had become one of my favorite places on the mountain. I'd been fishing down at the lake a time or two with Hoover Hall and I reckon we'd explored every inch of what seemed to me a vast and endless space. I figured a campsite might put it to good use for whatever the YMCA might be. I was curious why they would want a campsite but didn't want to appear ignorant in front of everyone. I decided I'd ask my Aunt Bessie when we got back home. She had a way of telling me things that made me feel smart.

I glanced down at Fritz trotting beside us, his tongue lolling, and smiled at him. That dog had become my constant companion and I couldn't imagine going anywhere without him. I wondered what would become of him if Mama decided she wanted me back home. I loved my Aunt Bessie, Uncle Fletcher and Fritz, and felt part of a family with them. I realized I didn't want to leave them. But how could I convince my aunt and uncle to let me stay? I prayed they would want me to and I would never have to face that problem.

It didn't take long to reach the top of the mountain. Uncle Fletch led us onto the property using a game trail and dismounted at a clearing not too far in. From here, the mountains around us loomed large and beautiful against the backdrop of the late summer sky, just beginning to darken as the sun dipped behind the mountain to our west. But not dim enough that you couldn't see the shimmering surface of the lake, reflecting the green trees around it.

Uncle Fletch turned to Mr. Fesperman and said, "I'll let you walk where you want. Aunt Mintie Jane's got about 50 acres here, some of it cleared but most wooded, as you can see. There's the lake over yonder."

Mr. Fesperman nodded. "I reckon that's where we'll start."

Uncle Fletch fell into step with him as the two men who had accompanied Mr. Fesperman trailed behind, stepping off the trail to look at this or that.

When we reached the lake, Mr. Fesperman nodded in satisfaction. "Ever fish this lake?"

Uncle Fletch smiled as he turned to me. "John here's the fisherman of the family. I reckon he's been here a time or two."

Mr. Fesperman gave me a questioning look. "Catch anything?"

"Oh, yes, sir. There's plenty of fish in the water."

"You ever take a swim in it?"

"I can't swim but my friend Hoover likes to swim here. Says the water feels real good, nice and cool."

Mr. Fesperman stooped down and cupped water into his hand, then swirled it around. "He's right, John, it feels nice and cool." He stood, stretching his back. "Not used to horses," he muttered. We watched as he looked around for a bit. "We could make a beach here." He gestured to the grass at our feet then pointed across the lake. "Put in a dock over there." He turned to a small clearing to the right. "Maybe some cabins there." He then looked at a small rise to our left.

"More cabins up there and maybe even higher going up the mountain. And right above us, overlooking the lake, our headquarters and the canteen." He smiled at me as he ruffled my hair. "Sure is pretty, isn't it, John?"

"It's my favorite place on the mountain," I said. I didn't mention it was a place that seemed mysterious and mystical to me and one I thought just might be haunted. Stone Mountain Baptist Church's graveyard backed up to the property and there was a family cemetery on this parcel of land not far from the lake. Hoover told me he figured the ghosts from the church and Aunt Mintie Jane's land wandered around out here because it was so pretty and peaceful, his reasoning being that that's what he'd do if he was a ghost. As if to prove his point, early one evening when we were fishing, we both heard a woman scream something awful from the direction of the church's graveyard. When the shrieking sound drew closer, without a body attached to it, we didn't look at one another, didn't even say a word, simply dropped our poles and ran off faster than salts through a widow woman. By the time we reached Hoover's house, which was closest, it was full dark. I had no intention of stepping foot outside to go home so spent the night with Hoover. When I got back the next day, Aunt Bessie was a bit put out with me for not coming home. I couldn't work up the nerve to tell her what happened although later came to realize it probably wouldn't have bothered her at all to know ghosts walked Aunt Mintie Jane's property.

"Let's walk some more," Mr. Fesperman said, interrupting my thoughts, and off we went. He didn't tour the entire acreage because it soon became too hard to see but as we returned to the horses said to Uncle Fletcher, "I knew the minute I stepped foot on this property it was the place for us. You reckon I could talk to your aunt?"

Uncle Fletcher rubbed his hand over Pet's muzzle. "I reckon so but might be best to speak to the rest of her family as well. Could be her eight children will feel they should have a say-so in this." He hesitated, studying Mr. Fesperman for a long moment. "You any idea how much you want to spend for the lease?"

Mr. Fesperman glanced away and I wondered at his expression. Was he embarrassed? He finally met my uncle's gaze. "Well, now, that's the problem. We don't have any money to spend but we would develop the land for you, bring in young men to help clear it and build cabins. We'll create jobs and buy produce and meat from local farmers. When the lease is up, of course, the cabins would be yours to use as you like. I assure you, Mr. Elliott, we will take care of this place, treat it as if it were our own."

Uncle Fletcher rubbed his chin, thinking. "Let me talk to my family, Mr. Fesperman, see how they feel."

Mr. Fesperman nodded. "I know the chances are slim they'll agree to it, but this is the perfect place for us. I don't think I'll find anything better in these mountains."

"It is a right pretty place," Uncle Fletcher agreed. I watched the two men shake hands, excited at the prospect of a whole group of people I didn't know coming onto the mountain. Maybe there would be boys my own age to fish and hunt with.

On the ride back, the men were mostly silent and left us at the turnoff to our farm. "I'll be waiting to hear from you, Mr. Elliott," Mr. Fesperman said.

"I won't make you wait long," Uncle Fletcher promised with a wave.

Aunt Bessie was excited when Uncle Fletcher told her about Mr. Fesperman's interest in the acreage. "This will be good for the economy here, Fletcher, maybe encourage some of our young ones to stay put instead of going off to the cities to work in factories."

Uncle Fletcher nodded. "I sure hope so, Bessie. Seems more go off every year to seek their fortune elsewhere. We'll be seeing the family at church tomorrow. I'll talk to Boyd and Lewis about getting everyone together afterward for a family meeting."

The next day after morning service, Uncle Fletcher drew his cousins Lewis and Boyd apart and told them about Mr. Fesperman's proposal. They agreed for the family meeting to take place at the Stone Mountain Baptist Church shortly before evening service since the family would be in attendance anyway. Preacher Justice offered the chapel which proved to be a Godsend as a fierce thunderstorm roared through just as my uncle stood to address his aunt and cousins. The adults had gathered at the front of the church while the children played in the rear. Interested in what the Elliott family would decide, I stayed close enough to hear what was being said, my excuse being that I needed to watch Fritz, who was terrified of thunderstorms.

Uncle Fletcher began by telling them of Mr. Fesperman's visit and their tour of the acreage on top of Round Mountain. He recited Mr. Fesperman's comment about knowing when he first stepped onto the property it was perfect for the YMCA campsite then went on to explain it could produce jobs and a way for the farmers on the mountain to sell their produce and meat.

Lewis interrupted, "That's all well and good, Fletch, but how much did he offer for the lease?"

Uncle Fletch glanced at Aunt Bessie before saying, "Nothing."

Some of the adults looked confused while Lewis said, "I don't see how that can help the family, Fletch."

Aunt Bessie stood. "We all farm, we all have chickens and hogs and some of us have beef. We can sell them vegetables from our gardens, milk from our cows, eggs and whatever meat they need. They have to eat after all and they won't be able to grow their own food right off."

Lewis's wife nodded in agreement. "I think that's a right good idea. Lord knows, our garden produces more than we need and we could sure use the money."

"That's well and good but I'd rather have the money in hand up front," Lewis said.

Most of the men agreed with this, nodding their heads and making low grunts of approval.

Uncle Boyd stood and everyone turned their attention to him. He was a big man, more taciturn than verbal, but when he spoke, people listened. Although he wasn't my uncle, I called him Uncle Boyd like all the other children in the family, and of all my relatives, he was one of my favorites. As a child, he had been called Boy by his family, but when he enlisted in the Army during WWI, was told that wasn't a legitimate name so a D was added to Boy and from then on he became Boyd. He had a mischievous side to him and liked to tell people who didn't know him that he was an orphan and never had a name so everyone called him Boy when he was young. I'd believed him until Aunt Bessie told me different. But come to find out, there was one thing I knew about my Uncle Boyd my aunt and uncle didn't, and that was that he served a more universal role on the mountain. Uncle Boyd's property sat about halfway between their farm and Stone Mountain Baptist Church, fronting both sides of the road that ran over the mountain. In front of his house, he had a water wheel with a wooden rabbit perched on top set down into the creek that I admired every time I visited. I liked the way the wheel collected water from the creek then spilled it back in as it rotated, and the way the rabbit seemed to be running when the wheel spun. I asked Uncle Boyd one day why sometimes the wooden wheel turned and the rabbit ran but at other times it would be wedged so it couldn't spin. He grinned but didn't answer, which made me wonder what secret that rabbit held. I figured that out at a later time when I heard Thorney Dalton tell Hoover Hall's pa that when the rabbit was running, the moonshine was flowing. I decided not to relay this information to Aunt Bessie or Uncle Fletcher, who was a teetotaler and held my Uncle Boyd in high esteem.

Uncle Boyd waited until he knew he had everyone's full attention. "Let's hear Fletcher out. He wouldn't have come to us with this proposal unless he thought there was something to it."

"There will be jobs there," Uncle Fletcher said. "They'll need people to help run the camp, cooks for their canteen."

"There's no guaranty any of us will have jobs there," Lewis said. "Why, for all we know, they'll bring in outsiders to cook and clean and run the place."

Everyone began talking at once then, some arguing, others speaking while nodding their head in agreement. Uncle Fletcher banged his fist on the podium. They all quieted, looking at him. "Since we all can't agree, I think Aunt Mintie Jane should be the one to decide this. After all, this property belongs to her so let's leave it with her."

They all looked at Aunt Mintie Jane, a frail woman who sat hunched over, one hand, wrinkled with skin as thin as tissue paper, clutching a cane. She was a mystery to me, a woman who seemed as old as God and about as wise, someone who commanded respect from all those around her. She looked at her children and their wives and husbands and smiled. "Why, I think it's a right nice idea, don't you? Doing something for these people who are in need of what we have. It's the Christian thing, ain't it? Besides, that property has sat vacant for years now and needs developing. It will do me good to see it properly restored to its beauty."

"But what about payment, Mama?" Lewis said. "Even though that Mr. Fesperman says he don't have the funds, it's the State, and I bet they've got enough money to burn a wet mule just laying around waiting to be spent."

She shook her head. "Maybe so, Lewis, but that property ain't been put to good use in years. I reckon it'd be just as good to give the property to the State for this campsite. I don't see the need for money to change hands."

The adults started arguing again, some acting horrified at this notion, others as if they agreed. Aunt Mintie Jane let them talk awhile then banged her cane on the floor. They immediately fell silent and turned to her. "Y'all can get mad, get glad or scratch your ass, it don't make no difference to me. Like Fletch said, it's my property, it should be my decision."

Most everyone burst out laughing at that. Although a devout Baptist, Aunt Mintie Jane had been known to use salty language to get her point across.

She looked at Uncle Fletcher. "You agree with me, Fletch?"

Uncle Fletcher nodded. "Like you said, it ain't being used anyway and it will be put to good use. Plus it's a way for all of us to make some extra money."

She looked to Aunt Bessie. "Bess, you're more educated than the rest of us, you agree with what your husband says?"

Aunt Bessie smiled at her. "I do, Aunt Mintie Jane. If I know one thing about my husband, it's that he's got a good sense for making money. And like I told him, this is a way to help keep our young ones home instead of going off to the cities to find jobs for income."

Aunt Mintie Jane turned to her son Julius. "You're my oldest, Julius, and you ain't said what you think one way or the other. Let's hear from you."

He studied the ceiling as he thought. "If it's your wish, Mama, I won't go against you. Let's just hope they can prove to be the economic boom Fletcher and Bessie think they are."

She looked at Lewis. "Lewis, you seem to be the one opposed to it the most. You changed your mind?"

Lewis looked about to object but glanced at his wife who glared at him. Everyone in the Elliott family knew Lewis might be loud and boisterous and opinionated but the one who ruled his roost was his wife. He shrugged. "It's your decision, Mama. I'll accept whatever you decide."

She turned to each of her other children and all agreed it should be her decision since she felt so strongly about the matter. Aunt Mintie Jane smiled and I could see then the beautiful woman she must have been. "It's done, then. We'll let them have the property at no cost." She thought then continued, "Might be a good idea to put it in their heads we'd expect a bit of business back and forth for that right." She winked. The adults laughed at this, the tension in the room fleeing like an evil thought chased away by an angel.

Chapter Six

Late Summer 1924

Don't let your mouth overload your tail.

Every year, Stone Mountain Baptist Church held its annual Decoration Day on the second Sunday in September following church services. Everyone was expected to attend and do their part cleaning up the cemetery and placing flowers on each of the graves. After we finished, Preacher Justice would gather us together in the shade of the big oak trees surrounding the graveyard and say a few words in honor of all those departed souls.

Decoration Day seemed to always fall on a beautiful day with the worst heat of the summer behind us and the cold of winter far off in the future, and this year was no different. The asters and the goldenrod were in their glory, backed up by the fading Joe Pye weed blooms and the stunning red berries on the dogwood trees. The leaves of the deciduous trees were just showing a hint of the splendid color they would take on in the next month or so when, I imagined, if seen from above, the mountain would greatly resemble a multi-colored quilt. The air was clean and crisp and the sky, oh, the sky was a clear, beautiful blue with fluffy white pillows of clouds spattered here and there.

With fall, my favorite season, fast approaching, I

considered it the perfect time to honor the ones who had gone before. Elisi's story about how the cedar tree came into being was foremost in my mind whenever Decoration Day rolled around, and I always cut a huge bunch of cedar sprigs and placed one or two in with the flowers we put on each of the graves. It was my way of honoring not only Elisi, Mama and Green, but all of my Cherokee ancestors.

I shared the story with John that year as he helped me tuck the sprigs in with the little bouquets of flowers on the graves. He laughed at the way the People went back and forth over whether they wanted all daylight or all darkness but sobered when I talked about the ones who died and how the Creator decided to honor them with a new tree.

Brushing a finger over the cedar twigs, I breathed in the fresh, clean scent before holding them under John's nose so he could smell. "The Cherokee name is atsina tlugv, John, and whenever you see it or smell it, you should remember that you're looking at the spirits of your ancestors and that life always works best when it's in balance."

Though I suspected he was too young to completely grasp what it meant to be part Cherokee, he seemed to enjoy my stories. Or so I thought until he said, "Aunt Bessie, why do the Cherokee always talk about death? Don't they know any stories about happy things?"

I laughed as I ran my hand over his dark hair and gave it a tug on the too-long ends, thinking it would need to be trimmed soon. "They don't always, John. Your ancestors loved to tell stories, and in the many years they lived in these mountains, they told countless ones, some happy, some sad. Almost all of them were a way of enlightening their children, of teaching them about how to live their life. They have hundreds of stories about creation and living. I just haven't shared many of them with you yet."

Fletcher came up then and grinned at John. "Careful, boy, or she'll talk your ear off with those Cherokee stories of hers." He lowered his voice and winked at me. "Better run, Bessie-girl. Nettie Ledbetter's headed this way, says she wants to talk to you."

I kept the smile firmly on my face and bit back the groan

that wanted to escape at that bit of news. Nettie had recently purchased a radio and loved nothing more than telling everybody she saw everything she heard on that thing. I likened it to nothing more than her newfound way of spreading gossip and often wondered if she ever read a newspaper or a book or even a magazine anymore now that she had that talking machine to keep her informed of what was going on out in the world.

John grabbed Fletcher's hand and pulled him toward the front of the church, complaining about being thirsty. I quickly fell into step with them, linking my arm with my husband's, hoping against hope I could escape Nettie's notice.

It wasn't to be. I gritted my teeth when Nettie called after me, "Bessie, yoo-hoo, Bessie."

At Fletcher's chuckle, I sent him an evil look then sighed and turned to greet her. "Hello, Nettie. I didn't see you there. The Lord certainly sent us beautiful weather for Decoration Day this year, don't you think?"

She smiled sweetly at me, though the gleam in her eyes let me know she had some juicy gossip to impart.

I sighed again and held out my hand. "How are you, Nettie, and your family?" I looked around but didn't see her husband or her boys anywhere.

"Oh, I'm doing as well as can be expected this time of year. Busy, of course." She put her hand to the small of her back. "And my back is giving me fits but that seems to be my life's burden. I tell you, Bessie, I dread this winter 'cause I know I'll be down more than I'm up with the cold and all. It pains me something awful when the cold weather sets in. Why, some mornings I can't even get out of bed."

Though it was a complaint I'd heard many times before and I wanted badly to say, as I sometimes did with my students, "Nobody likes me, everybody hates me, gonna go to the garden and eat a worm and die. Gonna eat a wiggly worm, gonna eat a slicky worm, gonna eat a wooly worm and die." But I had a feeling Nettie wouldn't smile or laugh as the young'uns often did so bit my tongue and restricted myself to the same advice I'd offered many times in the past. "I'm real sorry to hear that, Nettie. Have you tried the willow bark tea like I told you before? It's not a cure but it will help with the pain."

As expected, she ignored my advice. "Oh, I'll get by, I always do."

"I reckon you will but the tea would help. I hope Merle and the children are doing all right."

"Well, Merle's down with a cold, coughed and hacked all night long. I didn't have the heart to insist he come to church this morning, much less to Decoration Day, and spend all afternoon out in this cool weather. The boys are around here somewhere, probably tagging after those no-good Dalton boys. I swan, Bessie, I do everything I can to raise my boys up right and all it takes is one afternoon with those Dalton young'uns and mine are spitting and whooping and hollering like they haven't been taught better. Why, I even heard the oldest curse the last time they played with those Daltons, and let me tell you, I washed his mouth out with soap 'til he looked like a rabid dog." She nodded her head firmly. "I won't stand for that kind of behavior from my boys."

Though I thought it a rather heartless punishment for a phase that every young boy, and even some girls, went through, I smiled. "Thorney's young'uns can be a handful. Vera does a good job with them but sometimes I wonder how she keeps her sanity with so many of them running around. Still, they're well-behaved in church and school so she's doing something right."

Nettie frowned and hummed deep in her throat as she took my hand in hers, squeezing my fingers tight enough to have the bones rubbing together. I stifled a yelp while struggling to keep the smile on my face.

"Well, I suppose she does at that. I reckon that's all any of us can do." She squeezed my fingers again. "Bessie, I wanted to tell you how sorry I was to hear of your cousin's troubles and ask if there's anything I can do to help. I imagine you'll be going up there to Madison County to help with his children."

I had no idea what she was talking about. "My cousin? Which cousin is that, Nettie?"

She squeezed my fingers again and this time I didn't

bother to contain the yelp of pain.

"Oh, did I hurt you?" She waved that away as if it wasn't important but did gentle her grip a bit. "Don't tell me you haven't heard. Why, it's been all over the news, at least on my radio, but I was sure the papers would have covered it too." She shrugged. "Well, maybe not, after all it just happened last week and the newspapers can be slow at times. That's one of the reasons I love my new radio. Anyway, your cousin Frank Henderson from, oh, my, what is the name of that place?" She tapped her index finger against her forehead. "Stackhouse, yes, that's it, Stackhouse, up there in Madison County. That is where you come from, isn't it, Madison County? And wasn't your mama's maiden name Henderson?"

I nodded as I searched my memory for the name Frank Henderson. It wasn't familiar, but with all the Hendersons running around up in Madison County, I supposed he could be a cousin on Mama's side of the family. I shrugged. "Well, I reckon he could be a cousin, Nettie, but I've never met him. What happened?"

She lowered her voice and stepped closer. "He killed his wife, strangled her off in the woods somewhere then carried her back to the house and left her on the front porch. And with their three children right inside the house, not five feet away. I declare, it's downright shameful. Then he ran off with another woman to South Carolina, a," she leaned in and whispered, "a harlot people say he was living with instead of being home with his family."

Her hand tightened on mine as her eyes gleamed with the pleasure of being the first to break the scandalous news to me. I stepped back and drew my hand away, shaking it to get the blood flowing through my abused fingers as my mind frantically went through the people I knew from Mama's family. There were so many, but try as I might, I just couldn't place a "Frank" in with them.

I shook my head. "I don't know a Frank Henderson, Nettie. Are you sure you have the name right?"

"Oh, yes, as sure as I'm standing here. It's been all they're talking about on the radio for the last few days. Frank

Henderson from Stackhouse who strangled his wife then ran off to South Carolina on the train. Why, I bet Sheriff Nanny has a wanted poster in his office right now, offering a reward for capturing him. Do you have any family down in South Carolina that he could run to?"

"Are you thinking of strapping on a gun and going after him, Nettie?" I regretted the words almost as soon as they left my lips. I reached out and touched her arm. "I'm sorry, Nettie. This is a shock, to say the least. I'm not sure if he's a member of my family. If he is, I don't recall ever meeting him or hearing Mama or Aunt Belle talk about him or any other member of the family from that area, for that matter."

"I only asked because I thought if he was kin you'd want to go up there and see about helping with those poor children and I wanted to offer to take over your teaching duties while you're gone."

"That's sweet of you, Nettie, but I don't think it's necessary. I don't know him and don't even know if he is kin. And besides, there's a slew of Hendersons up there in that area. I'm sure they'll find someone who can take the children in."

She shook her head. "I can't imagine what evil got into the man, killing his wife that way and then carrying the body back to leave it on the front porch with his babies right inside the house. Why, it's, it's ..." She shook her head again. "I just don't know what this world is coming to. All these people killing people for no good reason, like those two boys, what were their names? Leopold and Loeb, that's it, up there in Chicago who killed their neighbor last year just because they were bored and wanted to see if they could commit the perfect murder. Well, they didn't but now everyone is calling it the crime of the century." She pursed her lips. "We can only hope but I'm sure it's not. There will be worse things to come, I'm certain of that. Why, it seems like every time the news comes on the radio, they're talking about something tragic like that. It's shameful, absolutely shameful the way those people in those big cities treat each other."

I patted her hand, trying to console her. When Nettie got worked up over something, she could go on for hours. "I reckon the best thing for us to do is stay right here in our peaceful little corner of the world surrounded by the safety the mountains afford us and let the rest of the world take care of itself."

"If you ask me, we should think about building a fence around our mountain instead of around Hell like Preacher Justice says. That way we could keep out all the riff-raff." She lowered her voice and leaned closer toward me to whisper, "You know, like the Negroes and all those foreigners from over there in Europe. They're the ones that cause most of the trouble."

My back went stiff at that. Riff-raff, Negroes and foreigners? It sounded too close to the eugenics program Doc Widby had told me about. What was the world coming to, indeed?

I wanted to argue the point with Nettie, but to tell the truth and shame the devil, I felt the need to get away from her so much I just couldn't bring myself to try. There was only so much of Nettie Ledbetter I could take in a day and I'd reached my limit. I began looking around for an excuse to escape. Glancing over her shoulder, I smiled when I spotted Fletcher and John coming around the corner of the church. "Well, you're certainly entitled to your opinion, Nettie," I said as I raised my hand and waved frantically. "Oh, look, there's a couple of handsome men coming my way." I patted her shoulder. "You give Merle some wild mint tea with honey for that cold and tell him I hope he gets better soon. You should give the boys and yourself a dose too just to be safe."

"But, Bessie, what are you going to do about Frank Henderson?"

"Nothing I can do, Nettie. I don't even know him."

"But what about the children? What's going to happen to them?"

I sighed. "Like I said, I'm sure with all the Hendersons up in Madison County, someone will step forward and take them in. I'll write to a friend of mine in Hot Springs tomorrow and ask him to check to make sure they're all right." I patted her hand. "Don't you worry. I'm sure they'll be taken care of."

With that, I waved again at my two men just as Fletcher

leaned down and spoke in John's ear then nudged him forward.

Smiling, John started running in my direction, yelling, "Aunt Bessie, Aunt Bessie, look what me and Uncle Fletch got for you." He waved a bouquet of wildflowers in his right hand, bright purple asters and a few sprigs of goldenrod slightly bedraggled but still sweet enough to make my heart turn over and to keep me from correcting his grammar.

Chapter Seven

Spring 1925

What in tarnation?

John's introduction to winter on our mountain proved to be a mild one, graciously giving us days where no coats were needed and we could go about doing our chores without freezing hands and faces. I was glad for this, because it seemed wherever my husband went, there went John too, followed by Fritz. I had never experienced cold weather in Knoxville but from what John told me suspected the winters there weren't nearly as severe as ours could be. Oh, we had our fair share of snow and ice but it didn't linger and before too long the weather would be fair once more with the sun, although weak, shining down upon our world. Winter being my least favorite season, I was thankful when the trees began budding and the grass once more showed signs of the lush green it would be in summer.

With my jelly safe almost depleted, I began going into the woods to gather herbs to supplement my medicinals, accompanied by John when he wasn't with Fletcher helping with chores or cutting timber. He was an intelligent boy and liked learning about plants and their uses. As we would go along, I would tell him the Cherokee words for plants if I knew them.

This morning, we were in search of early dandelions, a plant I knew would brave the chilly night temperatures. As we passed a cluster of violets, I kneeled down and showed him their pretty purple blooms. "Do you know what these are, John?"

"No, ma'am, but they sure are pretty."

"These are violets, but the People call them dindaskwateski."

John knelt beside me and touched the velvet petals. "They look so delicate, Aunt Bessie. Is that what dinda," he hesitated, "that word means, violets?"

"Actually, it means they pull each other's heads off."

He gave me a questioning look.

I smiled at his expression. "If the heads are interlocked, like this, when you pull the stem, it pulls the flowers off."

"Oh." He pointed to a large patch of Mayapple. "What's the Cherokee name for that? It looks kinda like an umbrella."

"You have a good eye for gathering, John. That's Mayapple or uniskwetugi which means 'it wears a hat' because the flowers grow underneath, sheltered by the umbrella-shaped cluster of leaves on top." I lifted up a leaf and showed him the tiny bud just forming beneath it.

John smiled. "It's hiding under the hat."

I ruffled his hair.

We moved along and I pointed to a plant which I knew John was familiar with even without the flowers.

"Joy Pye weed," he said proudly. "Does it have an Indian name?"

"I don't think so since it's named for a person. Do you know why it's called that, John?"

"No, ma'am."

"It's named for an Indian medicine man in Colonial times. He used the roots to treat typhus. Some call it queen of the meadow. Do you remember when I showed one to you last summer, tall with pinkish-purplish colored flowers in a big cluster on top?"

He nodded.

"It looks like a queen, don't you think, when it blooms with its pretty, regal-looking flowers."

"It sure does." A bird trilled nearby and we both looked into the trees. John pointed above me. "Look at that pretty redbird, Aunt Bessie."

I shaded my eyes against the sun as I looked in the direction he was pointing. "He sure is a handsome fellow."

"How do you know it's a boy, Aunt Bessie?"

"See the black mask around his eyes and beak? Females have a gray mask. And males are a more vibrant red while females are more of a dull red-brown color."

John watched the bird for a bit. "Don't seem right a boy being prettier than a girl," he finally said.

I laughed. "I agree, John."

"I like that thing on top of its head."

"Oh, the crest. I do too." I sat down on a fallen log and gestured for John to sit by me. We watched the bird for a moment, admiring its pretty red plumage. "Would you like to hear the story of how the redbird got its color?"

He smiled with pleasure. "I sure do. I was hoping you'd tell me one of your stories, Aunt Bessie."

I put my basket on the ground and made myself more comfortable. "In the early days of our People, there was a little bird who was of an earth-tone color and so plain he wasn't easily seen by the others. He thought if he was colored red, he would be recognized for his power and beauty and that the female birds would notice him. So he talked to one of the Elders in his clan council who told him he had to earn that privilege, that the color red was sacred like the color black and it had to be earned in a special way, through a vision.

"Many moons passed without the vision to tell the little bird what he had to do to earn the color red. One day, Raccoon and Wolf had a disagreement over Wolf playing tricks on Raccoon. Raccoon really enjoyed playing with his friend but he decided that he was tired of Wolf always getting the best of him. He knew that Wolf was very quick but sometimes not so smart about things so said, 'Hey, Wolf, come chase me. I bet you can't catch me.' Wolf replied, 'Raccoon, I can always catch you. I'll even give you a running start.' So Raccoon ran as quickly as his little legs could take him toward the edge of the water, knowing that the water was very cold and Wolf was afraid of the water's rapids.

"With great speed and agility, Wolf chased after Raccoon, who ran as fast as he could toward the water's edge and grabbed onto a yellowroot plant, holding on so he wouldn't fall into the water. Wolf didn't see him and thought Raccoon had jumped into the cold water. He was running so hard that by the time he saw Raccoon, he was headed into the water's rapids. 'Oh, this water is so cold, Raccoon, help me,' he said, 'you know I can't swim.' Raccoon knew that Wolf would be all right floating down the rapids but Wolf clawed at the clay edge until he finally pulled himself out onto the clay bank. Exhausted, he fell asleep in the warm sunshine, and while he slept, Raccoon quietly packed the soft red clay on Wolf's eyes, which hardened in the warm sun.

"The little bird had been sitting on a small tree branch watching his friends play when he heard Wolf cry, 'I can't see. Please help me, I can't see.' Little bird went over to help Wolf and said, 'I will help you but you must promise to always play nice with Raccoon and not to play tricks on your friends.' Wolf said, 'I promise. If I can just see again, I will also tell you where you can get a beautiful red color.' Little bird pecked and pecked at the hard clay until the dried clay was gone and Wolf could see again. Wolf kept his promise and told the little bird where to find a plant in the mountains called Red Paint Brush. The little bird used the plant to paint himself red and to this day Wolf plays fair with Raccoon and the little bird is now called the cardinal or redbird and, as you can see, is clearly a bird of distinction."

As if sensing the story was finished, the redbird flew away with a great fluttering of wings.

I rose to my feet and held out my hand to John to help pull him up.

"That was a good story, Aunt Bessie." He nodded. "I'm glad redbird figured out how to make himself a prettier bird."

"He sure brightens up the forest, doesn't he?" I said as we began walking again. A bit farther along, I spied what I was looking for, a clump of dandelions at the root of a large tree. Taking out my spade, I knelt beside them. "We want the entire plant, John, and that means we dig. But we only take every third one and leave the others untouched." I explained to him the Cherokee way of leaving two and taking one so that the plant would continue to thrive.

"What do you want with a dandelion, Aunt Bessie? They ain't nothin' but weeds," John said as we dug.

"It's a good all-around healing herb, John. It can be used to treat or prevent liver problems or given to someone to increase their appetite or to make them use the outhouse. The green leaves are loaded with all kinds of vitamins and minerals that are good for us. And they taste good."

He made a face. "I don't want to eat no weed."

I only smiled and said, "We'll see. Right now, we want to gather some roots for a liver tonic so keep digging. The roots go pretty deep and we don't want to break them."

"You reckon I'll ever learn all these herbs and their uses?" he asked, giving me a serious look.

"If you want to, John. You can do anything if you only put your mind to it."

His smile was so bright the sun seemed to pale in comparison.

As we walked back home, I pointed out a cluster of white puffball fungus growing near a tree. "The People call this Nakwisiudsi, which means little star."

John knelt down to study the plant then stood up and backed away. "I reckon it does from a distance. It's kind of pretty, don't you think?"

"It sure is and will be even prettier when the outer layer peels back making it look even more like a star."

John looked around the forest. "I reckon there's beauty all around us, Aunt Bessie."

I smiled at him. "There sure is, John."

By the time we returned home, we had a fair amount of dandelion roots. As we walked into the yard, I spied Hiram Henderson standing near the porch, talking to Fletcher. He smiled and waved when he saw us.

"Who's that?" John asked.

"That's Hiram Henderson, our local tooth jumper."

His eyes lighted with interest. "What's a tooth jumper?"

"I'll let Hiram tell you," I said, leading the way onto the porch where the two men now sat waiting on us.

Hiram was the sort of person who always made one smile upon seeing him. He was a short man, round through the middle, with spindly legs and large hands and feet. His hair, which had once been black as midnight, was now a beautiful snowy white, and he wore it tied back with a rawhide strip. His eyebrows and whiskers matched his hair and called attention to eyes as dark as sapphires above bright red cheeks. He always seemed such a jolly fellow and I often wondered how a man came to this state of mind, especially one like Hiram who had had more than his share of bad luck in life. Hiram had lost his first wife in childbirth and his only son died overseas during World War I. He had been buried there, which had taken Hiram years to come to terms with.

"Hello, Hiram, it's been a good while since we've seen you. I hope you're faring well," I said, setting my basket down near the door.

"Fair to middlin', I'd say, Moonfixer." He turned his attention to John. "Who's this little feller you got tagging along after you?"

I put my hand on John's shoulder but he introduced himself before I could, holding out his hand and saying, "I'm John, Uncle Fletch's boy."

Hiram shook John's hand, grinning. "Well, it's a pleasure to meet you, John. I heard you was from Knoxville. You planning on staying awhile?"

John glanced at Fletcher and me. "Oh, yes, sir, I plan to stay as long as I'm welcome."

I smiled at him. "We're hoping he stays with us forever."

The look on John's face nearly broke my heart in two but I was happy to see he felt about us the way we did about him.

Hiram nodded at my basket. "You got any 'sang in there, Bessie?"

"You in need of ginseng?"

"Yes'm. I got a patient with a gum that won't stop bleeding." He smiled at John. "I'm a tooth jumper, John." I couldn't help but grin at Fletcher. Hiram was in much demand and very popular on the mountain. Since we didn't have a dentist nearby, when someone needed a tooth pulled, they called on Hiram who basked in his status and necessity. I do have to say he was the best tooth jumper I'd ever seen.

"What's a tooth jumper, Mr. Henderson?" John said, going over to stand by Fletcher, who put his arm around his shoulders.

"Why, I take out teeth." He leaned forward, his eyebrows raised. "As your Aunt Bessie will tell you, John, there's an art to removing a tooth. Do it wrong and you're liable to break someone's jaw or bust out a whole mouthful of teeth."

"Really?" John said, leaning forward as well.

"Yep. You see, what I do is I use a hammer and chisel the size of a big nail when I have to knock someone's tooth out. I place the chisel against the ridge of the tooth, just under the edge of the gum, and give a quick, hard lick with the hammer, and the tooth jumps out like it was shot out of a rifle." He snapped his fingers." Just that quick." He winked. "That's why I'm called a tooth jumper."

John's eyes grew wide. "You don't ever pull 'em?"

"Nope. Too much can go wrong. Why, the tooth could break off or not come completely out. The way I do it's best and easiest."

John nodded, his expression contemplative.

"What happened?" I asked Hiram.

"Ol' Joe Harris had a tooth that was ailing him something awful. I got it out all right and packed it with salt to keep it from bleeding and so it'd heal up without being too awful sore, but it's still leaking. Figured I'd get some ginseng root from you to mash up and pack it with."

"That should do it, Hiram, but I don't have any fresh. It's the wrong time of year for that but I have some I gathered last fall and dried. Will that do you?"

"Dry's fine, works just as well as the fresh, if you ask me."

"All right. How much do you need?"

"A good handful, I'd say. Just enough to make a paste thick enough to pack that tooth and stop the bleeding."

"A handful of fresh? Or dry? With the dried root, it'll take about a third of what you would normally use of the fresh."

He shrugged. "One of them half-size jelly jars ought to do me, I reckon."

I nodded. "You leaving now or are you going to stay and talk a while?"

"I can sit a bit."

"All right. I'll get the ginseng for you before you leave."

"I do thank you, Moonfixer. How much do I owe you?"

"I'm sure we'll need your services one day, Hiram, so let's trade it out when the time comes."

"That's fine with me, Bess." He leaned back and eyed me speculatively.

"What is it, Hiram?" I asked, a little unsettled by his scrutiny.

"Bess, you're what my granny used to call a wise woman."

I smiled at that. "Oh, Hiram, I think I've a ways to go before I'd be considered wise."

"A wise woman, Bess, is a woman like you who possesses knowledge passed down through the generations of healing with what my granny called folk medicines. A healer who uses herbal remedies from plants."

"Well, Hiram, I'm honored you'd consider me a wise woman. I still don't have half the knowledge my great-grandmother Elisi possessed but I hope one day to be like her."

"And no doubt you will." He slapped his thighs, rose to his feet and walked a bit stiffly over to John. "Let me see your teeth, young man."

John opened his mouth wide. "Hmmm," Hiram said, cocking his head this way and that as he studied his teeth. "You got you a good set of teeth, John. I reckon I won't be seeing you for a good while."

"I hope not, Mr. Henderson," John said with such seriousness it made me smile. "I don't know that I'd like somebody putting a hammer and chisel in my mouth."

Hiram winked at John. "I reckon I feel the same way you do, John, although don't tell anyone that." He threw his head back and roared with laughter. Hiram had an infectious laugh and soon we all joined in.

Once the amusement passed, he cleared his throat and gave me a serious look. "I got called over to Black Mountain the other day to see to old Jebediah Slater. Had him one terrible infected tooth and the son of a gun wouldn't let his daughter fetch me till it almost killed him." He shook his head. "Couldn't eat anything and lost some weight and you know Jebediah was thin as a stick to start with. But now, he's so skinny, he'd have to stand up twice to cast a shadow."

I nodded. Jebediah was tall and lanky and I didn't think there was an ounce of fat on his body. He claimed he had inherited his body shape from his mother's side of the family but I suspected Jebediah would rather drink his supper than eat it. "It's a wonder he's still standing if he lost much weight."

"I told him the same thing. Told him he might ought to come see you, Moonfixer, see if you can give him a tonic to help him gain that lost weight back." He shook his head. "He looks like a scarecrow that's been left out in the field all winter long. Ain't got no color to him, why you can practically see his skull beneath his skin."

Hiram's description concerned me mightily. "I have just the thing." I pointed to my basket. "Dandelion roots will give him his appetite back and I'll be sure to take him some the next day or two. Did you treat the infection, Hiram, or should I take something over to him for that?"

"Well, I packed the gum with salt, you know, like I always do, which is good for an infection, but told him he might try putting honey on it if that don't work. Most people, once the tooth's out, the infection clears up pretty quick. I reckon his daughter will come fetch you if it gets worse or take him to Doc Trenton." He leaned against the porch railing. "Speaking of Doc Trenton, after I got that tooth out of Jeb's head, I decided to pay him a visit. He's fixing to retire you know."

"Yes, Dr. Widby told me that. Did you meet his replacement?"

Hiram's usual cheery, friendly expression changed. His mouth tightened and the lines around his eyes grew more pronounced. "I met him all right, feller by the name of Richard Denby, although he told me to call him *Doctor* Denby. Can't say I like the man any, though."

"Oh? Why's that, Hiram?"

"Started spouting off about eugenics, telling me how much he supports its premise. Said he intends to research the mountain people here, use us as an argument for its implementation."

I sat up straight. "He actually said that?"

"Yep."

"What did Doc Trenton say to all that, Hiram? Surely he doesn't agree with the man."

"Looked to me like he didn't but he held his tongue. I figure the man is so het up about retiring, which is more than likely due to his wife's constant nagging more than anything else, he don't-want to do or say anything that's going to interfere."

"I wonder why in the world he chose our mountain to base his research on," I said more to myself than Hiram.

"You know how them Yankees are about us, Bess. They think because we keep to ourselves, they's got to be something wrong with us. He's probably got it in his head we're all related to one another and don't marry outside the family, that there's all kinds of inbreeding going on." He shook his head. "I swear, nothing makes me hotter than that kind of ignorance."

Hiram was right. There was prejudice about the people of the Appalachian Mountains. Of course, there were instances of inbreeding in other areas but none on our mountain that I was aware of. Mountaineers were an eclectic sort, the kind of people who took care of one another and didn't easily let an outsider in. But that was no reason to lump us all together as an incestuous, illiterate group. I made a promise to myself to meet this doctor and set him straight.

Hiram straightened up. "I reckon I best be getting on afore the sun sets. Why, I'm liable to go off the side of the mountain, it gets so dark up here, and not even realize I've stepped off the road 'til it's too late."

I stood as well. "You're welcome to stay for dinner, Hiram. I figured I'd fix us some fried chicken."

"That sounds awful good, Bess, but my sister Winnie's liable to throw me off the mountain if I eat somewhere else. Whoo-wee, that woman can get madder than a mule chewing on bumblebees when she's cooked my dinner and I eat elsewhere. So, I best stay out of trouble and get on home."

"All right, I'll go get you some ginseng root. You think a half-pint jar will be enough?"

"Yep, that should do me right well."

I hurried into the kitchen to get the ginseng root then carried it back out on the porch. "There you go," I said as I handed it to Hiram.

"Looks good. I thankee, Moonfixer."

"You're more than welcome, Hiram. It's good to see you. Let me know if you need more ginseng or any other herbs."

"Will do." Hiram shook Fletcher's hand then patted John on his head and took his leave. I watched him amble off, saying a silent prayer none of us would need his services for a good while.

.

Chapter Eight

Summer 1925

Your face looks like it caught on fire and was put out with a bag of nickels.

The 1920s was, for me, at least, a time of hope, love and laughter, and I would in later years look back on that stretch of time when John lived with us as the happiest time in my life. I suppose that could all be credited to the fact that Fletcher and I finally had a child of our own to care for and love—Lord knows that alone would have been enough—but more than that, it was a time of serenity and calm on Stone Mountain and in the little town of Old Fort.

While the 1920s would later become known as the "Roaring Twenties" to the rest of the world, they didn't roar so much on Stone Mountain and in the little town of Old Fort. Mayhap they growled a time or two, but for the most part, they were calm and peaceful.

That's not to say there weren't changes on the mountain, but nothing drastic, and change is a part of life, after all.

Hoyt and Maude Berryhill had more or less made their home with Sally Laughter and her children. As they'd recently rented their own house to a man named Sawyer Eldridge and his family, it seemed they didn't have any plans to move back into the small cabin their sons and neighbors had rebuilt for them after their home place was struck by lightning and burned to the ground.

The Eldridge family consisted of Sawyer, his wife Susan, and their two boys and three girls. Fletcher hired Sawyer now and then to do some handiwork around our farm and gave him acreage to sharecrop. But there was something about Sawyer that Fletcher didn't trust and it wasn't long before he began to suspect Sawyer had placed a still somewhere on our property. The boys put on a good-as-gold front when their parents were around but were terrors in my classroom. Susan and the two older girls were shy and reticent and never had much to say for themselves. Sadly, the baby girl showed signs of becoming just like them. It made me wonder what kind of treatment they received at home from their father and two brothers.

Preacher Justice had the congregation of Stone Mountain Baptist Church firmly in hand. While our membership, for the most part, was static, it did fluctuate in tiny increments when someone new moved onto our mountain or someone decided to try their luck in Asheville or another of the bigger towns where work at the factories or lumber companies could be more easily found.

Old Fort gained a bit in population, thanks mostly to people moving away from the rural life to live in settled towns which offered more amenities and substantially more job opportunities, but it didn't grow so much or so fast that the township had problems accommodating all the new people. The Ragle Hotel in town, located across from the train depot, was under new ownership and underwent a bit of sprucing up to better accommodate those visitors who came while they either looked for a more permanent home or conducted whatever business had brought them to our town.

I suppose the biggest change was that Colonel Daniel W. Adams, a local resident and World War I veteran, purchased the land surrounding the Catawba Falls and built a hydro-electric dam to supply the town with electricity. The project took Colonel Adams and his crew three years to complete. It didn't concern me overly much. Electricity might be something city folk craved but I couldn't see it coming up on our mountain any time soon. When it finally did make it up the mountain some years later, Fletcher and I opted not to have it installed in our house.

The '20s did prove to be a challenge to most farmers with more than a few of them simply giving up and moving away to the towns and cities to find work in the factories. But thanks mostly to the hard work of my husband, our little farm prospered, and Fletch proved ingenious at coming up with new ways to make money. As for me, I had a teaching job I loved and enjoyed. We felt blessed to be surrounded by friends and loved ones whose company we enjoyed and friendship we cherished.

Outside Old Fort, the world itself was changing by leaps and bounds, at least as far as society was concerned.

Women were behind most of the changes during that time, campaigning and, in a few cases, actually being elected to state and city governments. In January, Nellie Tayloe Ross of Wyoming was sworn in as the first woman governor in the United States. North Carolina, though it hadn't ratified the 19th amendment yet and wouldn't during my lifetime, already had a woman elected to a seat on the state legislature. Though Lillian Exum Clement only served one term, retiring to take care of her family, she paved the way for women in North Carolina politics. Sadly, Mrs. Clement, or Ex as she was called by friends and family, died of pneumonia during the winter of 1925.

And many more women throughout the country were standing up and making changes, too. They went after and held jobs that were typically only filled by men, got involved in politics now that they had the vote, wore clothes that in my earlier days would have gotten them arrested, and even smoked cigarettes and drank hard liquor in public, habits that as a rule were formerly only indulged in by men.

Although 1925 turned out to be a year that wasn't particularly noteworthy in the historical sense at the time, the events that occurred proved to have long-lasting effects.

On May 27th, an explosion at the Carolina Coal Company in Coal Glen, North Carolina killed 53 miners. The explosion helped to spur the state's Worker's Compensation

Act, though it took four long years for it to pass. Atrocious as it was, the tragedy didn't impact us much on Stone Mountain other than to garnish prayers for the dead and wounded during Sunday services but it left us feeling both horrible at such a terrible loss to our neighbors and thankful our loved ones had been spared.

That summer, most of our country was enthralled with our neighboring state, Tennessee, and what came to be known as the Scopes Monkey Trial, never suspecting the manipulation used to bring the trial about.

In March, Tennessee became the first state to pass the Butler Act, an anti-evolution law, outlawing the teaching of Darwin's theory of evolution in its schools. Many other states soon followed, but Tennessee led the way. Unbeknownst to most everyone, including myself, a few people gathered in a drugstore in the small town of Dayton decided the Butler Act would be a grand way for the town to make a profit if they could find a teacher who would admit to teaching Darwin's theory, have him arrested, and arrange for the trial to be held in their little town. In May, they found their man in John T. Scopes, a coach at the local high school who occasionally filled in as a substitute teacher.

Mr. Scopes was arrested early in May and indicted a few weeks later. His trial, with Clarence Darrow representing Scopes and William Jennings Bryan as opposing counsel, began on the 10th of July and was the first trial to be broadcast on the radio. Needless to say, Nettie Ledbetter was in her heyday. She kept everyone informed of what was happening and when people didn't ask promptly told them anyway, never forgetting to add that she'd listened to the entire trial on her Westinghouse radio. I suspect she was telling the truth, only leaving during the broadcast to make trips to the privy. Mercy, that woman talked of nothing else and I admit I was a bit relieved when it concluded on July 21st. Scopes was found guilty and fined $100 but the conviction was later overturned on a technicality.

It all seemed silly to me, to waste all that time and money convincing people of something most of them already believed.

In July, a man named Adolf Hitler, head of the German National Socialist Workers Party, published *Mein Kamph*, calling for a national revival and war against communism and Jews. Hitler, though not well-known at the time, would, in the next decade, become infamous for his ruthless and vindictive actions and would play a key part in leading our country into another world war.

Back in America, the Ku Klux Clan held their first national congress and planned to march on Washington, DC in August. It was reported they had 200,000 members and intended to burn a cross in Virginia. Thankfully, that was avoided because of inclement weather but 40,000 made it to our capital, spewing their hatred and intolerance as they went.

I followed the story about their march on Washington, DC in the papers and even found myself wishing I had access to Nettie's radio so I could hear more about their doings. I often wondered if the radio ever relayed news about the Red Shirt Democrats, who had brought heartbreak and loss into my life, but Nettie never said so. I diligently searched though each newspaper I read for news about this secret organization but it seemed their activities remained covert. Their goals seemed to be in line with that of the KKK and I feared the two groups would join together in an effort to become more powerful. As far as I knew, that never happened, but I always thought it a possibility.

But at that time, those events seemed far away and were things I couldn't do much about, and since life on my mountain was currently running as smooth as silk, my thoughts didn't dwell on them overmuch.

After teaching John for the past year at home, my decision not to enroll him in my school that year was of utmost concern to me. I flip-flopped several times before I told myself to make up my mind one way or the other and stick with it. What finally decided me was the fact that John was so happy spending time with Fletch, who was teaching him things he would need to know later in life, skills he couldn't get out of books or in a classroom. And so, come September, John would be staying home with Fletcher and I would continue to teach him in the afternoons and evenings. I could enroll him during the school year, perhaps after Christmas break, if I changed my mind. But I didn't think I would do that since he was making good progress without going to school.

John's reading had improved greatly. I'd taught him using syllables rather than sounding out individual letters and he'd taken to it like a duck to water. Of course, that may have been more to Fletcher's credit than mine, as Fletch would have him read a verse or two from the Bible each night and always praised him mightily when he did. As for writing and arithmetic, I had tested him here and there on what he would need to know when he entered the second grade and found his skills to be more than adequate. He had beautiful handwriting, a wonderful and curious imagination about nature and science, and a love of history. At such a young age, he already showed an impressive artistic talent, drawing better than anyone on the mountain. I couldn't know it then, of course, but that was a talent he would carry with him and improve on throughout his life.

One Saturday in early August, John was home with me since Fletcher was busy cutting hay, a chore that could be dangerous for an easily distracted young boy. It was one of the few times I remember thinking Papa had been right when he said raising a young'un, especially a bored one, is sometimes like being pecked to death by a chicken. On Saturdays, I usually made my weekly check on Bob Bartlett, Jr. so told John I needed him to come with me to help carry things. I had yet another herbal remedy to take for Bob Jr. as well as some green beans and corn from our garden and a couple of jars of sausage I had canned last year after our annual hog-killing. Fletcher had mentioned the night before that hog-killing time was nigh so I wanted to clear my shelves.

Fritz trotted alongside us and we passed the time on the walk over by singing hymns and reciting some poems I'd had John memorize over the past year. He told me about a dream he'd had the night before where he and Fritz had been swimming in a pond on a hot summer day.

"Was the water clear or muddy?" I asked.

"Clear. I could see all the way down to my toes and Fritz must've drank about a gallon of it. I told him he better stop or he'd be sicker than a dog." He looked up and grinned at me. "But he just kept on drinking until, sure enough, he sicked all that water back up. It was nasty."

Fritz, as if understanding him, barked in agreement.

I laughed. "Maybe next time he'll listen to you. I don't know what Fritz getting sick means but Elisi once told me that clear water in a dream is a good thing. It means something good is going to happen to you."

"What, Aunt Bessie?"

"Hard to say. I guess we'll just have to wait and see what happens. Maybe you'll meet a new friend or find a penny or something like that."

"Aw, a penny's nothing to get excited about. Maybe I'll find a silver dollar." He looked intently at the ground. "That would be something real good."

"Why, what would you do with that much money?"

"Maybe I'll buy a fancy postcard and send it to Grandpapa John. I could tell him about fishing with Hoover or hunting with Uncle Fletcher."

"It could happen, I suppose. Meanwhile, you better look where you're going or something bad might happen instead." I put my hand on his shoulder and nudged him to the right. "This is the cutoff to the Bartlett farm, John."

Maisie and her youngest daughter Sari were standing on the front porch waiting for us when we arrived.

Sari's face lit up with a smile and she raised a hand to wave when she saw John. "Hey, John. Wanna go slide down the haystack with me?"

John looked up at me. When I nodded, he shrugged his shoulders in Sari's general direction.

"Mornin', Maisie," I called as we approached the porch steps. "How's our boy doing this morning?"

The lines between her eyes deepened. This was all taking a toll on Maisie. She had always been a thin woman but had lost so much weight over the past year that she was now so skinny she could, as I'd once heard Aunt Belle say, use a clothes-line as an umbrella. And her pretty face showed signs of the constant worry too. Her complexion had turned sallow, her lips seemed to be stuck in a perpetual frown, and her hair had gone from a lustrous red to a dull russet with threads of grey running through it. Today, she looked more tired than ever and I wished I could give her something that would bring back her once radiant smile.

"He's 'bout the same." She wrung her hands together. "Why don't he wake up, Bess?"

I stepped up on the porch and took her hand in mine. "I wish I could answer that question, Maisie, but I can't." I smiled at Sari. "Good morning, miss."

"Mornin', Miss Bessie. Can John go with me to slide down the haystack? Papa and the boys have it almost up to the loft window."

"That sounds like fun." I looked back at John. "I need to speak with Mrs. Bartlett, John. You run along with Sari and I'll call you when it's time to leave. Take Fritz with you and try to keep him out of Mr. Bartlett's pasture."

"Yes, ma'am. Come on, Sari." He took a couple of hesitant steps then turned and yelled, "Race ya'," before taking off around the side of the house with Sari in hot pursuit.

I turned back to Maisie. "I know I've said this many times, Maisie, but I'll say it again. You have to have faith that Bob Jr. will get well. Doc Widby and I are going to keep trying until we can look into those warm brown eyes of his and see him smile again."

She sighed. "It's been almost a year, Bessie, and my faith is wearing a little thin right now."

"Yes, I know. And I know it's hard but I'll bet if Bob Jr. could speak he'd tell you not to give up on him. I think he's trying as hard to wake up as we're trying to get him to."

A solitary tear trickled out of her right eye. She wiped it away with her apron, took another deep breath, and squared her thin shoulders. "I'm sorry, Bessie. Of course, I believe that you and Doc Widby are going to make my boy well. It's just that lately, I have times when I'm sure he'll never wake up." She waved a hand. "And then not three minutes later, I'm sure he will. I don't know what's wrong with me these days."

I smiled. "How old are you, Maisie, if you don't mind my asking?"

"I reckon I don't mind. I'm 51."

I lowered my voice, knowing that some women were reluctant to share personal facts about themselves. "And are your monthlies still regular?"

She blushed and took a quick look around before answering. "Not as regular as they used to be. A few months ago, long about Christmas or thereabouts, I reckon, I was convinced I was carryin'. But a couple of weeks later, that notion was put to rest. Thank goodness. Can you imagine dealing with a baby now what with Bob Jr. needing all my care and time?"

"No, I can't and I'm glad you don't have to." I gentled my voice, knowing that some women reacted badly to hearing they were getting older. "I think it's possible you're going through the change, Maisie."

"The change? Why, whatever are you ..." Her eyes opened wide and she gaped at me. "Oh, well, the change. Don't know why I didn't think about that what with the way my mood changes on a dime these days."

"Do you get so hot sometimes you feel like you're on fire?"

She nodded and then slapped her forehead. "Stupid as a bag of rocks, that's what I am."

"Oh, I don't think so. You've had a lot to deal with in the past months." I winked. "And I've heard it said that menopause sometimes makes a woman a bit, well, flighty."

She laughed. "Well, it looks like I have all the symptoms. Thank you, Bessie." She pulled her hankie out of her sleeve and waved it in front of her face as her cheeks went fire red. "Speaking of being hot. That sure does take a load off my mind. I was afraid it might be something serious."

"No, not serious, at least health-wise, but you do need to take special care of yourself. I know some herbs, black cohosh extract, red clover leaf extract, and ginseng root, that might help."

"I'm willing to try anything. Bob Sr. will sure be happy to hear this. Why, I liked to snatched him bald this morning and all because he topped off the coffee in my cup without asking me first." She shook her head. "And I can't tell you how many hissy fits I've pitched with Bob Jr. trying to make him sit up and pay attention to me. Reckon I'll have to apologize to him for those when he wakes up."

It did my heart good to see her smiling and thinking more positive thoughts, and I said a quick prayer that her hope wouldn't prove false. I winked at her. "I won't tell him if you won't."

She hooked her arm through mine. "It's a deal. Now let's go see to my boy and then we'll have a cup of tea and you can tell me all about those herbs."

I gave Sari an infusion made with St. John's wort and hawthorn berries, sweetened with a bit of honey for Bob Jr. Normally used for anxiety or to lift someone's spirits, St. John's wort was one of the many remedies Elisi had taught me but I'd never prepared this particular infusion before. I worried that I may have made it too weak to do any good but thought if we started with a weaker version of the infusion first we could watch for any adverse reactions before I gave it to him full strength. I had discussed it with Doc Widby and he had agreed with me, saying, "Even them fancy doctors over in Europe don't have any idea how to treat this, Bessie. Hellfire … excuse me, Bessie … anything's worth trying right now, if you ask me."

I instructed Maisie on how to give the infusion to Bob Jr. I also told her it was safe for her to use herself to treat some of the symptoms she might experience from the change. Then we settled in the kitchen with a cup of tea and discussed the other herbs and wildflowers that might help with her symptoms, primarily black cohosh to ward off the hot flashes, St. John's wort to help with her moods, and passion flower for sleeplessness.

On the way home, John was unusually quiet. He'd spent the entire morning playing with Sari and I wondered if he might be suffering from his first case of "puppy love". I toyed with that idea for a few minutes, but luckily before I had them walking down the aisle, John said, "Aunt Bessie, I feel sorry for Sari."

I glanced down at him. "You mean because her brother's sick?"

"No, Sari says he's going to get better soon and when he does she's going to miss going into his room and making funny faces at him."

I laughed. "She does that?"

"Yep, she says she's trying to scare him awake."

"Does her mother know?"

He shrugged his shoulders. "I don't know. You're not going to tell her, are you? I don't want to get Sari in trouble."

I crossed my heart. "Her secret's safe with me. So why do you feel sorry for her?"

He cocked his head to the side and buried his hand in the scruff on Fritz's neck, a sure sign he was feeling nervous. "Well … when we were sliding on the haystack, a couple of times I beat Sari to the bottom, and when I turned around to watch her slide down, her dress flew up and she didn't have any underwear on and, well, she doesn't have a, a, you know, a *thing*."

I had to bite my cheek to hold in the laughter. Not at John, but from the delight I felt knowing that he felt comfortable enough to ask me such a question rather than waiting to ask Fletch.

And so, we spent the trip home talking about the difference between boys and girls and why God had made us that way. I tiptoed around the birds and the bees, but when I noticed John's little face turning red, I decided I'd leave the more intimate facts for his uncle to share with him when the time came. I figured he'd be a mite more comfortable talking to another man about what happens when a man and woman are in love and get married.

Chapter Nine

Fall 1926

He's so crooked you can't tell from his tracks if he's coming or going.

Even though John didn't attend school, he would at times accompany me part of the way in the mornings and in the afternoons would meet me along the pathway to walk me home. This little boy, who favored his grandfather so much an ache of longing to see my father would shoot through me when I looked at him, had quickly ingrained himself into our lives to the point that it seemed he had always been part of our family. That tiny seed of love I felt when first I saw him had quickly taken root when he came to live with us, unfurling and blossoming into something so deep and profound it frightened me at times. For I couldn't bear the thought of ever losing anything so precious.

Walking along one morning, the ever loyal Fritz at his side, John would from time to time step off the path to touch a tree then proudly name it for me. I noted the respect he showed each one and knew my husband had something to do with that. Fletcher held all things in nature in great awe and it pleased me he had relayed this to this small boy.

"Mercy, John, you can identify more trees than me. How is that?" I asked, knowing the answer.

"Uncle Fletch tells me their names and shows me how to tell them apart." He rubbed the bark of a lofty oak. "I like trees, Aunt Bessie. Sometimes it seems to me they're alive just like us."

I smiled at him. "They are alive, John, and serve God's purpose by helping to purify our air. Why, if it weren't for trees and plants, we wouldn't even be here on this Earth."

His eyes went wide. "Really?"

I nodded. "Yes."

"I guess that makes 'em one of God's creatures, just like us."

"Maybe not a creature but certainly one of God's beings. The People say the Plants had a special relationship with Mother Earth to give life and oxygen for the animals and humans to breathe. But the Plants serve another purpose, to help teach the People how to heal from illnesses and disease. So the Plant Clan held a council and decided it would be helpful to have different tastes and colors because the humans were still young and had a lot to learn. In the presence of the Sun, the Plants developed many varieties with different shapes so that humans could recognize them and the humans did very well at giving them names based on their shapes. One plant said, 'I will be bright purple and make myself like a horn so the humans can see me in the dark.' We call those nightshades. This was a very long council, as the plants decided ways to have presence for the humans to learn the Medicine. After all, the Great One intended the humans to be keepers of Mother Earth and it was decided in the council of the Plant Clan for all plants to be helpers to the human spirits from that day on."

His eyes widened. "Really?"

"Yes," I said, trying not to smile too widely.

"Well, then, I reckon I'll try to be as good a keeper as I can, Aunt Bessie."

"Me too, John."

Fritz spotted a squirrel, barked once then took off after it. John whistled and he came trotting back, a sheepish look on his face. Giving him a scratch between the ears, John praised him for obeying his call then pointed to a towering pine tree beside the path. "That's a pine, Aunt Bessie. I like the way they smell."

"I do too, John." I studied him for a moment. "Do you know how the pine tree came to be?"

He thought about this, his face so serious and studious, and shook his head. "Nope, don't reckon I do."

I smiled, glad to share another one of my great-grandmother Elisi's stories with her great-great-grandson. "According to the Cherokee, very early in the existence of our People, there were seven boys who did nothing but play the Indian ball game of moving a round stone across the ground with a stick. This did not please their mothers because the boys would rather play than work in the cornfields. One evening, the boys went home to eat after playing ball and were very hungry. Their mothers put the ball stones in water and told them since they wouldn't work, they could have the stones for supper instead of corn. The young boys were very upset and left, saying, 'We will never come back home again.' They began to do the Feather Dance, which is a dance using smell steps and moving around in a circle, praying to the spirits to take them away. Suddenly, their feet lifted off the ground as they continued to dance around and around. Their mothers went to find the boys and saw they were going higher and higher in the air toward the great skyvault. They tried to pull them down but the boys kept going upward. They let go but one mother hung onto her son and he finally fell to the ground but the other six were pulled higher and higher until they went into the skyvault.

"Some say you can see them at night as the Pleiades or 'The Boys' as they are called by our People. The seventh boy who struck the ground fell so hard, he was covered by the earth and never found again. The mothers were very sad and grieved every day, their tears falling on the ground where the boys once were. And one day, they noticed that a small tree had started to sprout from the place where the seventh boy struck the ground."

I hesitated, watching as John smiled. "Was it the pine tree, Aunt Bessie?"

I tousled his hair. "It sure was, John."

He nodded as if contemplating this and simply said, "That's good to know."

I grinned. By this time we had reached the place where he usually turned back, and my nephew, who seemed shy and not one to show affection, surprised me by throwing his arms around my waist and giving me a quick hug before leaving, calling bye over his shoulder and hurrying away as if embarrassed at this display. I threw a kiss his way and walked on, a smile on my face and a glowing warmth in my heart.

That afternoon, disappointed John wasn't waiting at the place in the path where he sometimes met me after school, I found myself a bit surprised to realize how much catching sight of his smiling face brightened my afternoons. I walked on, hoping to see him standing on the path but figured he was probably still helping Fletch with chores or they had gone on one of Fletch's long walks. I swan, that man loved to walk more than anyone I've ever known and seemed happy when John accompanied him.

As I crossed the bridge over the creek on our property, I spied Fletch and John talking to a man near the barn, the man gesturing at the mountains around us. When I drew nearer, Fletch's disgruntled expression told me this was not a welcome visit. Curious as to the man's reason for being there, I joined them. I kissed my husband and John on their respective cheeks, gave Fritz a pat on the head and nodded hello to the man. He was tall and gangly with a prominent Adam's apple that looked as if something had gotten stuck in his throat. He wore a rumpled suit topped by a felt hat which he continued to take off his head so he could blot perspiration off his forehead with a soiled handkerchief. His face was long and narrow, a bit fox-like with reddish whiskers covering his cheeks and upper neck that closely matched the long curls cascading over his scalp. I suspected he kept his hair long to cover his large and protuberant ears but his effort seemed only to emphasize their size. His green eyes were wide and set far apart, giving him a somewhat startled look, set above a large hooked nose which dominated his face. As Fletch made the introductions, I noted this stranger was assessing me as I had him. I wondered for a moment how he would perceive me then decided it didn't matter one way or the other to me.

"Bess, this is Mr. Evans," Fletcher said. Without lowering his voice, he added, "He's a timber cruiser."

I drew myself up, narrowing my eyes, and raised my eyebrows at Fletch, mentally asking him why in the world he'd let this man on our property.

"I was just about to ask him to leave," Fletch said.

"Now, now, let's not act too rashly," Mr. Evans said in a deep, melodic voice which belonged in a church choir.

"You have no business here, Mr. Evans," I said, more harshly than I meant to. It was because of men like him and the companies they represented that the forests had been severely damaged from overharvesting. My favorite tree, the American Chestnut, was close to extinction, felled by zealous lumber companies which sprang unscrupulous men like Mr. Evans and an Asian fungus introduced into the chestnut trees at the Bronx Zoo in New York back in 1904 which quickly spread throughout the Appalachians. I had recently read there was no saving them and they would one day soon be extinct. Oh, I wish you could have seen the mountains when one of every four trees was a chestnut and they dominated the Appalachian landscape. They towered 100 feet above the forest floor and bore an acre full of leaves, I'm told a million or so in all. Though not the loftiest trees in the mountains, only half the height of the tallest eastern pines, their weight and mass were unlike the others. At ground level, a full-sized Chestnut tree could be as much as 20 feet around. Their abundant blooms in June were beautiful to behold which I read naturalist Donald Culross Peattie akined to "a sea with white combers plowing across its surface". I thought that a very apt description.

Mr. Evans gave me a beguiling smile. "Nice to meet you, ma'am. First name's Seth, if you prefer informality."

"We're not interested in selling our land," Fletcher said, "and I reckon it'd be best if you just went on your way."

Mr. Evans acted as if he hadn't heard. "Well, now," he drawled, looking around at the forest surrounding us, "I had a look at your deed, seen you have about 400 acres here of what used to be the Zachariah Solomon plantation." He eyed the ridge behind us. "That the one they call Flinty Knob?"

When Fletch didn't answer, he continued as if he hadn't asked the question. "Looks to me like most of your acreage is hardwood." He paused to spit a stream of tobacco juice on the ground. "I'd say, from a cursory glance, you got about 3,000 board feet per acre here, and that's nothing to dismiss. Economy's starting to sour, as I'm sure you know." He took a moment to eye John, wearing pants, no shirt and no shoes. Why, he thinks we're poor, I thought, with a surge of anger. "All that prosperity after the Great War is on the decline. Even cotton's been hit. Sold for 35 cents per pound back in 1919 but its quickly declining. I bet it'll be below 10 cents a pound afore too long." He leaned toward us and winked. "And you know I'm right, don't say you don't."

"Mr. Evans, we have enough to sustain us, even with a poor economy," I said, "though it's no business of yours."

"Logging's gonna be gone from this area afore too long, you know," he continued, ignoring me. "Most if it's moving to the virgin forests of the Mississippi Delta, where there's plenty of hardwood just for the taking. But I'm giving you the chance to make some money here, something to sustain you through the hard times that are coming our way." He smiled with certainty.

Fletch stared at him long and hard, as though considering his words with much sincerity. Then, finally, he leaned toward Mr. Evans and said in a low voice, "How much you reckon I can get from all this timber I got?"

I stifled a gasp of horror. Surely Fletcher wouldn't sell our land.

Mr. Evans' eyes lit up like he'd just landed the biggest fish in the ocean. "Well, now, I'd have to do some figuring. But we can talk about that later. All I need is you to sign this agreement I got with me here and we can get down to business."

Fletcher tipped back on his heels. "Oh, no need for that, Mr. Evans."

"Well, a handshake will do me if it'll do you," Evans said.

Fletcher shook his head. "I reckon I've seen what the lumber mills have done to these mountains. Why, if it wasn't for George Washington Biltmore and that German forester he brought in to manage his woodlands, the Pisgah Forest would probably be as bald as a baby's bottom. Now, the way I see it, I've worked for sawmills before, know the what and the how of it, and if I wanted to sell timber off my land, I'd set up my own sawmill and work it myself and keep the money, not give it to some greedy lumber company that doesn't care a whit about what kind of damage they leave behind." He swept his hand at the mountains around us. "This is God's beauty, and he didn't put humans here to lay it bare, erode it, skin it like a dead carcass." He pointed his finger at Mr. Evans. "And this here is my land and my responsibility. I'm here to protect it, you see, and to keep marauders like you out. Now, you don't get off my land, I reckon I'll have to help you off it, and not in a nice way either." He stood straight, his eyes hard, his mouth set in a firm line. I glanced at John, wide-eyed and open-mouthed, and imagined this was the first time he had seen his amiable uncle in a snit. My eyes returned to my husband, looking solid and strong and a bit put out, and I smiled, thinking how proud I was to be his wife and how much I loved him.

After a few moments of staring back, Mr. Evans cleared his throat. "Well, I reckon this is something you need to think about so I best be getting on now." He nodded in my direction and began walking backward. "But don't think this is the end of it. I'm just the first person you'll be meeting. Them mountains up there," he raised his eyes to the ridgeline behind us, "they're exactly what we're looking for. You ain't seen the last of us ..."

Fletcher started toward him and the man turned around and fled.

I laughed when Fletcher rejoined us. "You had me scared for a moment there. Why didn't you throw him off when you knew who he was?"

Fletcher shrugged. "Sometimes, Bess, it's a bit fun to play with them, see what happens."

I shook my head, smiling at John, who was laughing.

Mr. Evans made good on his promise. The next Sunday, I spied him sitting in the back of the church during morning service. I glanced around for Fletcher and when our eyes met cast mine toward Mr. Evans. Fletcher looked that way and with a grimace gave me a curt nod of acknowledgement. I turned my attention back to the piano, curious why the timber cruiser had shown up here at Stone Mountain Baptist Church. I strongly suspected it wasn't to worship.

After the service was over, as per usual on a temperate day, the congregants gathered around outside, visiting with one another, catching up on the latest gossip and each others' lives. I made my way through the crowd, holding John's hand, smiling and pausing to speak to friends, trying to find the timber cruiser. I spied him standing under a large pine, a group of men gathered around him. Mr. Evans must have been giving his spiel, as he waved his arms around, and it concerned me that more than a few were nodding their heads in agreement with whatever he was telling them. I watched Fletcher, accompanied by Thorney Dalton, approach Bull Elliott and Possum Gilliam and hold conference with them for several minutes. Bull and Possum, not ones for subtlety, kept casting Mr. Evans ominous glances. When Fletcher finished speaking, they puffed out their chests, hitched up their pants, and ambled over to Mr. Evans. Although I didn't hear what they said to him, they must have made their point, because Mr. Evans stuffed his hat back on his head and hurried off. Bull and Possum gave each other curt nods of approval and, strutting like bantam roosters, made their way over to a group of giggling young ladies.

I couldn't help but laugh.

Fletcher joined me, smiling when he saw my amused expression. "What did you say to them?" I asked.

"Told 'em who he was, what he wanted, and suggested he might be bringing some handsome, muscular lumberjacks to the mountain to cut wood. Suggested they might not want such fierce competition for the young ladies' attention."

"I agree," I said with a laugh.

Bull and Possum were always chasing after the unmarried young women on the mountain and so far seemed to be fairly successful at securing dates, although neither one was particularly handsome or muscular. Bull had more fat around his belly than a pig and Gilliam looked like a miniature version of what a man should be. I imagined neither one would contend well with competition from handsome, muscular men outside the mountain.

I hoped that would be the end of the timber cruiser but at our weekly prayer meeting on Wednesday night, as the women were putting things to right in the kitchen, Nettie Ledbetter said to no one in particular, "Merle and I had a most interesting meeting with a Mr. Evans yesterday."

I turned to her. "The timber cruiser?"

The other women paused in their duties, ears perked with interest.

"What's a timber cruiser?" Melanie Nanny, the sheriff's wife, asked.

"A man sent out by lumber companies to try to get land owners to agree to sell them the timber off their lands," I said. "These companies move in and cause the worst kind of damage."

Nettie made a huffing noise. "You have a contrary opinion of these lumber companies, Bessie. From what Mr. Evans told us, they can provide economic growth to a community. Why, according to him, they create jobs harvesting the timber and milling it at their sawmill. Sometimes they're so productive, they even set up their own little town with its own store, church and school."

"While raping the land," I said.

Junior Hall's grandmother snorted her amusement as she struggled to gain her feet. I reached out to help her and she gave me a conspiratorial wink.

Nettie gasped, her hand flying to her ample bosom. "That's a strong word for such a mundane operation.

Certainly they cut timber off the land but I doubt they," she hesitated, unwilling to say the word, "do any sort of real damage. After all, trees can be planted again."

"Nettie, it takes years for a tree to mature. Look at these mountains around us, covered with all these beautiful trees and think what it would look like without them, all those gorgeous tulip trees, chestnuts, red oaks, poplar, basswoods and ash trees gone. The land would be not only bare but nonproductive. They think only of the money to be made while doing nothing but damaging the land by clearing it of trees and transporting the lumber to market by skidding the logs down the mountains to get them to splash dams they create on streams. It's bad enough they cut the trees down but even worse what they do to the land transporting the timber. Splash dams have been proven to be the most destructive logging technique ever devised. Look at what happened to the Pigeon River in Newport in '86 when the flood swept through. I read logs were scattered clear to the Gulf of Mexico. But that doesn't matter to them, all they care about is making money at the expense of the land and the people they leave behind."

"Mr. Evans assured us they won't use the splash dam method to transport the logs out of the mountains. We've got the railroad." She smiled with pleasure.

"But how will they get them to the railroad?"

"Oh I imagine by horse and wagon."

"They'll need to create roads out of the mountain to use for transporting the lumber," Melanie said. "If they cut most of the timber, Nettie, they'll create erosion of the worst kind. These mountains can't stand that kind of treatment. I've lived here all my life and pray to God I never see destruction of that sort."

Nettie huffed. "You're talking about a lot of ifs. Mr. Evans assured me they would not overharvest and any sort of damage they inadvertently cause they will restore. We have to look at this from an economic standpoint. We have such poverty on this mountain and think what it will do for our community if everyone has a job, a means of income other than farming or making moonshine. Our young people won't run off to a city once they're grown where they can work and make money. They can stay here. It won't be as terrible as you think."

"So far we've all managed to survive," I said.

She sniffed with disdain. "Well, of course you would say that, Bessie. You have a job teaching and Fletcher has all this land to farm." She gestured toward Melanie. "Melanie's husband's the sheriff. She doesn't have to worry about making an income." She leaned toward me. "I listen to the news on the radio every night and, unlike most of the people on this mountain, have been keeping up with what's happening in the world outside our mountain. Have you seen what's going on with the stock market? Up and down and out of control while prices go up, up, up. Why, they're saying on the radio that some economists are now predicting we're headed for a depression if things don't turn around."

I stared at her, wondering why she seemed so willing to leave the future of our community to a lumber company that had proven in the past it cared nothing for the mountain or mountaineers it would leave behind. Was it greed or were she and Merle in financial distress? They seemed to do well enough with Merle's tobacco crop. "Nettie, as you know, we help those who need it. No one on this mountain goes without unless it's in secret. That's not the kind of people we are."

"All I know is life could be a lot better for some on this mountain if we allow this lumber company access to the timber."

Mrs. Hall set the plate in her hand on the table with a loud clatter. We all turned to her, waiting for her to catch her breath. The poor woman suffered from emphysema and her gray pallor told me she was having a bad day. "I lived on this mountain my whole life," she wheezed, to no one in particular. "I ain't got much but I don't need much. But I got one thing to say on this matter then I'll take my leave." She pointed at Nettie and struggled to draw in a deep breath. "This is God's world and from what I've witnessed the past seventy plus years, it don't take man long to destroy what God creates. You let those men on this mountain, they'll do more damage than good and you know that in your heart. You're letting greed control your thinking and the Bible don't agree with that. Mayhap I'd like a prettier house, money to buy me some things that might make my situation a bit easier. But I won't do it at the cost of this mountain." She nodded for emphasis then waddled her way out of the room.

Nettie shook her head, glaring at me. "I see you've made up your mind. But there are other people who live on this mountain, Bessie, and I think once they listen to what Mr. Evans and his company can offer them, they'll be more than willing to let them cut timber off their property." She gave a curt nod. "I'll say good evening and hopefully the next meeting won't be so acrimonious."

Melanie and I looked at one another, both, I'm sure, sharing the same thought. We could not let this timber cruiser convince these mountaineers to give over their land to a lumber company that did not hold their best interests at heart.

It did not take Mr. Evans long to cause conflict among the mountaineers, promising those in need that they could live a luxurious life with more than they would ever want. As a teacher, I witnessed the poverty on the mountain firsthand. Many of my students came to school barefoot, dressed in clothes far too big for them, hand-me-downs from their brothers or sisters, or ones they had long outgrown. Many of the girls wore dresses made out of flour sacks. There was one family whose children went without clothes during the summer. I, along with other women in my prayer group, sewed shirts and pants and dresses for these youngsters, shared with their families the harvest from our gardens. I could understand the yearning for a better life, one not so hard, with full bellies all the time and more than one change of clothes. But I knew from what I had read and heard that the promises made by this lumber company were simply made to get what they wanted. The families would receive money for their timber, but it would be no more than a pittance, not what they deserved, and when the lumber company was finished with the land, they wouldn't even be able to plant a summer garden to bide them through the winter.

Chapter Ten

Fall 1926

Don't let the tail wag the dog.

JOHN

I reckon when Uncle Fletcher got mad at the timber cruiser that was the first time I'd ever actually seen my uncle angry and it was something to behold. Why, he looked like he could pick that man up and throw him clear across the creek. And he probably could. I'd watched my uncle do manual labor around the farm and thought he was the strongest man I'd ever seen. I felt safe and secure around him and was proud to be seen with him and each day wanted to be more and more like him.

My aunt and uncle had many conversations about Mr. Evans and his promises to the mountaineers. There were a lot of poor people on the mountain and they thought several families would believe him when he told them they would have plenty of money if they allowed the lumber company to harvest the timber. But Mr. Evans made it clear that the lumber company wanted the entire mountain, not just bits and pieces, so everyone had to be in agreement. It seemed the people of Stone Mountain were split two ways, either for or against leasing land to the lumber company. It got so bad that church services usually ended in arguments, some developing into physical altercations between men with opposing views. Uncle Fletcher and the other deacons kept busy trying to break up fights or stop them before they got started.

It was during this time that I began to have headaches along with aching muscles and feeling tired all the time. Aunt Bessie figured my blood might be low so had me drink a tonic made out of sassafras, dandelion and goldenseal. It perked me up a bit but not by much. I didn't want to worry her so tried to act normal, even though I had no appetite and would rather stay in bed than get up and go about my chores. But when I woke up one morning a couple of weeks later with swollen cheeks and a fever, I knew I couldn't hide this from my aunt. The minute she saw me, she told me I had the mumps and to get back in bed. Most of the next week is lost to me as the fever raged and my head ached and felt too heavy to lift. I remember my aunt encouraging me to drink soups and water, but the most profound memory I have is of her kneeling by my bed, praying for me. I had never had anyone pray for me before and was shocked by the thought that someone cared enough about me to ask God to look after me. Her prayers must have worked because within a day or two I felt much better and after another week was back to my usual self. I often wondered what would have happened if I hadn't been under my aunt's tender care.

By the next Sunday, Aunt Bessie thought I was well enough to go to church. I was happy at this news. I'd missed watching all the arguing going on over whether or not to sell timber off the mountain. At the end of church service, Reverend Justice announced a meeting for the following Monday evening about the timber company's offer. A lot of people started hollering, some thinking it was a good idea, others objecting to it. It got so bad, Uncle Fletcher and Thorney Dalton had to break up a couple of fistfights before they got out of hand and drew in more men. After all the hullabaloo died down, Reverend Justice said Mr. Evans would be there to speak his piece and everyone would get a chance to state their opinion if they so desired. He implored his congregants to act in a civil manner and not get carried away by their feelings to the point they would do something they might regret later. On the way home, Aunt Bessie told me that was probably the smartest thing to do, a way for the mountaineers to debate the issue and put an end to the discord once and for all. I was glad the mumps were behind me. I wanted to attend that meeting, hoping I'd get the chance to watch a fistfight or two.

The next evening, after dinner, Uncle Fletcher said, "I don't reckon it's a good idea for little John to attend the meeting, Bessie. I'm afraid things might get out of hand and I don't want him to witness any sort of violent confrontation which I'm sure is going to happen. The people on this mountain ain't been so riled since Sally Laughter..." he glanced at me but didn't finish.

I wondered briefly what had happened with Sally Laughter. I'd met her a time or two and thought her awful pretty. She always had a whole passel of children tagging along behind her but didn't seem to mind at all, even appeared happy about it. That thought was quickly replaced by an urgent need to beg them to be allowed to go to the meeting. I knew there'd be trouble and wanted to be witness to any sort of physical altercation that might go on.

Aunt Bessie untied her apron and set it aside. "Well, he's seen confrontation over this very issue during church services and it might be an important lesson for our John, Fletch, seeing the way a community tries to resolve a problem among its denizens. Besides it's liable to be awful late by the time we get back home and I don't want him here by himself after dark." She picked up her bonnet and settled it on her head. "I'm sure there will be other children there, and if things get out of hand, we can always send them outside to play."

Uncle Fletch considered that for a moment before giving her a curt nod. "I reckon since you're a teacher, you'd know better what to do than me. I'll go hitch up the wagon and we'll be on our way." He glanced at me. "You want to help, John?"

"I sure do," I said, following him out. I liked to help my Uncle Fletcher. It made me feel important and he always treated me as if I could do everything just as well as he could.

I reckon most of the mountain people turned out for that meeting. When we arrived at the church, a host of people stood outside talking amongst themselves but many more were already inside, some seated, some on their feet, speaking in loud voices.

Reverend Justice approached us as we walked up the front steps and drew Uncle Fletcher aside. "Fletch, I wonder if you and Thorney Dalton can find a couple of other deacons to help out? I'd like you all at the front of the church in case things get out of hand."

Uncle Fletch nodded. "I'd say that's a good idea, Reverend. I'm sure Merle Ledbetter's here and I saw Otis Berryhill outside. We should probably put a couple of men in the back too." He paused. "Sheriff Nanny said he'd be sure to attend the meeting and it might be a good idea to get Bull Elliott and Possum Gilliam to help out. They're good at breaking up fights."

"Causing them too," Reverend Justice said.

Aunt Bessie smiled. "Bull and Possum will do what you tell them to, don't worry about that."

I wondered how she knew that but didn't ask.

It took a good half-hour or so to get everyone inside and seated and another fifteen minutes before Reverend Justice could get them to be quiet. Mr. Evans stood at the front of the room next to Reverend Justice and I noticed he looked a bit nervous. I wondered if it was because he had to speak in front of all these people. I know I would have been. On the other side of the Reverend stood my uncle, Thorney Dalton, Merle Ledbetter, and Sheriff Nanny. I didn't see Otis Berryhill until I looked at the back of the church and noticed him standing by the door. Bull Elliott and Possum Gilliam lurked nearby, stony expressions on their faces. They didn't look too awful capable to me, to be honest, but if Uncle Fletcher said they could break up a fistfight, why, I reckon they could.

Reverend Justice banged on his podium for silence then said, "We're here tonight to discuss the potential lease agreement being offered by Mr. Reginald Evans here for the Champion Timber Company. As you all know, the timber company will not sign a contract for the timber unless every land owner on this mountain agrees to it. We'll hear Mr. Evans speak then y'all can ask your questions, after which we'll open the floor to anyone who wants to say their piece. All I ask is that you be civil to one another and not engage in hateful language or violence. Remember, this is the Lord's house. Respect that." With a curt nod, he stepped back and gestured for Mr. Evans to step up to the podium. Some people booed while others clapped.

Aunt Bessie leaned close to me and whispered, "It's liable to be a long night, John. If you get tired, let me know and we'll make a bed for you in the back of the wagon."

I nodded but was determined to stay. I wanted to see a fistfight.

I have to say Mr. Evans gilded the lily, as my aunt would have said. He made the agreement the timber company was offering sound like a lifesaver to the mountain people. He offered top dollar for their lumber, promised jobs to those who wanted them, to build a general store for the lumber company's employees and a schoolhouse for their children. Aunt Bessie made a disgruntled noise at that. He skirted around the issue of how to transport the lumber off the mountain, simply saying that they would do it the most feasible way.

"What's feasible mean, Aunt Bessie?" I asked.

She whispered, "His meaning is the easiest and quickest."

He spoke for a good fifteen minutes and everyone was attentive and respectful for the most part. There were a few mumbled disagreements and some shouts of support but nothing got out of hand. Afterward, a host of hands shot up and Reverend Justice took over, stepping forward and pointing out each person allowed to question Mr. Evans.

Junior Hall, sitting beside his grandmother, whose wheezes could be heard over the room, was the first to stand and speak. "You talked about paying us for the timber but never gave a dollar amount. I reckon it'll help us decide if we know how much we stand to make from this venture."

When he sat down, his grandmother slapped his arm, saying out loud, "Why do you even want to know, Junior? You know I won't abide by any kind of agreement with a no-good lumber company."

Several people laughed at this.

Mr. Evans looked a bit uncomfortable. "Well, now, I can't give you a set dollar amount right now. We got to get our people up here to take a look at the timber, calculate how much we can harvest and what it's worth. I promise you we'll be fair and compensate you for what we take. Like I told Mr. Elliott there," he turned and motioned to Uncle Fletcher, "the timber business is moving out west to the Mississippi Delta and I reckon this will be your last chance if you want to make any money off the timber on your land. So you got to decide if you want to make a decent living or continue living off the land like you are, farming and whatnot." He grinned and leaned forward conspiratorially. "And I ain't saying what the whatnot is." Several people laughed at this but there were more than a few frowns.

I tugged on my aunt's sleeve. "What's he talking about, Aunt Bessie?"

She bent down to me and whispered, "He's insinuating moonshining, John."

I turned back to Mr. Evans, who was speaking. "Way I see it, there ain't many jobs here to be had. I been told a lot of the young people move away once they've got an education under their belts for jobs in factories in the cities. I'm sure most of you in this room would like for your young'uns to stay home, get married, have their own children here." Several voices rose up in agreement at that. Mr. Evans nodded. "You want 'em to do that, you got to give them a reason to stay and we're offering a reason to stay."

Aunt Bessie held up her hand and Reverend Justice called on her. "A temporary reason, Mr. Evans. Isn't that right? Once you've cleared the timber off this mountain, your company will be on to the next mountain or forest and we're left to deal with the aftermath, all the damage created by your company to our creeks and our land. Most people won't even be able to farm their land after you're done with it, isn't that right?"

Some shouted in agreement at this but others booed my aunt.

Mr. Evans frowned at her then shrugged. "I reckon I'm not a farmer so I can't say anything about how skilled you might be at farming."

"It has nothing to do with skill, Mr. Evans. If the soil is gone, depleted, ruined, it can't be farmed so—"

"Look at this mountain," Mr. Evans said, loudly. "Not many here are able to farm it anyway. Why not put its natural resources, all this timber, to good use and make income from it?"

"Because once the timber is gone, it will be decades, centuries before it's able to come back, that's why," Aunt Bessie said. "What happens to these people when the money you promise them, which you can't set a dollar amount to, is gone and they're left with land that is unusable? The animals they hunt will be gone, erosion will take away homes and wash out farmland. This mountain will die."

Voices exploded at that and people began arguing with one another. Uncle Fletcher and Sheriff Nanny gave each other tense looks and stepped down into the crowd, hoping to stop a fight before it got started. Bull Elliott and Possum Gilliam edged into the maelstrom as well, their fists clenched. They looked to me like they wanted to start a fight if they couldn't find one to break up.

Reverend Justice banged his fist on the podium until it quieted down again. "Remember where you are," he shouted, raising his hand to the heavens above. "Everyone gets to state their opinion, even if we have to stay here all night, so there's no need to argue amongst yourselves. Give voice to what you're feeling but do it in a peaceful way."

Mr. Evans used a handkerchief to wipe perspiration off his forehead. "You claim we'll destroy the land, Mrs. Elliott, but you ain't got proof that's going to happen. I promise we'll only take what is harvestable and leave the rest."

"But how will you transport the logs, Mr. Evans? Will you use the splash dam method, damming up streams to raise water levels, destroying fish, moving boulders, eroding banks? Will you skid the logs down the mountains to get to the streams or roads or whatever method of transport you decide? You'll have to clear other less mature timber out of the way to do that, won't you?"

Mr. Evans shifted on his feet, glancing around the room. "I can't comment on what method of transportation my company will use but I assure you we will take only what we need."

Voices once more rose in argument and Reverend Justice banged his fist on the podium over and over until the room quieted. "Anyone else got a question for Mr. Evans here or want to state their opinion?" Just about every hand in the room shot up.

Reverend Justice did what he promised, gave those who wanted a chance to say what they thought the opportunity to do so. For the most part, the room remained passive but there were several outbursts over what someone said. Several pressured Mr. Evans to give a dollar amount for the timber but he either couldn't or wouldn't and I noticed this seemed to turn the tide away from the lumber company having access to the timber.

Hours later, Reverend Justice took back the podium. By that time, my eyes felt heavy and scratchy and I'd dozed off a time or two while people spoke, jerking awake when an argument broke out. "All right, I'll ask it for the last time. Is there anyone here who hasn't spoken who wants to?" He eyed the crowd but no one held up their hand. "I reckon it's time to move on and put the agreement to a vote. As y'all know, the timber company needs every land owner to join in the agreement so I'll simply ask those who don't want to grant the timber company access to the timber on the mountain to raise their hands." He leaned forward and raised his voice. "Without arguing about it or stating any more opinions." I reckon more than half the people in the room raised their hands. Reverend Justice turned to Mr. Evans. "You have your answer, sir. I don't see that there's anything else to discuss."

I heard a scuffle in the back of the room and turned around to see Sawyer Eldridge and Joe Harris punching at one another. Uncle Fletcher and Sheriff Nanny hurried that way but Possum Gilliam and Bull Elliott reached them first. Instead of breaking up the fight, they joined in and before long several other men had decided they wanted a piece of the action. It took my uncle, Sheriff Nanny, Merle Ledbetter, Thorney Dalton, Otis Berryhill and several other men a good while to break apart those men who were trading punches. They hustled them out of the church and down the steps and told them to get off sacred land. I heard Sawyer Eldridge promise Joe Harris he wasn't done with him yet before he stomped away.

I tried not to let my aunt see my excitement over the fighting but it was something to see, all those men hitting one another with their fists, hearing their grunts and curses. I didn't see much blood so doubt they did any sort of damage but they sure scuffled around a lot.

Aunt Bessie took my hand and led me outside. "I'm sorry you had to see that, John. Those men should be ashamed of themselves, fighting like that in church, and over what? Sawyer Eldridge doesn't even own land and Joe Harris doesn't have enough to bother with."

Mr. Evans left the next day but I heard he promised Sawyer Eldridge he'd be back with more men to try to convince the mountaineers to lease their timber. As far as I know, he never came back but just the promise put a rift in the peacefulness of our mountain and it remained split as to whether the timber should be sold or not as long as I remained on the mountain.

Chapter Eleven

Summer 1927

Happy as a puppy with two tails.

Spring of 1927 was quite possibly the most beautiful spring I lived through during the many years of my life. We'd had substantial snow fall during the winter and when it finally started to melt the world just seemed to blossom with beauty. Everywhere you looked, there were wildflowers blooming in abundance, creating a colorful carpet beneath our feet. The trees, not to be outdone, formed a brilliant, misty green canopy to walk beneath.

Many times, I caught myself coming to a dead standstill as I walked to or from school, just breathing in the fresh, flower-scented air and enjoying the birds as they serenaded the arrival of the new season. I even did it when John was with me, but he, knowing my penchant for enjoying nature's beauty, merely stood beside me and waited patiently until I'd breathed my fill. I so enjoyed having him walk part of the way to or from school with me and usually used the time to extend his lessons, but that spring I found myself putting all that aside and talking to him about this, that, and whatever else crossed our minds—which, in John's case was more often than not fishing tales about his good friend Hoover Hall and the fact that his Uncle Fletcher had recently promised to teach him how to shoot his rifle.

I would have preferred Fletcher wait a few more years for that but John was determined it would happen sooner rather than later.

The only thing that marred the brightness of that spring was the news of a bombing at the Bath Consolidated School in the little town of Bath, Michigan, killing 45 people, 38 of whom were children. The person responsible for that atrocious act, Andrew Kehoe, was a farmer and a member of the school board who was upset over the taxes the town put into effect after building the modern elementary school. Before setting off the bombs at the school, he killed his wife and destroyed his farm, which was under threat of foreclosure. After he set off the bombs at the school, he blew up his truck, killing himself and the town superintendent. The newspapers reported Mr. Kehoe had spent several months wiring the school with dynamite before setting it off.

Despite the number killed and the overall atrocity of Kehoe's actions, the story didn't remain in the news for long. Three days after the bombing, Charles Lindbergh took off in his airplane, The Spirit of St. Louis, from an airport in New York and flew nonstop to Paris, becoming the first man to fly a solo nonstop transatlantic flight. That, it seemed, was more than enough to push the deaths of 45 people off the front pages of every major newspaper.

Both events were discussed in depth on the mountain but they barely resonated in my life because I had received a letter from Loney asking if Papa could come stay with us for the summer. It seemed my father had been causing a little mischief of his own and poor Loney was at her wit's end trying to deal with him.

Papa, as happens to all of us, was getting older and Loney didn't feel comfortable leaving him at home alone while she worked at the mill so had hired a woman to come and stay with him while she was gone. Papa, being Papa, didn't think he needed anyone hovering over his shoulder, feeding him meals and watching his every move, so one day he got the brilliant idea to ask the woman if she'd go to bed with him. Insulted, she waited until Loney got home, told her what happened and refused to come back the next day.

This happened with two more women, and even after Loney wised up to Papa's ways and hired a fourth whom she told Papa was there only to help with the housework and wasn't expected to do anything else, Papa propositioned her too. She quit the very same day.

I wrote Loney back and told her to send him on, promising I would have a talk with Papa while he was here. Loney must have been in a hurry to rid herself of Papa as I received a telegram shortly after I mailed my letter that he would be arriving the next day.

John, of course, was excited to see his Grandpapa John and could talk of nothing else as we returned to the house after a visit to the Barletts' place.

"How long until he gets here, Aunt Bessie?"

I didn't own a watch so looked up at the sky and judged the time to be around 4:00 in the afternoon. "Why, if the train's on time, he should be rolling into Old Fort around 1:00 tomorrow afternoon. Judging by the sun, it's a little after 4:00 now which means he'll be here in ..." Never one to miss a chance to teach my nephew, I continued, "Can you figure that out, John?"

"Less than a day?"

I laughed. "Yes, but what I meant was can you figure out how many hours until he arrives?"

I stopped and waited while he worked the problem out in his head, enjoying the birdsong while I did a little figuring myself.

It didn't take long for John to come up with his answer. "Twenty-one hours?" he said tentatively.

"Very good, John. You beat me."

He grinned. "I did?"

Although it wasn't quite true, I nodded. I wanted him to feel confident in his math abilities, something he hadn't quite reached yet. "You did. Can you tell me how you came to the answer?"

"Well, I figured 4:00 tomorrow would be 24 hours since that's how long a day is. And one from four is three so I took three away from 24 and that equals 21."

I ruffled his hair. "Good boy. I was going at it the hard way, counting the hours between now and 1:00 tomorrow. Your way is not only quicker, it's smarter."

His face practically split in two with his grin. I wanted to give him a quick hug, but like all boys when they reach the age of 8 or 9, John had recently decided he was too old for that kind of nonsense so I settled for a pat on his back. "I think that calls for fried apple pies with supper tonight." Fried apple pies were one of John's favorite foods.

"Yummy." He turned at the sound of a sharp whistle from up ahead on the path and his grin grew even wider. Taking off at a dead run, he skidded to a halt when Fletcher and Fritz rounded a curve in the path. "Hey, hey, Uncle Fletch, I beat Aunt Bessie at math and she's making fried apple pies to celebrate."

Fletcher grinned at me as he gave John the hug I'd wanted to. "Good for you, John." He patted his stomach and winked at me. "And good for me too. Hello, Bessie-girl."

"Hello, Fletch. How was your day?"

"Oh, fair to middlin'. Had a visit from Bose Dalton. He came by to drop off a present for John and said for me to be sure to tell you hello." He winked at me. Fletch was convinced Bose Dalton was secretly in love with me, despite the fact the man was married and had several children.

John tugged on Fletch's shirt sleeve. "A present for me? What is it, Uncle Fletch?"

"Well, you'll just have to wait and see. It's in a box on the front porch if you want to go take a look."

"Boy, do I," John said as he took off running.

"What did Bose bring him, Fletch?"

"Cutest little hound dog pup you ever saw. Prettier even than Fritz here." He leaned down and scratched between Fritz's ears. "But I bet it's nowhere near as good a hunter."

"A dog? Why in the world would Bose bring John a dog?"

"I think he's taken a shine to the boy." He grinned. "Kinda' like with you."

I could only shake my head. No amount of talking would convince my husband that he was wrong on this point. "Why would Bose bring John a dog?"

He laughed. "Well, he said every boy should have a dog. Said he found her—it's a girl—in a hollowed-out sycamore log down by the creek when he was on one of his walks. Since his dogs, the females I mean, are either pregnant or nursing their newborn pups, he said he don't need no more dogs around his place." He took my hand as we followed at a slower pace behind John. "I think we should let John keep her if he wants. It'd be something else to make him feel at home here."

My heart simply turned over in my chest. My husband had such a tender heart when it came to the people he loved, and though he rarely expressed his feelings in words, they often shone from his actions.

"Well, of course, he can keep him. Like Bose said, 'every boy needs a dog'. And you're right too when you said it's something that will make John feel more as if this is his home. Maybe it'll help ease the hurt in his heart from what his mama did."

"I didn't think of that. Do you think that still bothers him?"

I nodded. "Yes, I do and I also think he'll always carry a sore spot in his heart from what Jack did." I started to say more about that but Fletch had heard it all before and it was something I should get over anyway. Jack didn't know it but her actions had given Fletch and me some of the happiest times we'd ever known and I would always be grateful to her for those.

"Dog's a little busted up, looks like maybe she had a couple of run-ins with a fox or a raccoon or maybe even an ornery possum, but I'm sure you can get her back in tip-top shape in no time."

"Busted up how?"

"Got a gimp foreleg and a couple of cuts and scratches but nothing's bleeding. Her fur's long and there's a bunch of burrs turning to mats on her belly. She's so skinny you can count her ribs but she's real affectionate and seems tame enough around the other animals. Barked a bit at Fritz but I think that was her way of saying hello 'cause when Fritz walked over to check her out, she dropped to the ground and exposed her belly." He reached down and gave Fritz another scratch between his ears. "You were only greeting her, weren't you, boy?"

The dog woofed happily in agreement.

As we crossed the bridge over the creek, we could hear John laughing. I squeezed my husband's hand. "Isn't that a lovely sound to come home to?"

He smiled. "Sure is, Bessie-girl, it sure is."

John sat on the porch swing, cuddling the little dog in his lap and smiling like a goat in a briar patch. He hopped up and ran to meet us to show off his new possession.

"Look, Aunt Bessie, look. Bose brought me a puppy." He squeezed the dog so hard she yelped in protest and he immediately loosened his grip. "It's a girl puppy. Can I keep her? Can I name her?"

"Of course you can, John, she's yours. Let's have a look at her." I frowned as I ran my hand up and down her back where I could feel every knob of her spine then took her in my hands when John relinquished her, holding her up to my face to get a closer look. "Hello there, little one," I said as I examined the shallow scratches on her back and one deeper and nastier on the side of her neck. They were all scabbed over and seemed to be healing just fine except the deeper one on her neck looked like it could easily break open again. When I examined her right front paw, she yelped again. "Well, she looks fine except for that paw and the scratch on her neck but we can fix those up in no time."

John smiled. "Will you tell me what to do, Aunt Bessie, so I can fix her and make her all better?" When I looked at him, he added, "She's mine. I want to do it."

I nodded. "All right, John, I reckon that's only right. We should start with a good bath, get these burrs out of her fur, and I'd bet my life she's got some fleas on her, maybe some ticks too, though I didn't feel any and that's something of a miracle if you ask me. You think you can give her a bath?"

"I sure can," he said as he reached out to cuddle her in his arms again. "Can I use the water trough, Uncle Fletch?"

Fletcher grinned. "I think the washtub would work better, John. If it's all right with your aunt, that is."

"Can I, Aunt Bessie?"

"It's fine. You get her all clean and I'll see about getting her something to eat. She looks like she could use a bit of fattening up."

John took off at a run, clutching the pup to his chest, calling over his shoulder, "Come on, Fritz, you can help."

Fritz looked up at Fletch, a long-suffering expression on his face. "It's all right, boy, she's the one getting a bath this time. Go on with John and make sure he doesn't accidentally drown the poor little thing."

As Fritz reluctantly followed behind John, I turned to Fletcher. "She's a girl and that could bring problems when she gets older. How in the world are we going to handle that?"

"As soon as we notice signs she's going into heat, we'll have to keep her and Fritz separated somehow. I'll ask Bose next time I see him what's the best way to do that. Could be it won't be much of a problem. Fritz is coming on to ten years old. That's getting to be pretty old for a dog. Could be he's lost that urge."

"I suppose but we'll watch her all the same."

"Better safe than sorry, I reckon, but I bet my boy and her would have a litter of right handsome pups."

"You looking to give Bose a little competition providing hunting dogs for everybody on the mountain?"

He laughed. "Nope, can't say that I am, and I know you, you'd want to keep them all. Can't have that."

"No, we sure can't. Why, I'd have to resign my teaching job just so I could stay home and keep them from getting into the chicken coop and chasing after Ginger and Bell."

He leaned down and kissed my cheek. "That's that then. I better go see how John's doing. He'll probably end up wetter than the dog by the time he's finished."

I laughed. "Won't hurt him to have his bath a day early."

The next day we went into Old Fort to pick up Papa at the train station. John wanted to take his pup with us but Fletch convinced him to leave her behind with Fritz. He dragged his feet and kept turning around to look at

Sycamore, the name he'd chosen to give her, curled up with Fritz on the front porch until Fletcher said, "Lands sake, boy, Fritz won't let her go anywhere. You don't hurry up, your Grandpapa John might just decide we don't want him here and take that train back to Knoxville."

Excitement over Papa's arrival warred with worry over Sycamore running away while we were gone had John as fidgety as a scalded cat. It wasn't until we approached the train depot and he saw Papa standing outside waiting for us that he settled down. He leaped from the wagon and ran straight into Papa's arms, laughing and talking a mile a minute. Tears filled Papa's eyes as he hugged his grandson so tight I thought John just might yelp as Sycamore had the day before.

Fletcher and I stood back and let them have a few minutes together before my own excitement propelled me forward for my own hug. John, cradled between us, did yelp then and I pulled back so he could slide out.

"Oh, Papa, it's wonderful to see you," I said.

A few tears spilled over as he held my shoulders and kissed my cheek. As always, his handlebar moustache tickled my cheek and I smiled. "It's wonderful to see you too, Bessie-girl." He pulled me back into a one-armed hug, holding the other hand out to Fletcher. "Good to see you, Fletcher."

"We're glad to have you, Mr. Daniels."

"Aw, pshaw, I thought we settled that nonsense back when you took in my John Henry. Call me John, boy."

Fletch nodded and gave Papa's hand a firm shake. "Yes, sir, I will."

"All right, then. Bessie-girl, I'm hungry. You got anything to eat in that wagon?"

I laughed. Knowing my father's appetite, I had packed a basket full of ham biscuits and the leftover fried apple pies from the night before to tide Papa over on the ride up the mountain. I had chicken stewing on the stove, a fresh-baked cherry pie cooling on the counter and I would make dumplins and cook the year's first peas when we got home. "Oh, I might have something. Why don't we go find out?"

John grabbed Papa's hand and tugged him toward the wagon. "Come on, Grandpapa." His voice dropped but not low enough that I couldn't hear him whisper, "I know where Aunt Bessie put the basket. If you ride in the back with me, I'll let you have one of my fried apple pies."

I laughed, realizing the three people I loved best were all here with me on this beautiful early summer day. I didn't think it was possible to feel any happier than I did at that minute.

I was wrong. As the summer progressed and Papa seemed to grow stronger with every day, even walking without his cane at times, my happiness increased until I wondered it just didn't gush out of me like the water in Andrews' Geyser.

During that wonderful summer, Papa and John were never very far apart and Fletch was usually right there with them with Hoover Hall sometimes joining in the fun.

One Saturday in early July, John finally talked Fletch into letting him fire his shotgun. I was in the house finishing up the breakfast dishes when John came in, holding Fletch's bandana beneath his nose which was bleeding profusely. Fletch and Papa shuffled in behind him. Fritz, always by Fletcher's side, trailed them, head down and tail tucked between his legs. Sycamore was the only one who seemed undaunted, jumping up and down beside John with a happy smile on her face.

"Laws-a-mercy, what have you done, Fletcher Elliott?" I quickly dipped the cloth I was using to wash the dishes into the cold water bucket, wrung it out and slapped it on the back of John's neck, tilting his head back and holding it there.

"Aw, it ain't Fletch's fault, Bessie," Papa said. "He was teaching the boy to shoot the shotgun and I 'spect John Henry was too excited to listen to what his uncle told him and went ahead and pulled the trigger. The gun kicked, hit him in the face, and he got a bloody nose for not listening. You learned your lesson, didn't you, John Henry?"

John mumbled something but I ignored him and tenderly

removed the bandana to check to see if his nose was broken. Though I tried to be gentle, he yelped in protest when I manipulated it from side to side. "Ow, that hurts, Aunt Bessie."

"I imagine it does. I don't think it's broken but you're going to have a couple of black eyes along with a good bit of swelling and it's going to hurt for a while." I took the cloth away from his neck, used it to dab away a trickle of blood then handed it to Papa. "Rinse that out for me, Papa. Fletcher, go to the spring and get me a bucket of cold water. This has warmed too much to do much good."

They both just stood there, mouths agape. I slapped my hands on my hips. "Mercy, do what I tell you, the boy's hurting."

"You ain't gonna yell at us?" Papa said.

"What would be the sense of that? It's not like you punched him in the face and deliberately broke his nose. I expect you're right, Papa. John here wasn't listening, and I agree, he's learned his lesson. So go on and do what I told you. I need to get this bleeding stopped so I can get him cleaned up and tend to the swelling."

"Yes, ma'am," they both muttered.

Fletcher picked up the bucket and walked out the back door but Papa only stood there watching me warily.

"Well, Papa, what is it now?"

He shook his head and looked down at the floor as if carrying on an internal debate whether to say whatever was on his mind or to keep it to himself. I stood there and waited. After about a minute he looked up and said, "I gotta say, Bessie-girl, you sure have mellowed. Used to be you would've pitched a hissy fit about something like this but ..."

I picked up my dishtowel and shook it out. "I reckon the credit for that goes to the love of a good man, Papa." He winced but didn't say anything. "Or, I should probably say, the love of three good men."

Papa's eyebrows shot up. "Damn, Bess, you got something you want to tell me?"

I laughed. "No, Papa. Three good men." I pointed at the door. "My husband," then nodded at him, "you," I put my hand on John's shoulder, "and John."

John smiled then groaned. Papa chuckled as he dipped the dishrag in the rinse water to wash it out then passed it on to me.

I looked down at John as I handed him the dishrag. "You sit down at the table and keep your head tilted back and use the rag if it starts bleeding again. I'm going to fix a pot of willow bark tea. It'll help with the pain a bit." I turned to my jelly safe where I kept the majority of my herbs. "And maybe a mullein root or partridge berry decoction to help with the swelling." I was mostly talking to myself at this point but I heard John say, "Yes, ma'am," as meekly as his uncle and grandfather.

On the second Monday in August, two weeks before Papa left us, he decided our house needed a coat of fresh paint on the outside. There was no talking him out of it. The house needed to be painted and he was the man to handle the job.

"What color you want, Bessie-girl? I noticed Fletch had a few gallons of white gatherin' dust out there in the barn. That suit you?"

"Oh, Papa, you don't want to be out in this heat painting. You'll probably have a heat stroke."

"Pshaw, I may be old but I ain't in my grave yet, missy. 'Sides, I want to do it to pay you and Fletch back for having me here."

"We don't need any payment since we've enjoyed every minute and wish you would consider staying on for as long as you want. You're family and family's always welcome here. You know that, Papa."

"I know that, Bess, but I reckon I've been in your hair long enough. I miss my friends and the rest of my grandbabies. Myrtle should be about ready to hatch me another one in a couple weeks and I'd like to be there when it happens. It's her eleventh and I have a feeling I won't be seeing no more grandbabies born."

I smiled. Papa had always loved having a new baby around. "All right. I'll have Fletcher buy you a train ticket when he goes to Old Fort on Saturday or did you want to leave before then?"

"Nah, I'm not in that much of a hurry. And your man doesn't have to be buying me a train ticket. I've got money of my own. Mayhap I'll go into Old Fort with him in a week or two and leave then. That be all right with you?"

"Of course. John's going to miss you."

"I know. And I'm going to miss him, too. Do you want me to take him back with me? Jack seems to have settled down some now that she's got old man Barrett dancing around her." He shook his head. "Don't know why she married him, he's 30 years older than her and poorer than dirt." His moustache lifted, a sign he was trying not to smile. "He was foreman at the mill where she works and Jack told me she figured he had a bit of money, but come to find out, he's so poor he couldn't jump over a nickel to save a dime." His smile widened to show teeth. "I reckon our Jack don't have the sense God gave a goose when it comes to finding a rich man."

I smiled. "I'm sure she thought she was doing her best, Papa, to find a good husband." I hesitated, debating whether to ask the question since I might not like the answer, but I had to know. "Since she's married, do you think she wants John back?"

"With Jack, it's hard to tell what she wants or what she'll do. I never would've thought ..." He shook his head. "Well, we've about talked that one to death so all I'll say is I hope she doesn't. I've never seen the boy so happy. Being with you and Fletch has been good for him."

"Yes, I think it has. And he's been good for us."

"Welp, I'm going to fetch the ladder and one of those gallons of paint and get started painting." He pointed at me as I started to object. "And don't you give me no lip about it, girl. I'll start over there on the side that's shaded this afternoon. I can probably get a side a day done and then Fletch can pick up some trim paint in Old Fort this Saturday and I'll do the trim next week."

"All right, Papa, but promise me you'll be careful and you'll come in if you get too hot or tired."

True to his word, Papa finished the house in four days with a little help from John. On Saturday, Fletcher picked up the paint for the trim and the next week Papa put on the finishing touches. He used the leftover trim paint to add a sign on the front wall beneath the window, "Painted by J. W. Daniels 1827," saying an artist always signed his work when it was finished.

That little sign made me smile every time I saw it.

The following Saturday, we all made a day of it and went to Old Fort to see Papa off on the train. We had a picnic on a little knoll on the banks of Mill Creek overlooking Spring Street with the large Union Tanning Company bark shed and the tannery boardinghouse in the distance.

It was a lovely day, marred only by the sadness of Papa leaving. It was hard for both John and me to let him go and we held on until the engineer blew the warning whistle. I tried to console both of us as we started back up the mountain by talking about the happy memories we'd made while Papa had been with us but it didn't do any good. John would smile fleetingly but it didn't take but a few seconds for it to fade away.

It was a long, silent trip after that, and as we crossed the bridge over Cedar Creek to the house, a shiver trickled up my spine followed by the unwelcome thought that I might never see my beloved Papa alive again.

Chapter Twelve

Summer 1927

He was mean enough to hunt bears with a hickory switch.

Around a farm, there are always chores to be done, but I never looked on gardening as such. I spent many happy hours outdoors planting my garden and watching it grow, my efforts rewarded with flavorful produce or beautiful flowers. I have always loved the taste of home-grown tomatoes but admit I found tending them about as much fun as kissing the back side of a bucking mule. I didn't mind the planting and loved the eating but weeding has always been, to me, a devil of a chore. But it had to be done, so there I was, my back aching from bending over so much, my arms tired from hoeing the hard ground, a stack of weeds growing behind me as I moved down the aisle between plants. I heard a mule bray and looked up to see John leading Jolly along on a harness, a sack of flour on his back. Sycamore trotted behind, occasionally barking at the two. Fletcher had given the red mule to the boy to break and John had fallen in love. He planned to enter him in an upcoming horse race at the county fair and had high dreams of winning first place. No one could make him understand Jolly didn't have a chance against swift horses. To John, that mule might as well have been a show horse.

I stood to stretch my back and glanced at the sky, willing a cloud to appear and cover the sun. Mercy, it was hot enough to peel house paint. I used my apron to blot my face and glanced toward the sky once more, my gaze moving over the ridge behind our house. I spied Sawyer Eldridge stepping out of the tree line at the edge of our property on Flinty Knob, leading a horse carrying something wrapped in a blanket. Fletcher suspected Sawyer had a still on our property and swore if he ever caught him, that would be the end of Sawyer sharecropping our farm, and it occurred to me he just might have hidden it on Flinty Knob. As Sawyer came nearer, I drew in my breath, the sight of that bundle over the horse's back bringing back memories of poor George thrown over the horse that had dragged him to his death. A cruel way to die, inflicted by the Red Shirt Democrats only because George was a Negro. I wished fervently that Fletcher was home but he had gone up to Sally Laughter's to help the Berryhills do some repairs and probably wouldn't be back until after dark.

Carrying my hoe with me, I stepped out of the garden and called to John. "Why don't you take Jolly into the barn and give him some corn and oats after you brush him down? He's worked hard for you today and deserves a treat, don't you think?"

John smiled with pleasure. "He's coming along, Aunt Bessie. Why, I reckon I'll be riding him before the week's over."

"I think you will," I said, hoping he would be in the barn by the time Sawyer revealed what he had thrown across that horse's back. I watched John lead Jolly into the barn, Sycamore trailing them, then hurried to meet Sawyer. Fritz, napping under the front porch, crawled out, sniffing the air. He trotted over beside me, stopping with a low growl when I drew up short as I neared Sawyer, the sight of blood on his shirt and pants and covering his hands giving me a shock. "Are you hurt, Sawyer?"

"No, ma'am, but I got ol' Joe Harris with me, Bessie, and he appears to be dead."

I stared at the blanket on the back of the horse then turned back to Sawyer. "Joe's dead? What happened to him?"

"Don't know. I was out huntin' and found him in the holler there on Flinty Knob, just layin' in the grass, covered with blood. Appears to me like he's been gored."

Fritz bared his teeth, the fur on the back of his neck standing. "Easy, boy," I said, knowing the scent of blood had gotten him riled. "Are you sure he was gored, Sawyer? Fletcher hasn't spied any wild boars up there in a good while."

"They stay hid pretty good, could be there's one or two running around. Anyway, I'm on my way down the mountain to see the sheriff in Old Fort. I reckon he'll know what to do with the body."

I dropped my hoe and rubbed the horse between her eyes. "Do you mind if I see him?"

"Now, there ain't no need for that, Bess. He's good and dead. I checked to see if he was breathing afore I wrapped him in my blanket and threw him over old Jezebel here."

"Still, I'm a healer, Sawyer. I need to make sure there's nothing I can do for him else I'll worry about it. Surely you can understand."

He studied me for a moment, his eyes hard and flat, and a chill ran up my spine. What in the world was the matter with the man? "Sheriff Nanny will either send for me or for Doc to make sure. He's done it before."

He shrugged then dropped the horse's reins on the ground and went around to the covered body. I watched as he reached over and pulled it off without care or any sort of gentleness. The corpse landed with a thud, the blanket falling open. The horse shied away, frightened, I'm sure, by the scent of blood and death. Fritz trotted over and sniffed at the body. I knelt beside Joe, placing my hand on Fritz's neck to still him. For a brief moment, I saw George, that dear, sweet man, lying in front of me, his skin colored brown and red from dirt and blood. It's not George, I told myself, closing my eyes for a moment then opening them, relieved to see Joe. I put my fingers over his neck, checking for a pulse, noting the blood covering his skin was sticky, not dry. "He hasn't been dead long," I said.

Sawyer didn't reply for a moment. When I looked at him, he lifted his shoulders as he glanced away. "I reckon he must've just died when I come across him."

I studied him for a moment, wondering about his demeanor which seemed aloof and hard, not the usual amiable and friendly one he had always portrayed to me. I stared at his clothes and hands. "Gracious, Sawyer, you're covered in blood. How'd you get so bloody?"

He looked down at his hands, spreading his fingers wide, seeming surprised at the blood. He wiped them on his pants but the blood had dried and remained where it was. "When I picked him up, I reckon. I tell you, Bess, I ain't never seen so much blood in my life, not even at hog slaughtering time."

I nodded as I looked away, thinking those shallow cuts on Sawyer's hands sure didn't come from picking up a dead body. I studied the slits in Joe's clothes, too numerous to count but too fine to be caused by a boar's tusk, then picked up his hands, which were covered with shallow nicks and deep cuts. "Doesn't look to me like he's been gored, Sawyer. Looks more like he's been cut by something and the condition of his hands tells me he put up a fight."

At that moment, John came out of the barn. "What are you looking at, Aunt Bessie?" he asked, walking toward us.

I glanced at Sawyer, watched his eyes narrow as they honed in on my young nephew. "It's nothing, John, just something dead Sawyer found. Why don't you go on out to the field and bring in Ginger and Bell so your Uncle Fletcher won't have to worry about fetching them when he gets home?"

John came closer, his eyes widening. "Is that Mr. Harris?" He hurried over. "What's wrong with him, Aunt Bessie?" Sycamore crept close to the body, sniffed the blood, and backed up, growling low in her throat.

I put my hand out when John knelt beside me and gripped his forearm. "Mr. Harris is dead, John. Looks like something got hold of him. Mr. Eldridge there thinks a wild boar gored him."

John's face paled, and when he looked at me, I could see he was frightened. "I ain't never seen a dead person before, Aunt Bessie. I sure am sorry this happened to Mr. Harris. He was always so nice to me."

"I'm sorry you had to see this, John. There's nothing to be done for him, so why don't you go on, now, while I help Sawyer. We'll have us some supper when you get back."

"You sure you don't need help, Aunt Bessie?" he asked.

"We're fine, son. You'd be more help fetching those cows for me."

He looked as if he wanted to protest but seemed to think better of it and turned around. "I'll be back soon. Come on, Fritz, come on, Sycamore," he called over his shoulder as he ran toward the rear of the barn.

"Go," I said to Fritz, wanting him with me for protection but knowing John would suspect something unusual was happening if I made him stay. I waited until they had gone around the side of the barn before turning my attention back to Sawyer.

It took all I could muster to meet Sawyer's eyes with a calm expression. "He must have just died when you came upon him, Sawyer. He hasn't started to stiffen up, the blood's still warm and sticky."

"I thought the same thing, Bess. I feel right sorry I didn't come upon him sooner. Maybe I could have helped him." The tone of his voice belied the concern he tried to show. He shifted his weight, glancing around. I spied my hoe on the ground next to me and inched my hand that way, thinking I could use it if he thought I might have suspicions about his actions.

He finally said, "You want me to tell Sheriff Nanny a boar got him or he's been stabbed?" pronouncing it the mountain way, stobbed.

"Well, it's not my call, Sawyer. I'm just taking a wild guess. Tell him what you told me since that's what you think happened to him. Sheriff Nanny will make his own determination or get Doc to if he isn't sure himself." I picked up my hoe and rose to my feet.

Sawyer nodded then spat tobacco juice on the ground. "Well, I reckon I best get to it then." He paused. "You say Fletcher's not to home?"

"He should be back any minute now. He's gone to Sally Laughter's to help the Berryhills with a chore." I swallowed then continued. "You're welcome to stay if you want but that body won't fare well out here in the hot sun."

"Naw, I reckon it won't. I'll just be on my way, Bess. Want to make it to Old Fort afore it gets dark."

I watched him wrestle the body onto the back of the horse, who shied away when she caught a fresh whiff of blood. I reached out, caught her halter, and held her steady so Sawyer could sling Joe's body over the mare's back.

"Good day to you, Bess," he said with a nod before leading the horse off.

I nodded back and stared after him as he made his way across the bridge to the road. I stood in the yard long after he had gone, watching for him while waiting for John, anxious for the boy to return home with Fritz and Sycamore. And only then did I go inside, locking the door behind us, something I rarely bothered to do.

Fletcher arrived home just as I was putting supper on the table. He greeted us with a smile, ruffling John's hair and kissing me on the cheek. I smiled at him but my face felt so stiff, I could barely move my lips. He stared at me a moment and I cursed myself for not being able to hide my feelings. He raised his eyebrows in a questioning way and I whispered, "I'll tell you later, after John goes to bed."

John, though, had news to share. "Mr. Eldridge brought Joe Harris's body down off of Flinty Knob, Uncle Fletch. He had him wrapped up in a blanket and poor Joe had blood all over him. That's the first dead body I've ever seen and it sure did scare me."

"Is that right?" Fletcher sat down at the table, looking at me then back to John.

"Sure is. Aunt Bessie said she couldn't do nothing for him so Mr. Eldridge was going to take him to Sheriff Nanny. I had to go fetch the cows and didn't see him leave, though."

"I imagine that was a bit of a shock, seeing poor old Joe like that," Fletcher said, glancing at me.

"Mr. Eldridge said a wild boar got him." John's forehead crinkled. "You think there's any wild boars around here, Uncle Fletch? I'd sure hate to meet up with one if they can kill like that."

Fletcher squeezed his shoulder. "I reckon I'll go on up to Flinty Knob the next day or two and have a look around, see if I can find any boar tracks, John. Don't you worry, son, if there is one, he won't come around the farm. Not with Fritz and Sycamore here."

Fritz barked his agreement and Fletcher rubbed his back.

"I was thinking the same thing," John said with more bravado than he felt, I'm sure.

"I sure do thank you for putting the cows in the barn for me," Fletcher said. "Saved me a chore I wasn't looking forward to when I got home. I swan, I think those Berryhills had a mountain of chores saved up for me to do. Why, I reckon I was busier than a one-eyed cat watching two rat holes and don't think I got half of them done. I was wishing I'd taken you with me, John, since you're such a big help. Reckon I will next time."

John puffed up at that and they started talking about what needed to be done at Sally's house. I was glad it took John's mind off poor Joe's body.

I waited until I knew John was good and asleep before telling Fletcher about Sawyer's visit. He listened quietly, reaching out to hold my hand when my voice got shaky. When I finished, he said, "You think he killed him, Bess?"

I shook my head. "I'm not sure, Fletch, but he had cuts on his hands, and as you know, anyone wielding a bloody knife, chances are it's going to slip and they're going to get cut themselves."

"That's a given."

"He had so much blood on him, Fletch, too much for simply picking up a body and placing it on a blanket, then throwing it over a horse."

"More likely he rolled the body onto the blanket," he said in a musing tone. His eyes met mine. "You're saying he come down from Flinty Knob?"

"Yes, that's where I first saw him, right at the edge there."

Fletcher sat back, nodding. "I've suspected awhile ol' Sawyer's got his still up there on Flinty Knob somewhere. I'd say what happened, Joe Harris came across that still and got caught by Sawyer. Maybe he was even helping himself to some moonshine. Joe did like his drink, you know."

"But why would Sawyer kill him?"

"Well, there's been bad blood between them ever since they got into that fistfight over the timber company. Could be they started arguing over that. But that may not be what happened. Mayhap Sawyer didn't want Joe to tell anyone where his still is. I've told Sawyer I don't know how many times I'd take away that acreage I gave him to sharecrop and kick him off our land if I find it here on our mountain. Or they could have argued about something else entirely. I doubt we'll ever know, Bess."

"But why bring the body down, Fletch? Why not just leave it up there to rot or bury it?"

"Could be he didn't have a shovel to dig a grave and he probably didn't want to leave it on Flinty Knob because it'd draw animals. We'd see buzzards flying over it, wonder what had died up there, might go inspect. He wouldn't want that if that's where his still is." He squeezed my hand. "I can tell he upset you. Was he acting threatening? Did he say anything?"

"No but he just seemed ... different. Harder maybe, definitely defensive. I tried not to let him know I suspected he was involved in what happened with Joe but I don't know if I succeeded."

Fletcher sat back. "I reckon I'll stick close to home the next few days, just to make sure he don't get the notion to come back and make sure you agree with what he said."

"Shouldn't we tell Sheriff Nanny our suspicions?"

"I'd say he'll be visiting you, Bess, if Sawyer tells him he saw you. If not, we'll go to Old Fort and tell him ourselves. And afterward, I'm going to walk every inch of Flinty Knob, looking for that still."

Panic raced up my spine. "Fletch, don't do that. The same thing might happen to you if he finds you up there."

"Don't you worry, Bess, I'll take my rifle with me, along with Fritz. He won't let anything happen to me." He ruffled the dog's fur. "Will you, old boy?"

Fritz barked his agreement and I couldn't help but smile, thinking talking to my husband didn't alleviate my fear but helped temper it somewhat.

Fletch stood, holding out his hand to me. "Let's go on to bed, Bess." As we walked toward the bedroom, he put his arm around me. "I won't let anything happen to you," he said in a low voice. "Don't know if I've ever told you, darlin', but you're my world."

I leaned into him, thanking God for this man.

Sheriff Nanny paid us a visit the next day. Fletch and I were standing on the porch watching John shout with joy as he trotted around the yard on Jolly. The boy had managed to break the mule in a short bit and Fletcher told him he had a future breaking horses if he had an interest in it. I could tell it pleased John to hear his uncle say this.

Sheriff Nanny got off his horse, watching John, then turned and smiled at us. "Didn't take him long, did it?"

Fletcher smiled proudly. "Plumb amazing he did it so quick. I figured it'd take him another week at least before he could mount that mule but here he is riding him like he's been broke a good while."

"He's got talent, I'd say," Sheriff Nanny said, climbing the porch steps. He nodded at me. "Good day to you, Moonfixer."

"Afternoon, Sheriff. What brings you out this way?"

I been up to see Bull Elliott about a matter and figured I'd drop by on my way back to Old Fort."

I smiled. "I'm sure if you were looking for Bull, you were looking for his sidekick Possum Gilliam." It seemed one went with the other more times than not.

He smiled. "Yep. Those two can't seem to stay out of trouble but it's usually not too serious."

"Why don't you sit and rest for a bit? Can I get you something to drink? I'm sure you're pretty dry if you rode up from Old Fort."

"Well, that'd be right nice, Bessie. Whatever you've got is fine with me."

"I just made some lemonade with lemons Fletcher traded for down in Old Fort. I'll be right back."

I returned with four glasses on a tray, handed one to Sheriff Nanny and one to Fletch. I set one aside for me and called to John. "I've got some lemonade for you when you're ready, John."

He grinned as he rode by. "In a bit, Aunt Bessie. I'm having too much fun to quit."

I smiled at him as I sat beside Fletcher and met Sheriff Nanny's eyes. "This visit have anything to do with Sawyer Eldridge finding Joe Harris's body?"

"Yep." He squinted his eyes at me. "Said he saw you when he brought him down from Flinty Knob. Said you told him you thought ol' Joe had been stabbed."

"That's right, Sheriff."

"Can you tell me why you thought that?"

"The slits in his shirt were too narrow and fine to have been caused by a boar's tusk. They looked more to me like those made by a knife."

"How'd Sawyer react when you said that?"

I shook my head. "He was acting strange, Sheriff. He's usually a friendly, amiable sort of fellow but he seemed, I don't know, distant, cold. He didn't want me to see the body at first but I told him either I or Doc would see it eventually just to verify what had happened to poor Joe."

"I told him the same thing, Bess. Called Doc in and he came to the same conclusion you did."

"That's good to know."

Sheriff Nanny watched John for a minute then turned his attention back to me. "Anything else you want to tell me?"

"Did you see the blood on Sawyer's clothes, Sheriff, and the cuts on his hands?"

"He tried to hide his hands but I saw 'em all right."

"It just seemed to me that was an awful lot of blood on his clothes from rolling a dead body in a blanket then picking it up and placing it over a horse's back. And those cuts reminded me of times I've treated people who have been using a knife, got it bloody, which as you know will make a knife slick, and it slipped and cut their own hands. I reckon I've treated hundreds of those kinds of wounds, Sheriff."

He nodded, staring off at John. "I agree." He looked at Fletcher. "You think Joe and Sawyer had bad blood between them? I know they got into that fight at the church when Mr. Evans spoke but I ain't heard of anymore animosity between them since."

Fletcher shook his head. "If I was to speculate, I'd say Sawyer's got his still up there on Flinty Knob and Joe must have come across it. They might have argued about the timber cruiser's offer, or maybe Joe got into the moonshine, or he could have wanted Sawyer to give him some in exchange for not telling about it, or told him he was going to show me the still. This whole mountain knows I've warned Sawyer about having a still on my property. In any event, I'd say something happened between them and they got into it and Sawyer ended up killing Joe. But I ain't got proof of it and doubt any of us ever will unless there was another person up there that saw the whole thing."

Sheriff shook his head, his mouth in a firm line. "You're right, Fletch. I could tell by the way Sawyer was acting, he knew more than he was saying, but I can't charge him with murder unless I have some proof." He sighed. "Too late to do it today but I reckon I'll go on up there tomorrow and look around, see if I can find any sign of what happened."

"I'd go with you," Fletcher said, "but I don't think I want to leave Bessie and John here alone in case Sawyer decides to come back."

I put my hand on his. "Fletcher, I know how to use a shotgun. Don't you worry about John or me. I'll keep an eye out."

"You just make sure you keep it close to hand, Bess. But I'll stay if you need me."

I shook my head. "You go on and go. We'll be all right."

Fletcher turned back to the sheriff. "I reckon I'll go with you then. I want to make sure that still ain't on my property. I'd say Sawyer's moved it by now if it was."

"I'd say you're right." Sheriff Nanny sighed then stood. "I reckon I'll get on back. I'll meet you here right after sunrise, Fletch, and we'll head on up Flinty Knob and have a look see."

Fletcher stood. "I'll be here waiting on you, Sheriff."

With a wave, Sheriff Nanny mounted his horse and turned it toward the road. He trotted over beside John and congratulated him on his success breaking the mule. John waved happily as he lightly kicked Jolly and rode him around the yard once more.

Fletcher watched his nephew with a smile. "He's gonna be disappointed the day of the race, Bess. I sure wish I could find a way to help him win."

I patted his arm. "He's having fun, Fletch. Maybe that will be enough for him."

"I sure hope so. I don't like seeing my loved ones unhappy," Fletcher said, then stepped off the porch to help John down off Jolly.

Chapter Thirteen

Fall 1927

Ain't seen hide nor hair of him.

JOHN

I got up early the next morning, well before my aunt and uncle, before the sky had even begun to show the first hint of lightening. Aunt Bessie had told me Uncle Fletch and Sheriff Nanny were going up Flinty Knob looking for the place where Joe Harris had died and I wanted to go with them. I figured from the way my aunt and uncle talked in low voices and that since the sheriff was involved, Mr. Harris must have died from some other means than a wild boar. I couldn't figure out what in the world had happened to him and was more than a little bit curious to find out. By the time Aunt Bessie started breakfast, I'd done most of the chores including milking the cows. Her eyes lit with delight when I came through the door carrying a full milk bucket.

"Mercy, John, what a blessing you are, child. I woke with a bit of a backache from all that hoeing yesterday and wasn't looking forward to bending and leaning off of a milking stool this morning."

I smiled at her. "I woke up early so figured I'd get started on the morning. I put the cows out to pasture too, along with

Pet and Jolly. I was hoping I could go up Flinty Knob with Uncle Fletch and Sheriff Nanny. That is, if you don't need me for anything else."

Aunt Bessie's mouth tightened. "I'm not sure that's a good idea, John. It's a rough path going up that mountain and you're not used to riding for any length of time."

Uncle Fletcher stepped into the room, stretching his arms. "Is our John wanting to take a trip?" he asked, grinning at me.

"He wants to go up Flinty Knob with you and the sheriff," Aunt Bessie said.

A look passed between her and my uncle.

"You need him here, Bess?"

After a long moment, she smiled at my uncle. "He's got his chores taken care of, so I don't reckon I do."

Uncle Fletcher glanced at me and cocked his head as if thinking about something. I realized I still had the milk pail in my hand and set it on the table. Finally he said, "I reckon John's old enough to know what's going on, Bessie. If he thinks he can hang on to Jolly going up a mountain, he's welcome to come."

"Thank you, Uncle Fletcher," I shouted. "I'll go saddle Pet up for you."

"Now hold your horses, young fella," Uncle Fletcher said. "We got to eat breakfast first. We're liable to be gone a good while and will need something hearty in our bellies to sustain us."

"You just be careful," Aunt Bessie said. "There's snakes up there, and if they spook Jolly, he's liable to take off. So you hang on tight when he's moving. You just broke him and he's still skittish, you know."

"I'll hang on, Aunt Bessie, don't you worry about that."

We were just finishing breakfast when Sheriff Nanny arrived. I was so excited, I could barely eat anything, so Aunt Bessie packed up a big lunch for us to take. I helped Uncle Fletch saddle Pet, threw my tow sack over Jolly, and mounted, using a stump to step on first. Uncle Fletch told Aunt Bessie to keep the shotgun close and I wondered what he meant, but that thought quickly fled as we headed off, riding toward Flinty Knob at a trot right as the first sunbeams broke over the mountain.

We slowed to a walk when we entered the pathway going up the mountain. The going was rough and we had to stop a few times to clear trees that had fallen down over the trail. We took a break after moving one particularly cumbersome oak tree, which had taken a good half-hour to shove off the path. Uncle Fletcher and Sheriff Nanny sat on the tree trunk, letting their horses graze, while I took the tow sack off Jolly and used it to dry the sweat foaming on his flank.

Sheriff Nanny took a drink from his canteen and handed it to my uncle. "If I didn't know better, I'd say somebody deliberately made this trail impassible."

"I was thinking the same thing," Uncle Fletcher said. "It ain't been that long since I've been up this ridge and the trail was pretty easy to travel then."

Sheriff Nanny nodded. "Sawyer said he found Joe's body in the holler, Fletcher. You any idea how close we are?"

Uncle Fletcher took a long drink and held it out to me. "You thirsty, John?"

I shook my head and went back to my chore.

He handed it back to Sheriff Nanny. "We're maybe a quarter mile away." He looked up at the sky, using his hand to shade his eyes. "Should be near lunch by then. Bessie packed us a mighty fine one, Sheriff. Hope you'll join in."

Sheriff Nanny smiled. "You know me, Fletch, when it comes to food I never say no." He paused. "Well, unless my sister-in-law cooks it. Laws, that woman can make a cold ham taste like sawdust just by putting it on a platter."

I smiled as they laughed over his joke.

Uncle Fletcher stood, using his hat to brush at the dust on his britches. "I reckon we might as well get a move on. You ready, John?"

"Yes, sir," I said.

"Here, let me help you up." He leaned over and formed a pocket with his hands. I put my foot in and launched myself onto Jolly's back. I waited for them to mount then we were off.

We didn't encounter any other obstacles and finally reached our goal. Unlike the mountain trail we'd been on which meandered amongst scrub trees, brush, wild vines and looming pine and cedar trees, the holler was pretty to behold. Although Uncle Fletcher told me no one had cleared it, it looked like a small meadow encircled by the forest, free of trees but bountiful with wildflowers and occasional mountain laurel bushes. We dismounted at the edge of the clearing and left the horses to graze by themselves. Sheriff Nanny led the way in, moving with care, studying the ground. As Uncle Fletcher and I trailed behind, I wondered what Sheriff Nanny was searching for. He finally stopped and held his hand up and we immediately came to a halt.

"Lot of dried blood here," he said in a low voice.

Uncle Fletcher and I moved forward slowly until we stood next to Sheriff Nanny. The grass here was stained a dark brown and it looked to cover a massive amount.

Uncle Fletcher shook his head. "Poor old Joe must have lost near all the blood he had," he said in a low voice.

"All those stab wounds Doc found on his body would account for that," Sheriff Nanny said. "Sure wish I could find evidence to tell me who killed him."

I raised my head at that. I suspected they thought something other than a wild boar had killed him but didn't know they thought Mr. Harris had been murdered.

"Was it Mr. Eldridge?" I asked.

Uncle Fletcher laid his hand on my shoulder. "All we know is that Sawyer says he found the body, son, and if there's no way to prove he killed Joe, why, there's nothing we can say about it."

I nodded.

My uncle started walking around the clearing, searching the ground again. "What are you doing, Uncle Fletcher?"

"Looking for evidence for the sheriff as to who murdered Joe but also searching for signs of a still up here. I'd bet you my life savings this is where he had it." He pointed to a small stream that ran along the edge of the clearing. "See the red horsemint growing there?"

I nodded.

"It takes the right kind of water to make moonshine. That red horsemint there means that ain't hard water and hard water don't make good corn whiskey. Wish I could find some still-slop." He nodded at the horses. "Cattle and hogs love it but horses won't drink it. It'd be the best proof he's had a still up here."

We searched that clearing for a good hour but didn't find anything other than some indentations in the ground my uncle thought was where Sawyer had had his still.

"Well, he's cleared it out now," Uncle Fletcher said. "But I'm going to keep an eye on this holler just to make sure he don't come back."

Sheriff Nanny sat down in the grass, leaning his back against a maple tree and wiping his brow with the back of his forearm. "Nothing gets my dander up knowing somebody did a terrible thing and is going to get away with it. I reckon I'll check here too from time to time just in case something shows up pertaining to Joe's murder."

Uncle Fletcher pulled his saddlebags off Pet. "What say we forget our troubles for a bit and eat some of Bessie's good fried chicken." He rummaged through the bag. "Got us some biscuits, canned peach jam, and, lawsy mercy, lookee here, a whole cherry pie."

When the smell of that fried chicken hit our noses, I think all three of us forgot what we were doing in the clearing as we realized how hungry we were.

After lunch, we walked the holler again, searching for some clue as to what had happened to Joe Harris, but didn't find anything. Mid-afternoon, Sheriff Nanny called a halt to the search and we packed up and left.

Over the years I lived with my aunt and uncle, Uncle Fletcher and I made many a trip up to Flinty Knob Holler which quickly became known among the mountain people as Joe Stob Holler, stob being the mountain way of saying stab, but never found signs of a still or anything to help Sheriff Nanny in his investigation. My uncle and the sheriff were certain Sawyer Eldridge had killed Joe Harris but without anything to back up their suspicions could never accuse him of such and I know it bothered both of them a great deal. My uncle warned my aunt and me not to go near the man and made sure Mr. Eldridge stayed away by confronting him and telling him he found some evidence of a still having been on Joe Stob Holler and to keep off his land. As far as I know, Mr. Eldridge never stepped foot on his property again.

Chapter Fourteen

Summer 1928

You gonna have to relick that calf.

JOHN

I reckon the friend I spent the most time with on the mountain was Hoover Hall. We liked to hunt squirrels together and spent a lot of time exploring what became the new YMCA camp, now called Camp Elliott, where we would fish in the lake and I'd watch Hoover swim. But we stayed away from the cemetery there, where Lum Elliott had buried the leg he lost in a sawmill accident several years before. Hoover was convinced that leg would pop out of the ground one day and go looking for its owner. I have to admit, his fear at times was infectious so I didn't argue the point.

Although I liked Hoover and we had a lot in common, I was a bit wary of him. His mother reminded me every time I saw her that Hoover was a diabetic and epileptic. She warned me if he ever had an epileptic fit to put a stick between his teeth so he wouldn't swallow his tongue, or if he got weak and close to passing out, to give him a piece of hard candy. I made sure to always carry a piece of hard candy with me but had never heard of anyone swallowing their tongue before and certainly had no desire to witness it.

So when I was with Hoover, I remained on alert for the first sign of a seizure, figuring as soon as that happened, I'd light out for the nearest place to get help.

One day shortly after Camp Elliott opened, Hoover and I were squirrel hunting on Sammy Elliott's old place in an area called Sammy Fields. I stepped off the path, searching for a squirrel I'd spied, and right there, sunning itself on a large rock was the biggest rattlesnake I'd ever seen. It was a beauty, its skin covered with what Aunt Bessie called yellow pides, or diamond shapes. I stopped abruptly, causing Hoover, who must have been looking the other way, to collide with my back.

"What's wrong?" he asked, his voice low. Hoover always thought there was danger right around the corner and had been known to bolt at the sound of a tree limb snapping. Of course, with bears and bobcats prowling around, along with several species of poisonous snakes slithering through the grass, he had good reason to think that.

I pointed ahead. "See that rattler?" I whispered. "I reckon I ain't never seen one so big or so pretty."

Hoover's eyes widened when he spied the snake. "Whoo-wee, that's a monster," he said in a voice so low I could barely hear him.

We stood there, both trying to figure out how to get around the snake without being bitten.

"Reckon we ought to backtrack and go around it?" Hoover finally asked.

I shook my head. "I been thinking, Hoover, there might be a way to make some money with that snake."

He looked at me like my head had popped open and my brains flew away. "You're crazy," he said in a loud voice then clamped his hand over his mouth. We both looked frantically at the snake to see if he'd heard us. The theory at the time was that snakes couldn't hear because they didn't have ears but Hoover and I figured there was a first time for everything.

"What if we catch it?" I whispered. "I bet you somebody at Camp Elliott would be willing to pay a dollar or two for it."

"How you reckon we can catch it, John?"

"Let's see if we can find a forked stick. We'll trap its head then I'll pick it up and carry it."

Hoover's eyes widened. "You reckon you can do that? What if he hears us coming? You know how fast rattlers are. They can strike afore you know it."

"Maybe so but I'm quick as a snake, or so my Uncle Fletch tells me. You just keep your rifle ready, and if he lunges, shoot him."

We tiptoed far enough away we figured the snake wouldn't hear us then searched around for a bit and finally found the perfect stick to use. I handed Hoover my rifle. "Okay, I'll pin it with this stick then pick it up. You carry my gun."

"Be careful," Hoover said, "if it bites you, as big as it is, it just might kill you."

I tread as quietly as I could toward the rattler, who appeared to be dozing in the sun, and with one big lunge pinned its head in the fork of the stick. "Got it," I said. I reached down and picked the snake up behind its head and started walking back toward Camp Elliott, Hoover following behind carrying both guns. I hadn't gone far when the snake started wrapping its body around my arm. I stopped suddenly.

"What's wrong?" Hoover asked, his voice going high.

"It's wrapping itself around me, Hoover. Help me get it off." I was in a panic by then and doing my best not to rip at its body and let go of the head.

Hoover threw down the guns and started unwrapping the rattlesnake. "Don't let go of its head," he said.

"I won't let go, Hoover, but hurry." I looked into the eyes of that snake and thought I was staring at the red devil himself. I just knew he was going to sink his fangs in me and I'd be dead before Hoover got me back to Aunt Bessie.

"He's off," Hoover said.

I flung that rattler as far as I could. He immediately oriented himself and headed back toward us at a speed that was astounding. Instead of running away like I figured he would, Hoover impressed me with his agility as he picked up his gun and shot that snake in one smooth motion.

I was a bit shocked at Hoover's bravery. In the past, he had proven himself to be a bit of a coward. I'd even heard his sister say he wouldn't bust a grape in a fruit fight and figured that pretty much hit the nail on the head. But this snake incident changed my mind about my best friend.

We watched pieces of rattlesnake fly into the air then stood there a moment, watching for signs of activity, both shaking with fear. Finally, we went over to see how much damage had been done. That snake was pretty much obliterated.

I shook my head. "Well, I reckon we won't be collecting our two dollars," I told Hoover.

That night, I told Aunt Bessie and Uncle Fletcher about the rattlesnake. Both seemed impressed I'd taken him on which made me feel kind of proud.

Aunt Bessie smiled at my uncle. "Your uncle had his own dealing with a rattler, John. Why don't you tell John about it, Fletch?" She patted his arm then got up to check the cornbread in the woodstove.

Uncle Fletch gave her an uneasy look. He was a taciturn man, not prone to telling stories, but like my aunt, had a talent for it when convinced to share. He gave me a resigned smile as he settled back in his chair. "Early in my teens, John, I learned to hunt with my dad's old Punch rifle. Well, one late, drizzly October day, barefooted, my breeches rolled to my knees, I shouldered the rifle and went squirrel hunting. Across wooded ridges, down into thickety coves I went. The leaves were down and dampened by the falling rain and it wasn't only easy to see squirrels but to slip up within shooting distance. To facilitate carrying them, I had strung them on a little forked sourwood stick and had killed just under a dozen squirrels. Wanting one more to even my numbers, I was pleased to hear one barking in a thicket not too far away. Slipping along and peering ahead to sight my squirrel, I came to a log. Intent on the waving branch of a nut tree, I didn't look down, just stepped my left foot over the log. Shifting my weight to this foot, I rested my right foot on top of the log. Still peering into the tree, I began to feel a tingling sensation going up my leg while my foot was taking on a shuddery chilliness. I looked down and my heart skipped a beat. I was standing in the precise center of a coiled rattlesnake. Now, John, you may not know this, but poisonous snakes, in coiling, have their head in the center of the coil, and this saved me, for my foot rested directly on the snake's head with my weight keeping him down. I expect the chill of that late fall day prevented any but a weak whir of his rattles so I hadn't heard him.

"I looked about for a place to jump, a clear place free from saplings and undergrowth. I found it and leaped, and whirling about, put a ball through the snake's head, puncturing some of the coils. This experience made me snake conscious and as it was now late in the day, foggy and dark in the woodland, I decided to dispense with the desire for the extra squirrel and go home. Reloading my gun and carrying my game swinging along, I retraced my way back down the high ridge. Halfway down, I heard soft footfalls behind me. Some animal was following me, presumably tracking the blood from my squirrels. When I hurried my steps, the footfalls behind hurried. When I slowed down, the steps behind me slowed their gait. Every few steps, I looked back yet the animal, whatever it was, stayed just out of sight in the fog or skulked behind bushes. It was a long and apprehensive three miles I traveled, and when I reached the top of the ridge above home and climbed to the top rail of the pasture fence, the footfalls ceased. I tell you what, John, the light shining from home was never so welcome as then."

"Did you ever see the animal that was following you?" I asked.

He shook his head. "It may be a good thing I didn't. I probably would have panicked and tripped over my own two feet trying to get away from it."

"I reckon I'd have dropped the squirrels and lit out of there," I said.

"Me, too, John," Aunt Bessie said, joining us at the table.

"Well, I figured I could do that if he got too close," Uncle Fletcher said. "But I reckon that wasn't as scary as what happened to my grandpap Noye."

"What happened to him?" I asked, thinking there wasn't anything scarier than a rattler wanting to strike.

"He was out hunting one winter day when there came a big snow storm. He was too far from home to go back so he looked around for a place to get out of the weather where the snow wouldn't cover him up. He soon found a log with a big hollow in it and climbed right in. And lo and behold, found himself right beside a bear. Well, it scared both him and the bear, and the bear ran off before Grandpap Noye could so he stayed in the log till the storm passed."

"I don't know which I'd rather run from, a bear or a snake," I said.

"If I had my druthers, it wouldn't be either one," Uncle Fletch said. He sniffed the air. "Bessie, supper sure does smell good. You reckon it's done? I'm awful hungry after all that talking."

The next morning, I was carrying a bucket of milk to the house for breakfast when I spied Howard Gilliam in the yard with his two oxen. Howard was built like a box with graying hair that seemed to go every which way and eyebrows that looked like two wooly caterpillars sitting on top of his eyes. He had a jolly way about him and was well-liked on the mountain. He sometimes plowed for Uncle Fletch and would stay with my aunt and uncle when he did. I smiled at Mr. Gilliam, glad to see him, and stepped over to pet his oxen. I liked to watch him plow with those two powerful animals. They fascinated me the way they moved so slow yet managed to get the job done.

"Good morning, Mr. Gilliam. Are you here to plow?" I asked as I approached.

"I sure am, John. We're raring to go, soon as your Uncle Fletch points me in the right direction."

"We're getting ready to eat breakfast. Why don't you come on in?"

"I reckon I will," he said, following me inside and into the kitchen.

"Howard, you're just in time for breakfast," Aunt Bessie said when she spied him standing in the doorway.

"Seeing as you're the one who made it, I reckon I can't say no," Mr. Gilliam answered, taking off his hat and shaking hands with my uncle, who had joined us.

As we ate breakfast, I listened to my uncle and Mr. Gilliam discuss which field was to be plowed and the crops that would be planted there. Finished with our meal, I followed them outside and stayed in the field all day, sometimes following along behind as the oxen pulled the plow or standing aside and watching them. I even trailed along behind when Mr. Gilliam took them to the barn.

He smiled at me as he unyoked them. "Something tells me you like my ox, little John."

"I sure do, Mr. Gilliam. I like to watch them plow. Is it hard to put the yoke on them?"

"Nope, not once you get the hang of it and they're trained to it. Here, watch me unhook them, then all you do is reverse that in your head to put it back on. If you watch closely, I just might let you help me put the yoke on them tomorrow."

"Really? I sure would like that." I made it a point to watch and listen closely as he performed this chore.

True to his word, the next morning, Mr. Gilliam allowed me to help him as he yoked his oxen and during the day let me walk behind the plow with them several times. I was amazed at how easy it was, the pace more suited to my short legs than the one set by the mules.

A month later, Uncle Fletcher returned from Old Fort with two bull calves. I was in the barn and, hearing him call for me, met him in the yard. I ran over to pet the calves. "They sure are pretty, Uncle Fletch. You going to pasture them then sell them?"

He smiled at my aunt, who stepped off the porch to study the two creatures. "Nope, figured I'd give 'em to you, see if you can train them to the yoke if you want, maybe plow a field or two for me once they're broke to it."

I laughed with delight. "Where do you reckon I can get a yoke?"

Uncle Fletcher scratched his chin, contemplating. "Seems to me Bose Dalton told me his son had an old one he wanted rid of a month or so back. We'll pay him a visit tomorrow, see if he's still got it and is willing to part with it."

Aunt Bessie squeezed my shoulder. "Looks like you got you a fine pair of oxen, John. What do you reckon you'll call them?"

I studied the two dark creatures, already stout and muscular. "How about Ezekiel and Zebediah, Zeke and Zeb for short?"

She smiled at me. "That sounds like two fine Christian names. I reckon they'll do. Dinner's ready. Why don't you and your uncle see to your oxen then come on in and eat? Don't forget to wash up first."

I could barely sleep that night, I was so excited about the possibility of having a yoke as early as the morrow so I could begin training my oxen to it. Sure enough, Reese Dalton still had that old yoke and I started breaking my oxen that afternoon. Before long, thinking they were fairly manageable, I began using them to haul things around the farm pulling a sled and practiced plowing on a patch of land Uncle Fletch gave me. One day, I was using them to haul manure and as we went through the creek something spooked them and they took off. The reins slid out of my hands and I watched in wonder as they hightailed it across the creek and straight through my Aunt Bessie's tomato patch. I admit to being a bit astounded. I had always thought them great, lumbering creatures and had no idea they could move so fast. Aunt Bessie watched them with a forlorn look on her face and I felt terrible. My aunt's favorite thing in the world was gardening and she spent many an hour doing just that. She was awful proud of her tomatoes with people from all over the mountain coming to our farm to buy or trade for them. After the oxen tired out and came to a stop, I corralled them and put them in the barn then joined Aunt Bessie, still staring in shock at her broken tomato plants.

"I'm awful sorry, Aunt Bessie. Something spooked them and they took off before I could get control of them."

She gave me a sad smile which did little to dispel my feeling that she must be terribly disappointed in me.

"I'll fix it," I told her and set about replanting the tomato plants that could be saved, shaking my head at the wide swath those two animals had cut through her garden. When I looked up, Aunt Bessie was nowhere to be seen. I hoped she wasn't inside, crying over her lost tomatoes.

When I finished, I went to find my Uncle Fletcher, cutting kindling in back of the house. He looked up when I approached and put the axe down.

"I feel terrible, Uncle Fletch. Zeke and Zeb tore up Aunt Bessie's tomato patch and I know she's awful disappointed in me."

Uncle Fletch ruffled my hair. "You put it right, didn't you?"

"I replanted the ones that could be salvaged. I don't think she lost a lot but they sure tore up that garden."

"I think she'd have been disappointed if you didn't replant those tomato plants, John, but she won't hold it against you for what those two bull calves did." He looked off in the distance. "What do you reckon we ought to do with 'em?"

I thought about it for a bit. "Maybe we ought to just pasture them. They spook too easy."

He smiled. "I reckon that's the right decision, John. I'm sorry it didn't work out for you."

I didn't say anything and went off to make sure I'd cleaned up the garden patch as well as I could, displacing any sign my bull calves had torn through it.

My Aunt Bessie never said a word about her damaged tomato patch or the fact that that ended my experience with oxen, and I was thankful for that.

A few days later, I heard the jangling of a harness and rose from the breakfast table to see who had come to call. I watched the horse as he trotted over the bridge onto Uncle Fletcher's property, thinking what a beauty he was. As a stallion, he could be cantankerous but he was truly something to behold. The driver yelled, "Whoa, boy," drawing the reins back, and the horse came to a sudden stop, snorting and stomping at the ground.

"Good morning, Mr. Murphy," I said, stepping down off the porch. The people of Stone Mountain referred to Mont Murphy as a jake-leg veterinarian. Although he had no schooling or certification as a vet, he did well enough and I suspect most of the mountaineers would have chosen him over someone with a valid education and experience and the right to call themselves a veterinarian. He supplemented his income by breeding his Percheron horse and one of his mules and, having taken a liking to me, would occasionally take me along with him on his rounds. I thought him as old as Methuselah with his stooped shoulders, stringy white hair and knobby hands, but he always appeared to be in good health and disposition. "What brings you out this way?"

"Well, John, seeing as how you're so fond of animals, I was wondering if you'd like to accompany me on my rounds this fine day."

"I sure would, Mr. Murphy. I'll go ask my aunt and uncle if it's all right." I rushed off to find them. Aunt Bessie and Uncle Fletch, of course, came outside to greet Mr. Murphy and ascertain he had, indeed, asked me to go with him. Once this was confirmed, I was sent off with a hug and kiss and told to behave myself. I climbed into the buggy, wondering what sick animals we'd be seeing that day.

Our first stop was at Thorney Dalton's small farm, where Thorney's milk cow had bloated after getting into some of his corn mash. Like my Uncle Fletcher had done with his cow, Mr. Murphy stuck a knife in the cow's side to relieve the pressure and afterward patched her up. "She'll live, I reckon," he told Mr. Dalton, "but you got to be careful with the corn mash, Thorney. Cows will get into it every time."

Mr. Dalton spat a stream of tobacco juice on the ground. "I reckon they will," he said amiably. "I set aside some of my Hurricane Juice just for you, Mont. You think that will be payment enough?"

Mr. Murphy slapped Mr. Dalton on the back. "Why, I reckon that's more than enough, Thorney. I am curious, though, why you call it Hurricane Juice."

Mr. Dalton winked at me. "'Cause it will blow you down if you drink more than a little of it." Both men laughed but I wasn't sure what was so funny.

Mr. Murphy collected his moonshine and we returned to the buggy. As we rode along, he took more than a few swigs of the liquor. After a bit, he gave me a contemplative look. "I got me a little business to conduct just over the line in South Carolina, John. You reckon you feel like accompanying me?"

I'd never been to South Carolina before and was curious if it was any different than its sister state. "I sure do, Mr. Murphy," I said, and settled back for what I hoped would be an adventurous trip.

We reached his destination about lunch time and I was a bit surprised to realize the scenery hadn't changed much from one area to the other. Mr. Murphy pulled up in front of a wooden-planked house with a red door and handed the reins to me. "I won't be long, Johnny boy, then we'll go have us some lunch. You look after the horse while I'm gone."

"Sure will, Mr. Murphy." I got down from the buggy, still holding the reins, and petted the horse while Mr. Murphy went into the house. I thought it awful disrespectful that he didn't knock before entering then thought maybe this was family and there was no need. It wasn't long after that I heard a woman screaming and looked up at the house to see her run by the window, closely followed by Mr. Murphy, who didn't appear to have much on in the way of clothing. I pondered that for a bit until Mr. Murphy came outside, a big smile on his face.

"What say we go get us some lunch, John?" he said as he climbed into the buggy.

I opened my mouth, intending to ask about the woman and what had happened to her, but then decided maybe it wasn't any of my business. So instead, I nodded my agreement.

When Aunt Bessie asked me how my day went, I told her I'd had a fun day but didn't mention the woman, fearing she might not let me go with Mr. Murphy next time he asked.

Chapter Fifteen

Fall 1928

***If you don't stop, I'll knock you in the head and tell God
you died.***

I don't think John slept a wink the night before the first day of
the county fair at Rutherfordton. The morning dawned bright
and warm, humidity already prickling at my skin when I
stepped outside to visit the outhouse. I made a mental note
to be sure to pack more than enough water to sustain us
through the day as I made my way to the kitchen to begin
breakfast. I noticed John had already been there, witnessed
by a partially eaten biscuit left over from dinner the night
before. I smiled to myself and said a silent prayer, asking
God to give Jolly a healthy nudge during the race. John was
sure his mule would win, but I feared instead of being the
first equine to cross the finish line, he would be the last.

Fletcher wandered into the kitchen for a cup of coffee,
scratching at the stubble covering his face. He gave me a
sleepy smile which widened to a grin when he noticed the
biscuit. "I reckon he's already in the barn," he said.

"Getting Jolly ready, I presume." I sighed. "Fletch, I sure
don't want him to be disappointed but I don't see how that
mule can win against some of those horses. Sheriff Nanny's

entered and you know how fast his gelding is. Why, no one's been able to beat him the past five years."

Fletch nodded as I spoke. "I sure don't want to see him lose, Bess, because he's worked so hard to win this race but he'll do all right. And even if he doesn't win, maybe just the fact that he entered and raced Jolly will be enough. John's got a good head on his shoulders, he probably realizes deep down he won't come in first place."

"I sure hope so," I said, my heart already hurting for the boy.

John came through the doorway, a big smile on his face. "Well, Jolly's as ready as he's ever gonna be," he said, washing his hands. "I reckon we've got a fair enough chance, don't you, Uncle Fletch?"

"Well, now, this is Jolly's first race, John. He might feel intimidated by all the other horses. He'll be up against some mighty fast ones so don't get discouraged if he doesn't win. There's always next year."

John thought about this, a serious expression on his face. When he looked at us, his eyes lightened. "I reckon you're right, Uncle Fletch. Jolly might not be sure what's expected of him, this being his first time. But I reckon he'll do well enough."

"Even if he doesn't, don't blame him for it," Fletcher said. "That mule loves you and he'll do his best for you and that's all that counts."

"Yes, sir, I reckon so." John smiled at me. "That sausage sure smells good, Aunt Bessie. You reckon I can have an extra helping at breakfast? I'll need all my energy today, you know." He puffed out his chest, just like a man, and I couldn't help but laugh.

"You can have all the sausage you want, John," I told him, ruffling his hair.

We had just finished breakfast when we heard the honk of a horn outside. Fletch and John hurried outside to greet Horace Manny, who was giving us a ride in his truck to the fair which was about 35 miles away. I picked up the large wicker basket I'd packed with plenty of food for our trip along with some canned jams and a quilt I planned to enter into contests, and went to join them. After saying hello to Horace and his wife Julia, Fletcher, John and I climbed into the wooden bed of the truck after John tied Jolly to the rear bumper. I noticed John watching his mule trotting along behind as we traveled along. I'm sure he was worried whether Jolly could keep pace with the truck, but Hiram drove so slowly, I figured John probably would get to the fair quicker if he rode Jolly there. I studied the mule for a moment, noting his sleek lines and muscles, and thought maybe there was a chance he could at least place.

John, noticing my scrutiny, smiled. "Jolly sure looks fit, doesn't he, Aunt Bessie?"

"I was just thinking the same thing, John. How come you didn't ride him to the fair?"

He shrugged his shoulders. "Didn't want to tire him out too much, Aunt Bessie. He needs to be fresh for the race if he's going to win."

"Well, I reckon you're right about that." I turned to my husband and lowered my voice. "Maybe you shouldn't have sold that saddle, Fletch. It might help if he had a saddle to ride."

Fletch shook his head. "John sits that mule like he was born to it. Besides, a saddle only adds more weight." He looked at John. "Ain't that right, John?"

John nodded. "Sure does. 'Sides, I don't need a saddle, Aunt Bessie. I'd rather ride bareback anyways."

"Well, I'm sure you'll both do very well, John." I hid my hand in the folds of my skirt and crossed my fingers for luck.

The truck dipped down and Fletch muttered something unintelligible under his breath as the truck came to a sudden stop. He leaned over the side and shook his head.

"What's wrong?" I asked.

"Looks like we're stuck in the mud. Hope we didn't break an axle or wheel." He jumped down from the truck, joined moments later by Horace and John. I started to get down but Fletcher waved his hand at me. "It's awful muddy down here, Bess. Wouldn't want you to get that pretty dress of yours all dirtied up. Why don't you stay put while we get us clear of this rut?"

I sat back down. "Well, let me know if I can help, Fletch."

"Will do." I watched as the men examined the muddy hole the wheel had fallen into.

Fletcher stood, stretching his back. "I reckon we're gonna have to put something in front of that wheel it can grip onto." He looked around, spotted a dead tree on the ground. "Help me gather up some of those small limbs. We'll place 'em in front of the wheel and see if that gives us some traction."

The sun beat down on my head as the men collected the wood, and I fanned myself, hoping we got going soon. The day was already warm and would only get more so as the sun climbed the sky. I wondered with irritation if cool fall weather would ever come to the mountain. It seemed we'd had nothing but hot weather for a coon's age.

It didn't take the men long to pile large sticks in front of the wheel, then Horace got back in the truck and stepped on the accelerator while Fletcher and John pushed on the back bumper. The truck seemed stuck for a long moment and I feared we would be there all day but with a great sucking noise it finally released and we were free.

"Good job, boys," I said.

John and Fletcher hopped in the back and settled down.

"It must have come a good storm to make that much mud," John said. "I like the rain but I sure don't like the mud."

Remembering a story my great-grandmother Elisi had shared with me, I smiled. "Did you know, John, that in the beginning, the Earth was nothing but mud and water?"

"What a pure misery that would be. How did it dry up, Aunt Bessie?"

"I told you the story of how land was made when the Little Water Beetle dove beneath the ocean to the very bottom and carried up as much mud as he could and spread it until it became the island Earth. In the beginning, the Earth was wet and soft, without any dry land, so the council in the Sky World sent Great Buzzard out to search for a place where all living things could go. Great Buzzard flew down from the Sky World and soared over Earth, searching for such a place. When he grew very tired, his great big wings struck the Earth, creating valleys, and when he rose to the sky, mountains grew behind him. This later became known as Cherokee country.

"Now, all the plants, animals and rocks, even the little spirits, had a place to live but the Earth was still very soft and wet so the council in the Sky World asked Grandfather Sun to help and he said he would. So the Sun moved around the Earth from the East to the West, providing light and warmth to the land. And he was so impressed with its beauty that he decided he wanted to live in this new place, but knew if he got too close, he would burn it up because he was so hot and bright. So he decided to stay in the Sky World but to continue to move around Earth, admiring her beauty while giving her light and warmth and protecting her.

"The plants and animals and rocks in the Sky World were excited about their new home and thanked Grandfather Sun, agreeing to greet him each morning when he rose in the East and give thanks to him. Soon, all the plants, animals and rocks and even some of the little spirits, who were the first people, came down from the Sky World to live on Mother Earth. And all lived together in peace and balance as one family of many things, and were thankful each day for life and for their beautiful Mother Earth. This is the Cherokee story of how our world was made, and so, it is good."

John smiled with delight. "I can just see that big ol' buzzard making valleys and mountains with his wings, Aunt Bessie."

"I can too, John."

"Why, if he was here today, I bet he could dry this road up with one flap of his wings," he added.

I laughed. "I don't doubt he could."

"I just hope the fairgrounds aren't muddy like this road," Fletcher said.

And when we arrived, we were happy to see the rains apparently hadn't made it to Rutherfordton and there wasn't a muddy area in sight although it would have been hard to find one amidst all the people and animals milling about. As Fletcher helped me off the truck bed, I caught an air of excitement and anticipation in the air, the buzz of conversation everywhere. John jumped off the back of the truck before it even stopped and began to untie Jolly. He ran his hands over the mule, talking to him in a low voice, making sure he hadn't gotten overheated or tired. Fletch joined him, and as I watched my two men discussing the strategy of the race, I thanked God for blessing me with these precious people.

Fletcher finally stepped back, placing his hand on John's shoulder. "I reckon you best go and register for the race, John." He fished in his pocket and pulled out a dollar bill. "The cost to race was a dollar last year and I imagine it'll be the same this year. If it's more, I'll make sure you have enough to enter."

"Thanks, Uncle Fletch." John beamed at me. "You gonna watch the race, Aunt Bessie? I think it starts in about an hour."

I couldn't help but catch his enthusiasm. "I sure am, John. After I enter my jams and quilt in the contests, I'll walk over to the raceway."

Fletch pecked me on the cheek. "I reckon I'll go with John, Bess. See you there."

"You sure will." I leaned down and kissed John on the cheek. "For good luck," I said.

He smiled, picked up Jolly's reins and led him off, Fletcher walking beside him. After I entered my jams and quilt in their respective contests, I made my way to the racetrack, set up on the edge of the fairgrounds. The horses were a menagerie of old plow horses and broken-in geldings, feisty stallions and skittish mares. I found John brushing down Jolly while Fletcher talked to some of the other men, each debating the likeliest horse to win. I figured if any money was being bet, most would be on Sheriff Nanny. I watched John throw a tow sack over Jolly's back, what would serve as his horse blanket, while others placed old and new horse blankets beneath tattered and fancy saddles. It didn't seem to bother John that his mule and his accouterments didn't meet the others' standards and I was proud of him for that. But the men who were racing, whom I'm sure were amused by John and his mule, showed my nephew nothing but courtesy and respect, and I was glad for that.

Sheriff Nanny approached us right before the race, saying, "I've seen you on that mule and I reckon I'm a bit nervous racing against you and ol' Jolly here, John, but I'll give it my best."

John smiled, seeming pleased by this. "I reckon I will too, Sheriff." He stuck out his hand. "May the best man win."

Sheriff Nanny laughed as he shook, then mounted and headed for the track.

The horses and Jolly lined up and I couldn't help but be proud of my nephew who sat that mule like he would have a thoroughbred stallion, his back straight and his expression fiercely proud. The gun went off and the horses and that one red mule took off. It pleased me to no end when I heard several of the people in the crowd cheer for my nephew and his red mule, yelling, "Go, John, go," or "Go, Jolly." I joined in with them, shouting as loud as I could. The race didn't last long and, as expected, Sheriff Nanny won, but John didn't come in last either, for which I was thankful.

After the race, I approached John, who was receiving laudatory thumps on the back from some of the other riders for his good race. John smiled when he saw me. "Congratulations, John. That was an exciting race. Sweet Jolly here sure did give those horses a run for their money."

"I think he might have won if I hadn't held him back at the beginning." John ran his hand up Jolly's muzzle and turned to the mule. "We'll know how to win next year, won't we, Jolly?" The mule moved his head up and down as if answering yes. Fletcher and I laughed along with several others who witnessed this.

I reckon there isn't a relationship any sweeter than that between a boy and his pet, and John sure had made a pet of Jolly.

I told John and Fletcher I wanted to see what time they were judging the quilting contest and bid my goodbyes. As I walked along to the tent housing the quilts, Sally Laughter caught up to me, holding her daughter Alice by the hand. "Miss Bessie, I'm so pleased to see you."

I smiled at her, thinking Sally was a different person than the young woman who had been so brutally abused by her husband. She looked healthy and happy, her eyes shining, her smile bright and at ease. I kissed her cheek, then Alice's. "Where's the rest of your brood, Sally?"

"They're back a ways with Mr. and Mrs. Berryhill. Alice and I saw you and I wanted to catch up to say hello."

"Well, it sure is good to see you. We keep hoping you'll join us at Stone Mountain Baptist Church one day."

"I mean to, Miss Bessie, I sure do, but it seems life stays so busy with the young'uns and the Berryhills. But we say our prayers daily and read the Bible each night, so I reckon we're not neglecting our duty to the good Lord."

"Glad to hear it, Sally. Are you enjoying the fair?"

"I sure am. Did you hear about the Beautiful Baby and Fitter Family contests? A Dr. Denby approached me and asked me to enter my sweet baby girl Amy in the Beautiful Baby contest and me and my family in the Fitter Family contest. He said we're sure to win a medal."

"Well, you have a beautiful family, Sally. I have no doubt you won't win. I haven't heard of either contest. Where is the tent?"

"It's at the far end of the fairground. That Dr. Denby says he's going to lecture this afternoon about ... oh, what did he call it? Eugennie something or other, I think."

Shock traveled through me. "Eugenics?"

"Yes. He's a doctor from Black Mountain and he says with our blond hair and blue eyes, we're exactly what he's lecturing about. He asked if he could use us as an example."

Oh, Lord have mercy, I thought. "Sally, maybe you should listen to what he's lecturing about before you enter the contests. It may not be something you would agree with."

Her face fell and she lowered her voice to a whisper. "Is it something illegal, Miss Bessie?"

"It should be, in my view. It's at least morally unethical." I patted her hand, sorry to disappoint her. "But maybe I'm wrong so I'll go listen to what he says. You go on, have fun at this fair with your young'uns." I leaned toward her conspiratorially. "John said he saw a sign for an ape man and bearded lady at one of the tents. I know they won't want to miss that."

She smiled, happy again. "They sure won't." She glanced behind her. "Here they come. Maybe I'll see you at the contest this afternoon, Miss Bessie." She kissed my cheek and hurried off. I waved at the Berryhills, who looked happy with their foster family. They had lived on our property for awhile and I at times found myself missing Mr. Berryhill's tall tales always followed by his question to his wife, "Ain't that right, Miss Maudie?" and her response of "Wuss than that, Little Berry, wuss than that." I imagined they kept Sally and her babies entertained now and was glad these people had found each other.

I made my way to the edge of the fairgrounds, easily finding the Eugenics tent. An exhibit with flashing lights was set up outside the tent proclaiming, "Some People are Born to be a Burden on the Rest". I noted the exhibit was sponsored by the American Eugenics Society and wondered who was actually behind it. I read the text beneath each flashing light, growing more repulsed with each one. The light flashing every 15 seconds marked the $100 in tax money spent on the insane, feeble-minded, criminals and other defectives with bad heredity. The 16-second flashing light marked how often a baby was born in the US with the 48-second light noting the frequency of babies born who would grow up with a mental age of eight or lower. The 50-second light noted the frequency with which Americans went to jail, stating that very few normal people would ever go to jail. I thought of Sally and the time she had spent at Sheriff Nanny's jail for killing her husband and wondered if Dr. Denby knew of this. And what would he say to her if he found out? Oh, I couldn't let him make her feel less than she was, not since she had come so far. At the far right of the exhibit was a light that flashed every seven and one half minutes which marked the birth of a high-grade person who would have the ability to do creative work and be fit for leadership, further stating that only four percent of the American population fell into this category.

I stood there in shock. This was so morally wrong yet it seemed it was being embraced by the rich and powerful and even the Ku Klux Klan, and I did not know what I could do to stop it. I was aware that eugenics groups had advocated for laws to attain their aims. In 1924, the Immigration Act was passed by majorities in the U.S. House of Representatives and Senate which set up strict quotas limiting immigrants from countries believed by eugenicists to have "inferior" stock, particularly Southern Europe and Asia. President Coolidge, who signed the bill into law, stated when he was vice president, "America should be kept American ... Biological laws show that Nordics deteriorate when mixed with other races." Such bias! I wondered what God thought about all this.

"Aunt Bessie," John yelled, startling me out of my thoughts, and I turned to see him running toward me, Fletcher not far behind.

I smiled when he caught up to me, noticing his happy expression. "You look to be having fun."

"I am." He grabbed my hand. "Do you want to go see the ape man and bearded lady with Uncle Fletcher and me? I heard there's also the world's fattest lady and world's tallest man."

I widened my eyes. "Really? I don't reckon I've seen any of those before. Let's go see." I smiled at Fletcher and grasped his hand as John guided me toward the tent.

I suspect the bearded lady had glued hair to her face and the ape man had glued what looked to be hair from the same lot all over his body. The fat lady was fairly obese, with rolls of fat covering her belly, so much so that she had no lap, but this could have been achieved with padding as well, although her stout legs and rows of chins caused me to question my opinion. The world's tallest man looked slightly irregular and seemed a bit unsteady as if he were standing on sticks. Fletcher later told me he thought he caught sight of wooden stilts underneath the man's trousers. But John was in awe of each one and I was glad my nephew seemed to be having a good time.

We next attended the quilt judging contest and I think John took it harder than me that I didn't place. But I hadn't expected to. After all, I was not known for my skill with needle and thread. Well, except for stitching up skin. Next we went to the tent where jams were being judged. I didn't expect to place there, either. I seemed better at growing fruits and vegetables than canning them although Fletcher and John assured me more than once that no one made canned squirrel as good as me. All that mattered to me was that my men were fed well and proper with food that at least had a bit of good taste to it.

John and Fletcher wanted to watch the judging of the livestock so I told them I'd catch up with them later and made my way back to the Eugenics tent. Several people were gathered around in front, reading the large sign with the flashing lights. I spied Sally Laughter exiting the tent, her baby on her hip, a flustered look on her face.

I fell into step beside her. She gave me a distracted smile. "Well, I reckon you know we didn't qualify."

"I read the sign, Sally, and wondered about that."

"I should have read the sign afore I went in," she said. "Instead, I was naive and stupid ..." She looked away, blinking hard to hide her tears.

"No, Sally, you weren't. He had no business promising you something he didn't know he could deliver."

"He made me fill out these forms, answer all these questions, Miss Bessie, asking all about my family. He said we may look like we're part of the supreme race—"

I put my hand on her arm. "He actually said that?"

She stopped and faced me. "He shore did. Said with our blond hair and blue eyes and healthy body type, we could be, but the fact that I didn't finish school and ended up in jail made me inferior and a burden on society." She spat that word. "And my kids too because of me." She burst into tears.

My fists clenched. "Oh, the nerve of him." I pulled her to me and hugged her. "Sally, you can't let him make you feel less than you are. That's what makes him feel so superior, is putting down people so that they will think they're not as important as he is. He's wrong, Sally, and you can't listen to what he's saying. He's ignorant and biased and doesn't belong here and I'm going to go tell him just that to his face." With a curt nod, I turned around and marched off.

I stepped into the tent, surprised at the number of people inside. Voices were raised, some in anger, and it seemed more than a few were arguing with one another. Nettie Ledbetter saw me and rushed over. "Can you believe such a thing, Bess?" Her cheeks were flushed and her eyes bright.

"I've heard of it but never thought I'd see it here, Nettie."

She shook her head. "I read some of the literature he has in here." She looked toward the front of the tent, her brow furrowed. "Did you know that Alexander Graham Bell was a eugenicist? He believed that deaf people should not be allowed to marry."

This must have hit a nerve with Nettie, whose niece had been born deaf and because of that was thought by most to be mentally impaired. But I had found the dear girl intelligent and curious about life. Nettie and her husband had scraped up enough money to send her to a school for the deaf in Asheville and had both learned sign language so they could communicate with her. In my eyes, Nettie had some despicable qualities but her care for her family was admirable.

"I can't believe a man of his renown would think that," I said.

"But he's not the only one," she went on. "The Carnegie Institution and Rockefeller Foundation are financing some of their projects." She shook her head. "When I heard on the radio about the Racial Integrity Act of Virginia back in '24, I knew we were headed for trouble. Now, I may have my biases, but in my view, people of any color should be able to marry, not just whites. Why, think of the hedonism that creates, Bessie, men and women getting together and procreating without benefit of marriage."

"It's beyond belief," I said. "Did you meet Dr. Denby and does he actually support these views?"

She snorted with disdain. "I spoke to him briefly, told him I might fill out one of his questionnaires, just to see what he'd say."

"And what did he say, Nettie?"

"He said I wouldn't qualify," she said with indignation. "Due to my dark eyes and hair." She leaned closer. "Even accused me of being," she lowered her voice to a whisper, "Jewish."

I knew my Cherokee bloodline showed clearly in my high cheekbones, dark hair and eyes, and was certain he'd consider me inferior as well. Well, we'd see about that. "Where is he?"

"After he judged the Fitter Family and Better Baby contests, he just disappeared." Nettie huffed. "Said he had to be back in Black Mountain to see to a patient." She looked around. "I suspect it was more due to the fact that he wasn't getting as good a response from the crowd as he thought he would. Many booed his lecture and only a few entered the contest after I encouraged them to read the sign out front."

"Good for you, Nettie. We can't let this sort of thing be encouraged."

She folded her arms. "I agree. When you came in, I was on my way out to take down that Godforsaken sign. You ask me, this entire tent should be burned to the ground."

I suspected Nettie was more upset over the fact that she didn't qualify for the contest rather than the moral issue of eugenics but didn't discourage her. I watched with a bit of amusement as she dismantled the sign, stomping on the flashing lights until each broke under her foot. Several of the mountaineers had gathered outside and cheered her on. I noticed a young woman standing nearby, a beautiful baby girl in her arms. I smiled at her but then saw the baby had a ribbon around her neck. She was blond and blue-eyed and chubby, the epitome of a healthy Anglo child, and must have been the winner of the Better Baby contest. The young mother watched Nettie with a horrified look and must have felt confused by the reaction of some of her friends and neighbors. She didn't return my smile but simply turned on her heel and hurried off. I searched faces, wondering who had won the Fitter Family contest, but didn't see any more ribbons. I made a mental note to talk to Doc Widby about Dr. Denby's exhibition. The man needed to be made aware that this sort of prejudice would not abide on the mountain, not in most of the mountaineer's eyes nor in God's.

Chapter Sixteen

Fall 1928

Put wishes in one hand and spit in the other and see which one fills up first.

JOHN

I was so excited about the county fair, I reckon I didn't sleep a wink the night before. I thought Jolly was ready for the race and figured he'd run a good one. Aunt Bessie and Uncle Fletch kept telling me he would be up against strong, swift horses and not to expect too much, but I had faith in my red mule. He might not win but he'd give those horses a good race, I was sure of that.

We set off at daybreak in Horace Manny's truck. I rode in the back with my aunt and uncle, and we tied Jolly to the rear bumper. I was afraid he might tire out, trotting behind the truck, but it didn't seem to bother him. Uncle Fletch assured me he'd have a good rest before the race started. Besides, Mr. Manny drove so slow, I don't reckon it taxed Jolly at all.

As it turned out, when we got stuck in the mud, Jolly had enough time to catch his wind and graze a bit, so by the time we got to the fairgrounds, he looked to be in pretty good shape.

I hopped down from the truck and looked around as I untied Jolly. What a different world it seemed. There were tents everywhere, big ones and small ones, and booths where men yelled at the people passing by to stop and partake in whatever they were offering. I smelled fried foods and something really sweet, mingled with horse manure and downtrodden grass. It was a good smell. Uncle Fletch gave me the dollar entry fee and walked with me to the racetrack on the outskirts of the fairgrounds. I hesitated once I got a good look at the horses that were going to race. Some were older and didn't look too healthy and one or two looked more like plow horses than race horses, but there were some that were sleek and muscular and I figured they'd give Jolly a good race. When I spied Sheriff Nanny's horse, I thought my chances of winning the race had just narrowed down a bit. Uncle Fletcher told me Sheriff Nanny had won the race the last five years. But he had to lose sometime, I told Jolly, and this just might be Jolly's year.

The men were friendly enough and Sheriff Nanny seemed concerned I was racing, although to tell the truth, I think he was either putting me on or trying to make me feel more confident. I didn't care. I intended to do my best to win this race and Jolly seemed energetic and eager to get started.

When the starter shot the gun in the air, it startled me and Jolly and I almost fell off the mule, but we got situated soon enough and off we went. By that time, we were trailing a bit but it didn't take my red mule long to catch up with the stragglers and pass them by. I swear, I felt like Jolly and I were one being as he raced by other horses, me yelling in his ear to keep going. Before I knew it, the race was over and Sheriff Nanny had won, but I consoled myself that if we hadn't gotten off to such a poor start, we just might have won that race. Uncle Fletch said not to worry too much about it, there was always next year, and I told Jolly we were going to have to work on getting used to a gun going off to tell us it was time to race. Aunt Bessie said there were several people cheering me and Jolly on during the race and that made me feel better.

Afterwards, I put Jolly in a pasture set aside for horses and Aunt Bessie, Uncle Fletch and I went off to the tent showing what the man outside was calling freaks of nature.

There was a man in there they called the ape man, who was supposed to be half ape and half man. Aunt Bessie said he could be but more than likely it was simply a man who had glued some sort of fur or hair all over his body. He had so much hair on his face it was hard to see his features, though, and it was fun thinking he might actually be half ape and half man. He made weird noises like he was trying to roar and some women screeched when he did. The bearded woman had a beard clear down to her stomach and Aunt Bessie said more than likely she had glued hair on her face. Although to be honest, I'd seen women in my short lifetime who had hair on their face just like men did although none with long, bushy beards. The fat lady was the fattest person I'd ever seen. She looked like her body was one big roll of fat after another. She had so many chins, you couldn't see her neck, and no lap to speak of. She sat on a chair they said was specially made, the width of two chairs and supported by metal struts so it wouldn't collapse. Her legs looked like two tree trunks ending in wide, splayed feet. She had no ankles that I could see. I wondered how many meals she had eaten to get that large and if she could even stand and walk or if they had to wheel her everywhere. Aunt Bessie said it could be that she was a smaller person who had been made to look that way by stuffing padding in her clothing. Maybe so but she sure looked real to me. The world's tallest man was so tall, his head nearly touched the top of the tent. The strangest thing about him was that his legs were long and thin but the rest of his body looked normal. Uncle Fletcher pointed to his ankles and I noticed when he shifted that his pants legs rode up to reveal what looked to be sticks beneath instead of actual legs. Uncle Fletcher said he was more than likely standing on stilts.

I was a bit disappointed by the time we left the tent but still, all in all, it was fun. Most of the people passing through with us seemed to think the people inside were actual freaks as they claimed to be, but after thinking on it a bit, I thought my aunt and uncle were right.

By then it was time to watch the judging of the quilting and jam contests. Aunt Bessie didn't win any of the contests she entered which really surprised me. In my eyes, no one could cook or can as good as my aunt. She didn't seem particularly bothered by it so I figured it must not have been that important to her.

While Aunt Bessie went to a tent that had something to do with a word I'd never heard before, Uncle Fletcher and I decided to go watch the judging of the livestock. As we watched the horse judging, I told Uncle Fletch it was a shame they didn't judge mules. Jolly would win a blue ribbon, without a doubt. Uncle Fletch said he'd suggest that to the judging committee and maybe next year they would have such a contest.

We walked around the fairgrounds after that, waiting for Aunt Bessie to finish with whatever she was doing. They had what Uncle Fletcher called a merry-go-round, with wooden horses mounted on a platform that turned round and round. A lot of small children were riding the horses, which went up and down, and seemed to be having a lot of fun. Uncle Fletcher asked me if I wanted to join in, but I shook my head no. I felt too old for that ride although it looked like a good one.

By the time Aunt Bessie caught up with us, it was time for supper. Uncle Fletcher treated us to hotdogs he bought from a vendor. I got to pick what I wanted to go on top of my hot dog and chose chili and mustard. That was the best hotdog I'd ever had. We drank lemonade and then Uncle Fletcher bought what he called funnel cakes which were sweet and soft and just right for dessert. By that time, it was dark enough for the fireworks display which only lasted a couple of minutes but it sure was pretty. Afterward, Uncle Fletch said we best fetch Jolly because it was time to meet Horace for the trip back home.

On the ride home, I looked up at the sky, and I swear the moon was so big and round, I felt like I could reach up and touch it.

Aunt Bessie, seeing my look, patted my arm. "I'll tell you a story about the moon and sun," she said, "to help pass the time."

I smiled up at her. I loved hearing these stories.

"There was a time when the Sun was very young. She lived in the East, and in the evening, a young man would come to visit her. The People think this perhaps was the beginning of courting. She thought it strange that the young man would always leave near daylight, but while he visited, they would talk and gaze in awe at the beautiful stars in the deep skyvault. While she could talk with him, she could not see him, and he wouldn't even tell her his name. She was greatly curious as to who this young man was and decided one evening to find out by touching him in the dark of the night when he came to see her. As on all other nights in the past, he said very nice things to her about how she was so round and perfect and how bright her smile was. In the dark, she reached her hand into some warm ashes from an earlier fire and said, 'You are very cold from the wind hitting your face. Let me warm your face for you,' and put ashes on his face. He didn't know she had ashes on her hands and at the first peek of daylight he abruptly left on his journey. When the Moon came up in the skyvault the next day, the Sun could see the ashes on his face and knew that it was her brother, the Moon, who had been coming to see her. While she was excited to learn who he was, the Moon was ashamed and to this day comes up at the other end of the skyvault to keep distance from the sun going down."

I drifted off to sleep, lulled by the cadence of her words, and don't remember the rest of the ride back. I woke up when Mr. Manny stopped the truck. I thanked him for taking us to the fair, and after putting Jolly in his stall and making sure he had hay and water, gave my aunt and uncle a hug good night and went to bed, barely aware of Sycamore and Fritz crowding into bed beside me.

Chapter Seventeen

Spring 1929

Either fish or cut bait.

One bright early spring morning, I set off to the Bartlett place to check on Bob Jr. Although he showed no signs of improving, I hoped one day to walk through the door and see his smiling face. Doc Widby and I had read all the research on encephalitis lethargica we could find and knew the results would probably not be good but, still, there was hope. Our church members prayed for him at each Sunday service and I strongly believed in the miracle of prayer, having witnessed it myself a time or two. My concern for his mother Maisie had not diminished, as her health continued to dwindle. I knew it was a huge burden taking care of a grown man who could not feed or bathe himself, along with the mental stress of worrying for her son. Each visit, I took her a tonic in the form of a tea made from sassafras, dandelion and goldenseal, in hopes that her health would not completely falter. But each time I saw her, she looked paler and thinner, and I feared stress would be her downfall if things didn't improve with her son.

Many times, John would accompany me to the Bartlett place and we would pass the time admiring the fauna of the forest or talking about his Cherokee ancestry. On this journey, we discussed the weather, which couldn't seem to make up its mind whether we were still in the throes of a fiercely cold winter or entering a warm, humid spring.

John shivered and moved closer to me as we walked along. I put my arm around his shoulders. "Do you want my shawl, John?"

"No, ma'am, I'll be all right, I reckon. I didn't bring my jacket 'cause I figured the sun would warm the day up pretty quick."

"It's early yet, John. Let's hope it does warm up soon," I replied, resisting the urge to shiver myself.

"Why doesn't the weather stay the same year-round, Aunt Bessie? It'd sure be nice if we had cool evenings and warm days all the time, don't you think?"

To take our minds off the chilly morning, I decided to tell him a story. "Well, the People have a legend about that, John. Did I ever tell you about the North and South?"

He looked at me and grinned. "No, but I'd sure like to hear it."

"Well, the North decided to take a trip so he figured he'd go to the South. He enjoyed himself as he headed in that direction and soon met the daughter of the South who was so beautiful, he wanted to marry her and take her home with him. But the South was not pleased with the North coming so far South because the North was too cold. So the South told his daughter that she would have to go back with the North because he couldn't stay very long in the South or the South would freeze. The South's daughter agreed to go back with the North to the ice houses and Ice People, but after a few days, the ice houses started to melt and the Ice People were hot and sweaty. They called for a council with the North to let him know that his beloved bride would have to return to the South. If not, the entire North would eventually melt away. The North knew the council was right but was terribly sad and didn't want to send her away so did nothing. As the days passed, the North became hotter and the council met again and said to the North, 'The South's daughter must return to where she grew up. Her nature is warm and that is where she belongs, not here in the North.' Although it saddened him, North sent her home to her family in the South. But to this day, the North sneaks a brief trip toward the South to touch his beautiful bride in the South. And sometimes she sneaks a trip toward the North but only for a brief time so as not to melt the Ice People and their houses. And they are always glad to see the North smile with sunshine, if only for a short time."

John contemplated this, nodding, and finally said, "Well, it makes sense to me."

I patted his cheek. "You're such a special boy, John, I hope you know that."

He only smiled at me and that near broke my heart. All children should feel special and unique and well-loved, and I hoped before this boy left my life, he would feel that way about himself.

I looked up and noticed we were near the Bartletts' place. "Well, John, let's hope Bob Jr. is up and about," I said as I led him toward their front porch.

Maisie met me at the door, wringing her hands in her apron, looking wretched. I rushed to her. "Is it Bob Jr., Maisie? Is he all right?"

Tears sprang to her eyes and she glanced behind her then eased the door shut. "Bob Sr. thought it might be a good idea to have that new doctor in Black Mountain take a look at him, Bessie, and he just left." She bit her lip. "He, he didn't have anything good to say. In fact, thinks it might be best if we put Bob Jr. out of his misery."

I stepped back, shock coursing through my body. "Did he actually say that, Maisie?"

She nodded. "Called it eutha something or other."

"Euthenasia?"

"Yes, that's it. Bob Sr.'s fit to be tied. He's out in the barn, tearing it apart, I suspect."

I clenched my fists. "Was the doctor on horseback or walking?"

"Appeared to be walking. He said he likes to walk."

I looked at the trail heading back to Black Mountain then turned to Maisie. "Is it all right if John stays with you for a little while, Maisie? I'd like to talk to that Dr. Denby. I'm sure he misspoke when he told you that."

She nodded as she held out her hand to John. The smile on her lips didn't quite reach her eyes. "I made some of them fried peach pies you like so much, John. You care to have one or two? I suspect Sari's gotten into them by now so we best make haste or they'll be gone afore you know it."

"I sure would," he said, smiling at me before being led off by Maisie.

I stepped off the porch and ran down the trail, my body tingling with the need to set this man straight. How dare he suggest such a thing to the Bartletts, who loved their son dearly.

It wasn't long before I spied a man ahead of me on the trail, ambling along, swinging a walking cane. "Dr. Denby," I called.

He stopped and turned around, his brows lifted inquiringly.

I rushed to catch up to him, studying him as I approached. He appeared to be of medium size, with a head full of curly, blond hair and eyes a watery blue, so pale they almost blended with his face. His lips were curled into an arrogant smirk and I briefly wondered if that was natural or practiced. I was curious why a man like this would be practicing medicine on the mountain then remembered what Hiram Henderson had told me. Well, maybe it was time someone set him straight.

"I'm Bessie Elliott," I said when I reached him.

He stared at me for a long moment, then realization seemed to come to him. "Oh, yes, the healer. I believe these mountain people also call you Moonfixer."

"Yes, that's right. I just came from the Bartletts' house. Maisie told me what you said to them about Bob Jr. and I am hoping Maisie misunderstood you recommended euthanasia."

He cocked his head. "I am sure I made myself clear on the matter, Mrs. Elliott."

"Surely you weren't serious, Dr. Denby."

He drew his head back as if surprised someone had challenged him. "Of course I was. I wouldn't have said it otherwise."

"That seems pretty severe to me. They're his parents and I don't see how you helped them by telling them he should be euthanized."

"What else is there to do? As you may know, this disease is not curable. There's nothing to be done for the lad and he's only a burden on the family. As I'm sure you have seen for yourself, it seems to be taking its toll, especially with Mrs. Bartlett."

"There is the chance he'll wake up, Dr. Denby. There's no need to end a life simply because a cure has not been found. There's always the possibility one will be and soon."

He shook his head as if dealing with an insolent child. "Mrs. Elliott, I understand you're also a teacher so you're not illiterate like most of these mountaineers. And as a healer, I'm certain you have your own opinions as to the best way to treat that poor soul. But I have much more experience than you and am, in fact, a medical doctor, unlike you. Although you may not agree with my recommendation, surely you can understand my diagnosis and the need for it."

"No, I cannot. Nor will I ever. And I certainly don't condone it."

We stared at one another for a long moment.

He sneered. "Well, you have that right, of course, but I fail to see that that makes any difference one way or the other."

I shook my head. "I can't for the life of me understand why any person, doctor or not, would choose to murder such a young patient."

"Mrs. Elliott, it's more of a mercy killing than murder, I quite assure you."

"Oh, I disagree. But I'm curious how you have come to this decision, Dr. Denby. Does it arise from your strong advocacy for eugenics?"

He smiled as if proud. "Yes, indeed. And if you know anything about it, you're aware it's a very strong movement, gaining ground daily."

"I only know that eugenicists are no better than the KKK," I snorted.

"Unlike the KKK, we have some very powerful people behind us as well as legal precedent, beginning with Connecticut as far back as 1896 enacting marriage laws incorporating eugenic criteria prohibiting anyone who was epileptic, imbecile or feeble-minded from marrying. Indiana enacted the first law allowing sterilization on eugenic grounds back in '07 and recently Virginia, with their Eugenical Sterilization Act. Universities and high schools across the nation are offering eugenics courses now as a branch of their biology curriculum. It will one day be practiced throughout this country."

"But from what I've read on the matter, most eugenicists don't advocate euthanasia, but rather, sterilization."

"Perhaps so, but there are those of us who think it should be included in the program. Bob Jr. is the perfect example of why."

"Either way doesn't justify the need for it that I can see; in fact, makes a strong case against it."

He leaned on his walking stick and studied me for a bit. "Perhaps you'll understand it if you consider the eugenics premise is based on the idea that we selectively breed our livestock for desired traits so wouldn't it follow we do so with human society to breed the perfect, pure race?" At my look, he continued. "The theories actually derive from Charles Darwin and his cousin Sir Francis Dalton who believed that if only the best and the brightest married each other and bore children, it would serve to elevate the human race."

I folded my arms, unable to believe someone could be so selective in their thinking. "And just who would make up the perfect, pure race?"

He sniffed with disdain, as if growing irritated with my questions. "I suppose you would say a Nordic race, tall, intelligent, talented, blond-haired and blue-eyed."

I eyed him up and down. "Well, you may qualify because you're blond and blue-eyed, but I don't see that you're particularly tall, and as for intelligence, I have to question that based on your beliefs."

He drew himself up. "I'm tall enough," he said as if offended.

"And who would you weed out through eugenics?" I asked, not trying to conceal the irony in my voice.

"Criminals, the mentally ill, developmentally disadvantaged, chronically indigent, alcoholics, basically any who are a burden to society."

"Indigents? Most of the people on this mountain are indigent, Dr. Denby, through no fault of their own."

"Perhaps if they had more intelligence, they wouldn't be indigent," he said with a smirk.

I could see there would be no persuading this man, who had embraced to the extreme a premise I found abhorrent. As far as I could see, he had no real supporters on our mountain and most, like me, felt he did not belong here. I strongly suspected that before long, that point would be made clear by the mountaineers one way or the other and saw no need to waste any more of my time. "Dr. Denby, I don't know what you're doing on this mountain, but you certainly don't belong here. I suggest you go back to Philadelphia and practice your beliefs there." With a huff, I turned on my heel and left.

"Your people on this mountain will prove the theory true, Mrs. Elliott," he called after me. "That's my reason for being here. And one day you'll agree with eugenics, mark my word."

"I don't think God would agree, sir, and that's what I live my life by," I called over my shoulder, sickened to my stomach by this man and his views.

As it turned out, eugenics never took a firm hold in America, losing favor when it was condemned by scientific communities in 1936, although it was practiced in my state well into the 1960s. Sterilization of people in institutions for the mentally ill and retarded continued into the mid 1970s in the rest of the country, and it shames me that the precedent allowing sterilization of the feeble-minded has never been overruled. It did come to fruition in the most evil way in a country called Germany led by a man named Adolf Hitler who embraced the premise, quoting American texts and using them as evidence to support his efforts to recruit others to his cause. In fact, Madison Grant, one of the leaders of the American eugenics movement, received a fan letter from Adolf Hitler praising his work as inspiring. The Rockefellers played a part not only in the American Eugenics movement but the European one as well by helping to finance a German branch that counted Joseph Mengele, known as the Angel of Death at the Auschwitz Concentration Camp during World War II, in its ranks.

Chapter Eighteen

Fall 1929 - Summer 1930

She's feeling as low as a toad in a dry well.

The saying goes that into every life a little rain must fall. I admit, I'd had more than my fair share of sunshine, but when things turned dark, they did so with a vengeance, proving the next couple of years to be two of the worst of my life, with great personal loss and a fearful doubt about the future.

The morning of October 24, 1929, we woke to a cool breeze with the sun shining brightly, promising a glorious day. The mountain was a wonder of color, reds and browns and golds against the dark green of the evergreen trees, with skies clear and blue. I remember looking out the window, praising God for such a beautiful day while thinking how wonderfully blessed we were, a feeling which soon shattered.

We had just finished breakfast when I heard horse hooves pounding over the wooden bridge across our creek. Fletcher and I rose from the table and stepped outside to see who had come to call, John and the dogs following along. We watched as Nettie Ledbetter pulled on the reins and her horse drew to a stop when she neared the cabin. Fletch helped her down from the buggy, and I noted her face was flushed, tears shimmering in her eyes.

"Is it Merle?" I asked, going to her.

She grabbed my hands. "Oh, Bess, I have terrible news."

I caught her panic, my spine tingling. "What is it? What happened?"

"The stock market crashed. The whole country is in an uproar and people are killing themselves."

I looked at Fletcher.

He shook his head. "Nettie, that's way up there in New York City. It won't affect us."

She nodded. "Yes, it will. They said on the radio the banks are closed, that we won't be able to get our money. They say everything in the banks is just gone." She sobbed into a handkerchief.

Fletcher looked at me and for the first time ever I saw panic in my husband's eyes.

Nettie clutched me, turning my attention back to her. "Merle's gone to Old Fort to see if he can get our money out of the bank, but if the radio is saying they're closed, how can he do that? Oh, Bess, we'll lose everything."

Fletcher began moving toward the barn. "I'm going to Old Fort," he said over his shoulder.

"Can I go, Uncle Fletcher?" John asked, catching up with him.

"You best stay with your aunt, John. I won't be gone long."

I watched my husband run to the barn, willing myself not to panic, remembering I had dreamed of this, oh, yes, but when I told Fletcher, he had convinced me something like this could never happen in America. But it appeared he, as well as millions of others, had been wrong.

It only took minutes for Fletch to saddle Pet and he was off, waving as he passed us.

I reached out to John and clutched his arm. All our money was in the bank in Old Fort, every cent we had saved for all our years on the mountain. What would we do if it was gone like Nettie said? How would we live?

As if sensing my worries, John said, "Don't worry, Aunt Bessie, Uncle Fletch will take care of it."

Bless that child. I tried to smile at him, tried not to let him see my panic but fear I was not able to hide my feelings.

Nettie climbed back in the buggy. "I've got to go warn everyone. Maybe if enough of us show up in Old Fort, they'll have to give us our money."

I watched her race back across the bridge then turned and looked at John, telling myself there was no sense worrying until I actually had something to worry about. And the best thing to do to take our minds off our troubles was to find some busywork. I squeezed his hand. "We've got apples left to pick, John. Let's get us a basket and get to the orchard. Won't do us any good to sit here worrying. Like you said, your uncle will take care of things."

Late afternoon, John and I were in the basement, storing away the apples we had picked, when I heard Pet neigh. We ran outside to the barn, where Fletch was unsaddling the horse. He turned to us when we stepped into the barn and I knew from the expression on his face that the news was grim.

His eyes darted to John and it was obvious he didn't want to share bad news in front of our boy. So I planted a smile on my face and kissed my husband on his cheek. "You take care of things, Fletch?" I asked lightly although I admit my voice shook a bit.

"Everything's fine, Bess." He ruffled John's hair. "How about you help an old man out and unsaddle Pet for me, John? I'm a bit tired from all that riding."

"Yes, sir," John said. "You go on inside and rest a bit. I'll take care of things."

I smiled at the boy, thinking how much he had grown since he came to us.

Fletch and I walked to the house, and when we were far enough away that John couldn't hear, he told me he had gone straight to the bank. Several men were gathered outside the building which was locked up tight, a sign on the door proclaiming the bank was closed indefinitely. Try as they might, they couldn't get anyone to come to the door.

Merle Ledbetter told the group that he had managed to talk to the bank's manager before he hightailed it out of town, who told him people had forced their way into the bank early that morning and closed their accounts until there was no money left. He told Merle if he hadn't shipped money off to the main branch the day before, he probably would have had enough so that everyone could have taken their money out. "Bad luck, I guess," was all he had to say when Merle told him it wasn't fair some got their money and others didn't. Merle told Fletch it was all he could do not to pull out his gun and shoot him. Fletch said the town folk were so riled, it was a good thing the bank manager left, else Sheriff Nanny would be dealing with a lynch mob.

"What are we going to do?" I said, my stomach clenching.

Fletcher squeezed my hand. "We'll get by, like we always do, Bess. We have your income from teaching, I can sell wood off our land, sell off our pigs and cows, and we have the tobacco crop. That should see us through the winter."

"But what about any seed money we may need for our garden next year? Money to buy calves and piglets?"

Fletcher shook his head. "We managed before, we'll manage again. We have to put our faith in the good Lord and do our best, that's all we can do."

I thought again about the dream I'd had foretelling this and the way Fletcher had dismissed it, laughing and telling me I had nothing to worry about. I wanted to scream this at him, throw it in his face, but refrained. Fletcher had been a good provider and had seen us through hard times. He would again. I kissed his cheek. "You're right, Fletch. We'll get through this. We've gotten through worse, I reckon."

He smiled at me. "Let's try not to let little John see how worried we are, Bess. I don't want him worrying about something he has no control over."

It was bad enough losing our savings but even worse when we lost our sweet Fritz that winter. We grieved his loss as deeply as we would a family member. Fritz lived a good, long life but at the end could barely walk and had trouble hearing and seeing. Although we knew his time was drawing close, we ignored that fact as we helped him get around as much as we could, telling ourselves he wasn't ready to leave just yet. Fletch found him late one morning beneath the front porch where he always napped, his body stiff and cold. We buried him beside the first Fritz, saying a prayer over his body with tears running down our faces. John sang a hymn over his grave in his beautiful voice, Fletch and I joining in as best we could, our voices wavering as we said goodbye to that precious soul.

But no financial hardship nor the loss of our beloved Fritz could ever devastate me as much as when we lost our sweet boy.

John stayed with us until the summer of 1930 when he was twelve years old. Since he had graduated the sixth grade, as high as I was qualified to teach, he would have to transfer to the school in Old Fort if he wanted to continue his schooling. And that meant he would have to walk three miles to catch the bus, ride to the school which took almost an hour, and in the afternoon do the same thing in reverse. A good four or five hours out of his day traveling which, in my opinion, and John's too, was too long. We had talked about him riding Jolly to the bus stop, which would cut off a little of that time, but what would he do with Jolly when he got there? Tie him to a tree and expect him to be waiting there when he returned? There was too much of a chance that someone would steal him what with the state of the economy in those days and John didn't want to risk that. The only solution seemed to be that John return to Knoxville to finish his schooling. He didn't want to leave and, Lord knows, Fletch and I didn't want him to go, but we couldn't see a way to keep him with us although I prayed over this constantly. I lost much sleep before he left, frantically trying to find a solution to this problem so that John could remain with us but there was nothing that could be done as far as I could see. And God saw no reason to answer my prayers.

There had been letters flying back and forth between Stone Mountain and Knoxville all summer long over this issue. Papa wanted John to come live with him and Loney and Jack, who had recently become a widow for the second time. When asked if he wanted to do that, John squirmed in his seat and after several minutes reluctantly admitted that he'd prefer not to. Roy and Alice and their family had moved to Memphis a couple of years before so that wasn't even considered. I didn't want John to go to Knoxville, much less all the way over to Memphis. It was finally settled that he would live with Thee and Myrtle since their daughter Etta would be enrolled in the same school so John would at least have one person he knew on his first day in a new school. I figured a friendly, outgoing boy like him would have no trouble making friends after that.

After the decision was made, I spent many an hour in the barn loft, crying over this upcoming loss, praying for the strength to let our boy go without becoming hysterical and clingy. I knew it would be hard enough on John to leave and was determined I wouldn't make it worse for him than it had to be.

About the only bright spot that summer was on July 27th when we went to Old Fort to watch the unveiling and dedication of the arrowhead monument to commemorate Davidson's Fort which gave the town its name. Sitting on a base of native river rock and chiseled out of a slab of pink granite from the Salisbury Quarries, the monument was placed on an old Native American trail, across the street from the train depot where I first arrived as a new bride. Before the unveiling, we were treated to speeches from local dignitaries about Appalachian Mountain pioneers and their descendents and one about the Indian influence. Chiefs and members of the Cherokee and Catawba tribes were present and smoked a peace pipe for the first time in history. The unveiling was performed by Marie Nesbitt, the great-great-great granddaughter of Martha Burgin, the only white child born in the original fort. The monument still stands today as it did on that festive day back in 1930, one of the few that summer when my mind wasn't consumed with thoughts of John leaving.

The day in early September when we took John to the station to catch the train back to Knoxville was the saddest day of my life up until that point. I wanted to be strong for

John and send him off with love and a smile but I was miserable thinking about the days without him when I would go back to my solitary walks to and from school. Fletcher would also miss having him to hunt and fish with and poor Sycamore would be heartbroken. She had already lost Fritz back in the winter and now she would lose the most important person in the world to her. And that wasn't all. John's red mule, Jolly, poor thing, would be grieving right along with Sycamore and us. There would be no more daily rides and no more horse races in his future.

I would miss telling John bedtime stories and hearing his beautiful voice when we sang hymns at night after Fletcher read from the Bible. I would miss seeing his grin when he told me about some mischief he had gotten into with his friend Hoover Hall, his bright laughter when he rode Jolly around the pasture, and his excited hugs when he accomplished some new project or chore he'd never been able to do before.

But mostly, I'd miss his presence and seeing the almost daily changes that signaled he would soon be a grown man. I had shared in so many firsts with him, but I was greedy, I wanted to be there for the rest of them.

I was glad John rode in the back of the wagon as we made our way to Old Fort, where he couldn't see me dab at my eyes with my handkerchief or put my fist against my mouth to stifle a sob. Fletcher, bless him, would reach over and squeeze my hand from time to time but that gesture of comfort only made my misery worse. I envied my husband's ability to staunch his emotions at times like this. I knew he was as sad as I was but he was so much better at putting his feelings away until he could grieve in private.

At the station, while we waited for the train conductor to give the signal to board, I clutched John's hand in mine and could not contain my emotions. I admit, I wept a good bit but managed to send John off with a fierce hug and kiss with promises to write every week. I watched him board the train, my hand to my chest, clutching at my heart, which felt rent in two. It wasn't right to be given this gift for six years then have to relinquish it. I prayed John would come back to me one day for good, and that prayer was the only thing I could grasp onto to keep me from running after the train, calling for John to come back.

"He'll be back next summer, Bess," Fletch said as he helped me into the wagon outside the Old Fort Train Depot.

I could only nod. Yes, he had promised to come back next summer and the summer after that but I would miss him terribly in between. "It seems such a long time, Fletch. How will we know he's doing all right or if he needs anything?"

"Well, you did insist on him writing at least once a week and he promised he would. And your Papa will be close by. He'll see to John's needs if Thee and Myrtle don't take care of whatever it is first."

I pulled my hankie out of my skirt pocket and dabbed my eyes. "I know I'm being foolish but that's our boy we've just sent off into the world ..." It hit me how silly I sounded. It wasn't as if he'd died and we'd never see him again. He would, as my husband reminded me, be returning to us next summer. I leaned against Fletcher and did my best to smile. "I'm just a sentimental old fool. I already miss him and I know I'll miss him more with every passing day."

"So will I. He's a good boy. You did a right good job raising him up, Bess."

"You played a part in his raising too, Fletcher, and he'll be all the better of a man because of your influence. Just think of all the things you were able to teach him in six short years, how to ride a horse, how to fish and hunt." I smiled. "How to shoot a shotgun."

Fletcher smiled too. "Didn't do such a good job with that one, did I? But he learned eventually."

"Yes, and he also learned the importance of listening before he tried something new." I sighed. "I'm being greedy, I know, but I wish we could have kept him with us until he at least graduated from high school."

"So do I but there's no way around it. We lost too much of our money when the bank crashed." He shook his head. "I'm sorry about that, Bess, I should've listened to you and taken that money out of the bank. You warned me."

I firmed my lips and reminded myself not to say, "I told

you so." Fletcher had apologized more times than I could count and it didn't do any good to beat a dead horse. And the truth is, after the dream, I'd mentioned it and then let it drop, and that was as much on me as it was on my husband.

Fletch flicked the reins over the mules' backs. "Ho, my ladies, let's get this rig moving. I reckon we could sell some of the land and buy one of those danged ol' automobiles to drive John to and from the bus stop or even to and from the school in Old Fort, but it would be a burden coming up with money to buy gas and keep the thing running. I don't think John would like being a burden on us."

I sighed. "No, no, he wouldn't. I hope he'll do all right with Thee and Myrtle."

"Why shouldn't he?"

"Well, they have their own children and I'm worried they might favor them over John. Not that I think Thee would do that but I don't know Myrtle very well at all so I can't say if she would or not."

Fletcher patted my hand. "He'll be all right, and if he isn't I bet he'll let you know about it. If that happens, we'll just bring him back here and we'll figure out some way to get him to school."

"I could try to teach him at home like I did the first few years he was with us but I'm not trained for that level and I'm not sure I'm up to the task."

"You could do it, Bess, but it'd be awful hard on you if you wanted to go on teaching at Crooked Creek."

"I'd give up my job in a minute flat, but like you said, we need the money."

Fletcher sighed. "I can't tell you enough how sorry I am about that, Bess. I should never have trusted our money with that damned bank. Shoulda done what I plan to do from now on, bury it in the back yard or under the barn or ..."

I patted his arm. "Hush now, enough of that. You did what you thought best, and there for a while, it was. Now that the money's gone, we'll figure out how to get by. It's not like we'll go hungry. We have our garden and you can hunt. We might have to scrimp on a few things like sugar and coffee for a while but I imagine with your horse-trading skills, you could trade for those if we need them. We have a roof over our heads and plenty of wood to keep us warm in the winter. And we own 400 acres of good land free and clear so they can't take that away from us."

"Guess you're right but I keep telling myself if I hadn't trusted that ..."

I smiled. "Didn't I tell you to hush? No use crying over spilt milk, Fletcher. We're going to be all right. I just know it. With the help of God, we'll get through this."

"I reckon you're right."

"Of course I am. We've been through hard times before and come through and we'll make it through this too." I smiled at him. "Besides, we have the most important thing already, and that's each other. We'll do just fine." I pointed up ahead where Thorney Dalton had stepped out of the trees and was waving us down. "And look, there's one more way we'll survive. I reckon I've treated Thorney for more things than you can shake a stick at. I wonder what's wrong with him now?"

Fletcher braked the mules to a stop and tipped his hat to Thorney. "Need a ride, Thorney? Hop on up here and we'll take you where you want to go."

I gripped Fletcher's arm as I saw I had been right. Blood soaked Thorney's pants leg and was beginning to form a pool around his foot. "Merciful heavens, Thorney, what have you done to yourself this time?"

He swayed as his eyes rolled back, showing the whites, and fell flat on his face. Fletch and I jumped down from the wagon, startling the mules.

Thankfully, Fletch hadn't released the reins and he jerked them to a halt again. "Whoa, girls, hold steady now."

I reached Thorney and knelt at his side, tearing the hole in his trousers to get a better look at his leg. I still had my hankie in my hand and pressed it on the wound to try to staunch the blood. "Fletch, please get my bag out from under the seat. His leg's in bad shape and I need to stop this bleeding so I can get a better look at what happened."

"Here you are, Bess. Let me get these mules settled and tied, then I'll help you."

"Do we have any water?"

"Nope, didn't think to put any in the wagon this morning."

"All right, as soon as you get the mules secure and I get a bandage on his leg, we'll get him in the wagon and take him home."

"Won't all that jostling make the bleeding worse?"

"I'll sit beside him and hold his leg in my lap and keep pressure on it. That might help a bit." I shook my head then looked up into Fletcher's eyes. "I don't see that we have any choice in the matter. We have to get him somewhere where I can treat the wound. I have some herbs in my bag but nothing that will stop the bleeding." I hesitated, looking back down at Thorney as I took a deep breath, trying to calm myself so I could see what to do. "All right. Give me your belt. It's tricky but I'll try a tourniquet around his thigh. That should help contain the bleeding enough to give us time to get him home. It's not that far."

Fletcher handed me his belt and I secured it around Thorney's upper leg. "That should do it." I scooted around to crouch at Thorney's feet. "I'll take this end, you get his shoulders."

He bent down and got a closer look at Thorney's leg. "That looks like a gunshot wound, Bessie."

I nodded. "It is but we don't have time to worry about who shot him right now. I'm afraid the bullet might have nicked the artery and I have to get this bleeding stopped. It went through, and that's a good thing, but he's lost an awful lot of blood which is why he passed out."

"All right. Let's get him into the wagon." He moved around to Thorney's head, lifting him slightly as he got a good grip under the shoulders. "You ready?"

"Yes, but be gentle. This is likely to hurt and he may wake up. I don't want him thrashing around and making it bleed even more."

We picked Thorney up and slid him into the back of the wagon. I climbed up with him and released the tourniquet for a few seconds to let some blood flow then tightened it again before lifting his leg and propping it up across my own, which, I hoped, might slow the bleeding. Fletch climbed up in the seat and took the reins, smacking them sharply against the mules' backs. "Yo, girls, yo." He glanced at me. "His house or ours, Bess?"

"His is a mite closer," I said as I blotted my handkerchief to the wound again. Thorney moaned but didn't open his eyes.

It seemed like it took forever to get to Thorney's place, but in actuality Fletcher got us there at a fairly good clip. I clutched Thorney's leg as tightly as I could, trying to keep it from being jostled too much as the mules made their way over the rocky road, sighing in relief when I caught sight of their home place.

Vera and all the children came running out of the house when they heard the wagon.

"You seen my man?" she yelled while we were still a good 20 feet away. As Fletcher braked the wagon to a stop, she asked again, "You seen my man?"

"He's in the back of the wagon, Vera. Bessie's taking care of him."

Vera clapped her hands to her mouth, taking several deep breaths to steady herself then walked to the back of the wagon. When she saw Thorney, her hands clenched into fists and she stifled a sob. After that brief sign of despair, she straightened her shoulders. "He all right, Moonfixer?"

"He's been shot, Vera. Do you have any idea what happened?"

Fletcher lowered the tailgate and jumped up beside me. "Let's get him inside first, Bessie. Stand back, Vera, and give us some room."

"Billy, Joe, you get on over here and help Mr. Elliott," she called to the two oldest boys. "I'll go in and clean off the kitchen table. Reckon that would be the best place to work on him."

I nodded as I jumped down from the wagon and took her hands, clasped so tightly in front of her that the knuckles showed white. "He'll be all right, Vera. The bullet went clear through, which is a blessing." I squeezed her hands. "A blessing, Vera, you remember that. He has lost a lot of blood but we can fix that." I squeezed her hands as she sobbed.

"He'll be all right, hold on to that."

She closed her eyes and shook her head. "We heard rumors that there were revenuers on the mountain. I warned Thorney to keep to home for a few days and not tangle with them, but when he heard gunfire coming from the direction of Julius Elliott's still, nothing'd do him but to hightail it out of here." She shook her head again. "Trying to be a hero." She gazed at her husband for a long moment. "Stupid old man."

I expected Fletcher to ask what had happened to his cousin Julius or maybe to go see for himself but he only directed the boys to take their father's feet. He guided Thorney's limp body out of the wagon, took his shoulders, and helped the boys carry him into the house. Vera rushed in ahead of them, yelling at the other children to stay out of the way.

I grabbed my medical bag and followed, shushing the children as they crowded around me, wanting to know if their father would be all right. "All of you hush now, your papa will be fine, but I need to get inside and take care of him." When that didn't help, I took the oldest daughter's hand. "Millie, you know what goldenseal is, don't you? And passion flowers?"

She nodded. "There's some passion flowers growing by the fence behind the barn and the pasture's full of goldenseal."

"Good, that's good. You take your sisters and pull up a good handful of both. Be sure to pull hard so you get the roots. I'm going to need them. Can you do that for me?"

"Yes, ma'am, Miss Bessie."

"Good. Go on now." As they hurried off, I turned my attention to the boys. "We're going to need plenty of water, boys. Find all the buckets you can and fill them up. Set them on the back porch so Fletch can carry them in as I need them. Can you see to that for me?" At their eager nods, I smiled. "Good, go on while I do what I can to help your papa."

As they hustled to do my bidding, I went inside and found Thorney stretched out on the kitchen table. It reminded me so much of the time in Hot Springs when Papa had brought home a dead man and laid him on our kitchen table—much to Mama's shock and consternation—and I took a moment to say a quick prayer. My old friend Death might be hovering over my shoulder right now but I'd do my best to keep Him from winning this encounter. Thorney had a wife and too many young'uns to care for to die at such a young age.

I saw Vera had had the good sense to spread an old sheet on the table as I set my medical bag near Thorney's knees and loosened the tourniquet. The bleeding had thankfully almost stopped but he had lost a lot of blood and his pants leg was soaked with it. I opened my bag and searched for nettle. "Vera, start some water boiling and add a couple spoonfuls of this nettle. Let it steep about three minutes then add a couple spoonfuls of molasses. Thorney will need a few cups of that every day until he's built his blood back up. The boys are bringing some more water." I turned to the two oldest boys. "Billy, Joe, can you help Fletcher get your papa's britches off?"

They both blushed furiously.

I smiled. "Be as gentle as you can. We don't want to move him too much and start the bleeding again. After that, y'all go out and help your brothers. And tell them and your sisters that everything's going to be all right."

"Yes, ma'am."

"I can cut them off if you'd like, Moonfixer," Vera said.

"No need to ruin a perfectly good pair of trousers, Vera. They'll probably carry the stain for a while but the hole's not too big that it can't be mended, if Thorney will let you mend it, that is. That hole and those bloodstains are going to give him another tall tale to share with all of his friends."

Smiling, Vera nodded. "That it will. 'Course, he'll be telling that tale every chance he gets, whether he's wearing these pants or not." She paused as she took my hand. "I want to thank you, Moonfixer."

I squeezed her hand. "Thank me later after Thorney's back to his old self and keeping you hopping, waiting on him hand and foot and whining like a cranky toddler."

She laughed. "Oh, I'm sure he will but you won't hear me complaining, at least not for a good long while."

"Millie and the girls are going to be bringing you some passion flower and goldenseal roots, probably the whole plant, but what I need first is the roots. Can you wash them good and then grind them into a paste for me? Best thing to use is a mortar and pestle if you have one, a wooden spoon and a bowl if you don't. I'll need them to make a poultice for his wound to stop the bleeding completely and help stave off inflammation. And don't throw the passion flowers out, the flowers themselves, I mean. We'll need them to make a tea to keep him comfortable and help him sleep later. Does he have any medical conditions I need to know about?"

"No, he's always been healthy as a horse. Doesn't even catch colds or anythin' when the young'uns bring them home from school. He claims it's the moonshine that keeps him from getting sick." She caressed her husband's cheek. "Don't you dare die on me, you stupid old man," she murmured.

"He's not going to die, Vera. Not if I can help it anyway." I looked at Fletcher as he held out Thorney's pants to Vera. Billy and Joe were already heading out the door, their faces still as red as a ripe tomato.

"Why don't you go and see what's keeping your girls, Vera? They've had more than enough time to pull up a whole field of flowers."

She stroked Thorney's cheek one more time and mumbled again, "Stupid old man," before walking out of the room, yelling for Millie.

I took a deep breath and smiled at my husband. "He'll be all right, I'm sure of it, but we need to get this wound good and clean so infection won't set in."

Fletch nodded. "What can I do to help?"

"Build up the fire then fill Vera's biggest pot with water and put it on the stove to boil. I may need you to hold him down while I clean out the debris from that wound. That's going to hurt and he'll probably come around when it does. I don't want him thrashing around and doing more damage."

As I expected, Thorney regained consciousness while I cleaned his wound. Fletch, holding his shoulders, leaned down and talked to him as if Thorney were one of his horses.

He was able to calm him down so that he didn't thrash around overly much. As soon as I deemed it clean enough, I took the goldenseal roots, which Vera had ground into a suitable mush, and smoothed the paste onto the wound. I followed that with the passion flower roots and as I worked instructed Vera on how to make the tea from the flowers.

Then I looked at Fletch. "We need to turn him over so I can treat the exit wound. Thank the good Lord the bullet passed through the fleshy part of his leg and didn't hit the bone or the muscle."

"All right, Bess, just tell me what to do."

By the time I'd finished, Thorney had regained consciousness. After Vera gave him a drink or two of his own white lightening, he was aware enough of what was going on that he could tell us what happened.

"I ran like a madman when I heard the gunfire. Didn't think about getting shot or nothin', I just wanted to get there and do what I could to help Julius. I suspected it was revenuers and damn if I wasn't right. I checked that old hollowed-out log where Julius keeps his stash first, figured if he'd gotten clear that's where he'd be, but didn't find nothin' so I headed off in the direction of his still. They'd found it all right and were chasing after Julius and that old hound dog of his.

"Julius had a good head start on them and when he saw me he yelled, "Revenuers comin', run," then scooted up a tree quick as a scalded cat. I hid behind a bush and them revenuers went past us as pretty as you please." Thorney shook his head and chuckled. "Probably woulda been all right except for that crazy dog of Julius's. Stupid hound treed Julius like a coon. Stood there at the base of that tree barking his fool head off and the revenuers, well, they tweren't as dumb as the ones I dealt with a few years ago. Remember that, Moonfixer?"

I laughed. "You led them a merry chase, Thorney."

"I shore did but these 'uns was smarter than those 'uns. They knew they had their man and they come back, thanks to that cussed fool dog barkin' like that. They walked right up to that tree and stood right there until the dog settled some then they started yelling at Julius to come on down, he was under arrest."

"But how did you end up getting shot, Pa?" Billy asked.

"Welp, I thought I might could help Julius out so I started making a ruckus. Stomping through the leaves, breaking limbs, just making lots of noise, all the time staying out of sight, hoping they'd think I was a bear or a mountain lion and hightail it out of there."

"Then what happened, Pa?"

"I couldn't see them from where I was but what I figure is 'stead of running away scared, one of them musta shot into the trees and got lucky." He sighed. "That damn fool dog's dumber than a bag of rocks."

I handed Thorney a cup of tea. He took it but looked at it suspiciously after he got a good whiff of the contents. "What's this, Moonfixer?"

I smiled as I nudged the cup up to his mouth. "Never you mind. It'll make you feel better. Are you in pain, Thorney?"

"Nah, hurts some but not too bad."

"Then drink up. That wound will probably give you some misery later but I'll leave some herbs with Vera that will help with pain if you need it. Vera, you'll need to change the bandage twice a day for the first few days, then leave it open to the air. And let me know if you even suspect infection." I took her hand. "We need to keep your man alive."

She leaned in and kissed my cheek. "I don't know how to thank you, Moonfixer. It seems a mite trifling to say it, but if you ever need anything, all you have to do is tell me."

I pulled her into my arms and hugged tight. "I'm the one who should be thanking you and Thorney, Vera."

She stepped back. "Why is that, Moonfixer? You did all the hard work. Only thing I did was boil some water and make a paste with those roots. Thorney didn't do nothing but get his fool self shot in the leg."

I nodded. "Yes, but you did help and Thorney getting shot took my mind off the fact that we sent John back to Knoxville today. I was miserable when that train pulled out of the station and I imagine I'll be miserable again but healing your man sure did keep me from missing John."

"I'm sorry, Moonfixer." She gestured to her children. "I got a couple I can spare if you want. Just take your pick.

I laughed for the first time that day.

Chapter Nineteen

1930 – 1958

She's got enough wrinkles to hold an eight day rain.

In the late 1950s, I heard a hymn playing on the radio in the general store in Old Fort that spoke to me so much I immediately ordered the sheet music so I could learn how to play it. The song, written by a man named Mosie Lister and titled, *Till the Storm Passes By*, fittingly profiled my life and I took to singing it whenever I was lonely or just needed something to make me smile. I played it for John the next time he came to visit and was pleased that he loved it as much as I did.

But I'm getting ahead of myself. Truth be told, after John left, my life was nothing to speak about. Oh, there were high points and low points as there always are in life but nothing like what had come before. For the most part, Fletcher and I lived a serene life on our little farm on Stone Mountain.

Money was tight for a while after the big stock market crash but Fletcher and I managed. I continued to teach, thus bringing in a steady paycheck that we sometimes had to fall back on to make it through. It wasn't every month that we had to dip into it and I can't recall a time when having that money made the difference between eating and going hungry because Fletcher, well, you know Fletcher, he did whatever he could to bring in a little extra cash. It sometimes amazed me the way his mind worked, thinking of so many different ways to make money, and I knew somehow we would make it through the hard times.

As Fletch had since we'd bought the farm, he bought what cattle he could in the spring and fattened them up during the summer months. Come fall, he'd sell them to people on the mountain or in Old Fort who were more than willing to pay for good fresh meat for their tables. If he couldn't sell them all, he drove them into Black Mountain and sold them there.

The first few years, Fletch killed only the pigs we needed to make it through the winter and kept the others to breed and build up our stock. After that, he sold some pigs too and we went back to having hog-killings every fall which gave us plenty of bacon, sausage and hams for the winter.

And as he always had, Fletch hunted almost every day to add even more meat to our table. He was a firm believer in having meat with every meal. With wild boar, squirrels, possums, and the occasional bear running free on our mountain, we managed to eat very well.

In my spare time, I took to sewing more, using the old machine Papa had received from the Sullivan family in lieu of taxes back in the fall of 1897. I guess it could rightfully be labeled an antique by that time but it still worked well enough for me to sew a great many flour sack dresses. I gave them freely to whoever needed them, enabling mothers to use any cloth they could afford to buy to make clothes for their children or husbands. And though I didn't charge anything for them, the women on the mountain always managed to pay me in some small way.

My services as a healer seemed to grow during this time as many could not afford a doctor. Although I never charged a fee, the mountain people compensated me by other means, whether it be produce from their gardens or something as simple as a thimble to add to my sewing basket. Whatever it was, I felt God was looking out for us as many a time I was given something I found Fletch and myself in need of.

The market for tobacco grew and became so competitive by the mid 1930s that the government decided they needed to step in and control supply and demand. They set up what they called allotments for the tobacco farmers, and we were lucky enough to be granted a small one that allowed Fletch to grow one-quarter acre of red leaf tobacco. He tended that quarter acre like a mother bear tends her cubs, checking it daily and keeping pests from destroying the crop. He harvested the leaves and hung them in our tobacco barn to dry and when he had a hogshead would take it to Old Fort to sell at the tobacco auction.

It wasn't much but it was enough to keep our heads above water every year.

Unfortunately, the Union Tanning Company in Old Fort was struck by lightning in 1930 and burned to the ground. The company decided not to rebuild and that took away a small but steady source of income for us since Fletch no longer had a place to sell the acid wood and tan bark he gathered on the mountain.

It was a difficult time, full of hard work and more than a little worry, but there were bright days too. As he had promised, John came every summer to stay with us. Seeing his smiling face and hearing all about what he'd learned in school and the new friends he made during the year was something to look forward to and helped to get me through the sometimes harsh winters on the mountain.

In 1933, Jack, a widow for three years, came to stay with us for a few weeks. While visiting, she met Fletcher's cousin, Boyd Elliott, and spent a great deal of time with him. After she returned to Knoxville, it wasn't long before she came back to the mountain and married Boyd. They lived in Boyd's house a couple of miles up the main road that runs over Stone Mountain, almost exactly half way between us and Stone Mountain Baptist Church.

John, who didn't like Mr. Barrett and stayed away from his mother because of that, only going to their house to visit his brother, elected to stay in Knoxville with Thee and Myrtle to finish high school. Jack's fourth boy Ken, whom she had placed in the John Tarleton Home for Boys several months before old man Barrett died because she didn't feel capable of caring for him, was rescued by Boyd and came to live with them on the mountain.

I enjoyed having another young boy around but I missed John, the son Fletch and I raised whom I considered a gift from God. I was happy to have Jack living nearby but often found myself struggling to deal with her cavalier attitude when it came to her children. But, like Fletch said, that was between her and the Lord and there wasn't much I could do about it. It was in the past, and while I was sure it still hurt John, the only thing I could do was assure him he was well loved by Fletch and me. It was good advice and I took it.

Things improved for us as they did for most people after the 1930s. Money wasn't so tight and we could breathe a little easier, which was a good thing since both Fletcher and I were getting older. I sometimes felt it hard to believe we'd been married for close to forty years but it was true. I didn't feel old, or at least most of the time I didn't, and Fletch showed no signs of slowing down either.

Over in Europe, despite World War I, or the war to end all wars according to President Wilson, another major battle was brewing. On September 1, 1939, Germany invaded Poland. Two days later, Britain and France declared war on Germany. Germany's leader, Adolf Hitler, who believed in a Master Race, was hell-bent on killing everyone he deemed unacceptable, mostly those of the Jewish faith. To our country's great shame, he modeled his plan after the eugenics movement in America, though it wasn't well known when all this was happening.

We managed to stay out of the conflict until Japan bombed Pearl Harbor, a military base in the United States territory of Hawaii, on December 7, 1941. The next day, President Roosevelt addressed the nation, saying December 7th was a day that would "live in infamy", and declaring war on Japan. It wasn't long before we were fully involved in the Second World War.

Men, mostly boys, enlisted in the military by the thousands and were sent overseas to fight. There were many young men from our mountain and the town of Old

Fort who went to war with quite a few never coming home again.

Women also served in various ways, filling jobs in the factories here in the states after the men left for battle. Over three hundred thousand enlisted in the military and were sent overseas to do their part in the war. They filled office and clerical jobs in order to free men to fight and also drove trucks and repaired airplanes, and even flew them from place to place, sometimes acting as flying targets to help train the pilots. They served near the front lines as nurses, helping to save the lives of our injured soldiers, and over 1,600 of them were decorated for bravery under fire and meritorious service. However they contributed, they were a great help to our country. Even General Eisenhower stated that the war could not be won without their services, "whether on the farm or in the factory or in uniform," while Hitler scoffed and said the "role of German women was to be good wives and mothers and to have more babies for the Third Reich."

It was a sad time for our country, indeed for the world, but a time when America and her allies all seemed to pull together to support each other and put a stop to our enemies. It would come at a great cost but in the end the Allied forces were the ones to declare victory, first on May 8, 1945, Victory in Europe Day, and then on August 15, 1945, Victory in Japan Day.

While the war raged on, most of my thoughts during those years were centered on my family, Papa especially, who was nearing 90 years of age and in failing health. The night of August 27, 1943, I dreamed of Papa standing on the banks of Spring Creek, the waters raging against the embankment the way they had that awful day when my little brother Green drowned. Papa's clothes were soaking wet, his hair plastered to his scalp. When I called to him, he turned and smiled when he saw me. "Bessie, look who I found," he said and moved aside. I gasped and put my hand to my mouth to stifle my cry. "Greenie?" I said. "Oh, Greenie, I thought we lost you." Greenie smiled at me, then raised his hands to Papa as he had so often done in life. Papa hoisted him up and hugged him tightly then turned and walked away. He glanced back and said, "I love you, Bessie girl," then looked ahead once more. Over his shoulder, little Greenie waved a pudgy hand at me. "Papa, wait," I said. I began to follow but soon lost sight of them and woke, tears streaming from my eyes, knowing my beloved Papa was dead.

Loney sent a telegram the next day telling us he had suffered a massive stroke. Due to limited funds, Fletcher and I decided not to travel to Knoxville for the funeral. Although I felt strongly that Papa should be buried beside Mama in Hot Springs, the place where he'd been the happiest, Sandy Gap Church had closed many years ago and they were no longer burying people at the cemetery. So I consented reluctantly to Loney's decision to have him buried in Bookwalter Cemetery in Knoxville, close to where they lived, a regret I would carry the rest of my days. Not only could I not visit Papa's grave, I simply couldn't imagine him being at peace so far away from Mama. My only consolation was that they were together in Heaven with Green and Elisi.

With the war and all, it seemed there were a lot of deaths during that time. And I suppose, a lot of that had to do with the fact that Fletcher and I, well into our sixties, were getting older. I had retired from teaching during the war and that left me with a lot of time on my hands. I filled it by returning to one of my youthful loves, writing articles for the Old Fort newspaper and even sending in a few of my teaching stories to the *Reader's Digest*. I never heard back from them but getting my stories published didn't matter all that much to me. It was enough that I knew John would hold on to them when I died. I had no idea what he'd do with them but hoped he would pass them on to his children and they to theirs.

And time kept flowing, easing my pain over the loss of Papa as I went about my daily life, until my mind was occupied once more with another war, or police action as the politicians in Washington liked to call it. This conflict, which took place from June 25, 1950 to July 27, 1953, went beyond the scope of freedom for American soil, focusing on American-occupied South Korea fighting the communist forces of Russian-occupied North Korea. Many saw this as a symbol of the global struggle between east and west, good and evil, or as the first step in a communist campaign to take over the world. Although this war didn't receive a lot of attention, it was more personal to me as John, who had joined the Navy, had been assigned to serve on a battleship and was sent overseas. Oh, those three years seemed to last forever, each day crawling by, praying for John's safe return, watching for letters from him, waiting for the dreaded news. And when I finally received a letter from him that he was back on American soil, I fell to my knees and thanked God for saving our boy.

Shortly after serving in the Navy, John married a woman named Margie, and by 1957, they had five children, three girls and two boys. He brought them all to North Carolina to meet me, of course, and it thrilled me to see him so happy and fulfilled. He was working for the newspaper in Knoxville in advertising and had developed his talent for drawing, moving into oil paints and watercolors too.

John visited whenever he could and often drove Thee over the mountains to Hot Springs where they tended to Mama's and Green's graves and visited with the few people Thee knew who still lived there. Many a time they would make the trip to Stone Mountain afterward and how I looked forward to those visits which gave me a chance to catch up on news of my family in Knoxville and see my sweet boy.

I look back on this time as a quiet, peaceful period of my life, one not filled with illness or death but, rather, simply being.

Chapter Twenty

Late Winter 1958

Precious in the sight of the Lord is the death of His saint. - Psalm 116:15

The morning of March 1, 1958 began like any other. Up with the sun, a visit to the outhouse, then milking the cows and back inside to fix breakfast for Fletcher and myself. I had just started the coffee and taken out the flour to fix biscuits when I heard a sound from outside. It was then I realized I hadn't seen my husband since I got out of bed.

A tingling sensation shot up my spine as I ran toward the kitchen door, calling his name. I found him on the ground in front of the porch, his eyes closed. Kneeling down beside him, I patted his cheek. "Fletch?" I said, my voice cracking. "Can you hear me, Fletch?"

He opened his eyes and moved his mouth but couldn't seem to speak the words. Tears filled my eyes. This man, whom I had always found so tall and strong and handsome, now seemed a pale, fragile shadow of his former self as he lay there in the dirt. I blinked hard as I stroked his cheek. "You'll be fine, Fletch. Just a little fall, that's all. Let's get you into the house and into bed."

I put my arms under his and lifted, alarmed that he was so weak, he had trouble gaining his feet and standing. With great difficulty, we made it onto the porch and inside, then at a slow pace struggled to the bedroom. I managed to help him to the bed, then eased him down. With a sigh, he collapsed onto the mattress. I lifted his legs and maneuvered them around so that he lay flat, then grabbed a pillow and placed it under his head. I drew the quilt up from the bottom of the bed and covered him, tucking it around his body. "There now," I said, squeezing his hand, "that's better. Let me just get Doc—"

I felt a slight pressure against my hand and looked at him. His eyes locked with mine and I watched him once more try to speak to me. "It's all right, Fletch, don't say anything. We'll get you up and moving soon, just you wait and see." My voice quivered and I cleared my throat. I didn't want him to see how frightened I was.

He moved his head side to side, just barely but enough for me to understand he didn't want me to leave. I sat on the bed next to him, his hand still clutched in mine. Don't leave me, my mind whispered, but I didn't voice this. I tried smiling at him but my lips were trembling and I couldn't quite manage it. I placed my other hand on top of his and patted it, waiting for him to let me go, fighting panic. I wanted to bolt out of the room, run down the path, over the bridge and straight to Doc Burgiss in Old Fort, who had taken over Doc Widby's practice when he died. Although Doc Burgiss was from up North, he was considered one of the good Yankees by the mountaineers, especially Thorney Dalton. Doc put Thorney's white lightening to good practice, using it as a way to steady his nerves, a general antiseptic, for cleansing wounds, and a mouthwash in Doc's dental practice. However unorthodox his treatments, I considered him a good doctor and trusted him. I knew that whatever had happened with my husband was serious, but unlike all the others I had treated before him, I had no idea what to do for him and it frightened me to the bone. I prayed Doc would be able to pull off one of his unconventional miracle cures.

Maybe it's just a spell, I consoled myself as I sat there. Maybe it will pass and he'll be just like before, strong and healthy and ready to go about his daily chores. But I knew, oh, Lord, I knew. I saw the dark cloud around him, one I had seen many times and one that was no stranger to me.

Knowing time was precious, I leaned down close to him. "Fletch, we need Doc. I'll go outside and ring the cowbell until someone comes, and have them fetch him. He can help you." My voice broke and I stopped a moment, trying to get control of my emotions. "I'll be right back. I promise." I started to rise, then turned back to him. "Don't you go and die on me, Fletcher Elliott," I said, my mouth against his ear. "I can't lose you, not yet."

Without looking at him, I turned and ran outside to the cowbell hanging from the eave of the porch and began to ring it, calling my neighbors to come. I was still ringing it when Sawyer Eldridge's oldest son Lucas, who lived in the Berryhills' old house, came running. And didn't stop until he lay his hands over mine and stilled them, looking at me with concern, saying, "What's wrong, Bess? Where's Fletch?"

I fell to my knees, wailing my grief, unable to say the words.

I was barely aware of Lucas running inside the house, then he was back. "I'll get Doc," he said, helping me up. "You take care of Fletch. I won't be long." With that, he ran toward the path leading to the bridge.

I watched him go, swiping at my eyes and biting my lip, trying to get myself under control. I didn't want Fletch to know how worried I was, how scared I was. I turned and walked back to the bedroom and over to the bed. I sat down beside my husband and tried smiling at him but my lips wouldn't move. "Don't you worry, Fletch," I said, holding his hand. "Lucas has gone for Doc, he won't be long. You just hang on, Doc will help."

He barely nodded his head as he closed his eyes. As we waited, different reasons for his physical state ran through my mind. My first thought was that he had had a stroke but I didn't see any signs other than he didn't speak. No drooping of one side of his face, no inability to use one side of his body. A heart attack? I rested my hand over his heart as if touching him in a reassuring manner and waited. Nothing. Telling myself not to panic, I moved my hand down his arm, placing my middle and ring fingers over his wrist, trying to find a pulse. I bit my lip when I finally felt it, thready and slow and irregular.

I leaned closer. "Are you in pain, Fletch? Or did you feel anything before it happened?"

He didn't answer. Did he hear me, I wondered, or had he passed out. The slow rise and fall of his chest reassured me he was still with me but I feared it wouldn't be for long.

I have no idea how much later, I heard commotion on the front porch. I stood as Doc hustled into the room, his face flushed.

Lucas was right behind him. "Lucky for us, Doc was on his way back from seeing Ewan Laughter," he said.

Doc glanced at me. "Ewan's gout's flaring up."

I nodded, watching as Doc pulled his stethoscope out of his bag and leaned over my husband, who didn't even open his eyes at this. Doc listened for a good while, moving the stethoscope over Fletch's chest, his mouth set in a thin line. He finally stood and met my gaze. "Let's talk outside," he whispered.

We stepped into the living room. Doc reached out and touched my hand. "Bess, looks like he's had a heart attack." He shook his head. "I'm afraid it's pretty serious. There's nothing can be done, it's only a matter of time."

I put my fist to my mouth and bit hard, trying to stem the sounds of anguish and pain.

"I'm so sorry, Bess."

Lucas, who had been standing nearby, stepped closer. "I sure am sorry, Moonfixer." He nodded at Doc. "I best go pass the word. There'll be those who will want to come by and pay their respects."

Doc patted my shoulder. "Bess, I wish I could stay but Junior Hall's fallen and needs to be looked at. I'll go see to him then come right back here quick as I can."

I nodded then turned on my heel and went to my husband. I sat beside him and stroked his cheek with my hand. After a bit, he opened his eyes and looked at me.

"I love you, Bessie, girl," he said, his voice barely a whisper.

I managed a genuine smile this time as I rose up and cupped his face with my hands. "I love you, Fletcher Elliott. I will never love another the way I love you."

He closed his eyes and hissed a breath. I waited, watching for the rise and fall of his chest, but it remained still.

I jerked to my feet. "No, please, no," I cried. "Not now, not like this." I put my head over his chest, listening for a heartbeat but all was still. I licked my finger and placed it beneath his nose but no breath light as a feather touched my skin. I lay down beside him and nestled into him, as I had done thousands of times over our years together, and cried for a loss so great I felt as if my heart would truly break. We'd been married 56 years but it wasn't long enough for me, nowhere near long enough for me.

After a bit, I got up, kissed my husband on the lips for the last time, and began the process of releasing him into God's hands.

I removed Fletcher's clothes, washed his body, then dressed him in his finest suit, one he rarely wore, saved for funerals and weddings. I stood back, admiring my husband, thinking back on the day we had married and all that had happened since. It seemed to me time had gone by with the snap of my fingers. I had no regrets over marrying him and hoped he knew that. My mind turned to the night before. What had we talked about? Nothing of substance that I could think of. Was anything profound said, any declaration of love made? I didn't think so. He knew, I told myself. As I knew with him, although the words were not spoken until he died. But if only I had had a sense of what was coming, I would have spoken those words over and over again.

I covered Fletcher's eyes with coins, used his favorite handkerchief to tie his chin to keep his mouth closed, then placed my fingers to my lips and laid them against his. "You were the best man I've ever known, Fletcher. I'll see you one day soon." And I sat back down to wait for Doc.

I don't remember what happened after that, lost in a haze of heartache, only people coming and going, speaking to me in low voices, guiding me here and there.

I was told a telegram had been sent to John but he was in Nashville and couldn't make it back for the funeral but would come as soon as he could.

Much of the next few days is lost to me. I remember bits and pieces of the funeral at Stone Mountain Baptist Church but couldn't tell you who spoke or what was said, who attended or who didn't. At that point, I didn't care. I only wanted to retreat to a darkened room and sleep, dream of Fletcher and our life together. I wanted people to leave me alone, not speak to me or bring food for comfort. I only wanted to be lost in a haze of remembrance.

Until John came. My John, the boy Fletcher and I helped raise, the only son we had.

Although I was glad for Fletch's sake that his death had not been a lingering one, it took me a good, long while before I could sleep in our bed again. And an even longer time until I could laugh once more and really mean it. But as it has since the beginning, time proceeds onward and wounds which at first are so raw and festering begin to heal until one day the heart is open to new worlds, perhaps even new love.

Fletcher had never liked Jimmy Davis, usually referring to him as Old Sanctimonious. Jimmy proclaimed to love God and as testament attended church more often than anyone else but Fletcher always suspected Jimmy loved himself first of all with God coming in a poor second. And since Jimmy had stolen from Fletcher after he provided a home for him to live in and acreage to farm, Fletcher never trusted the man and had little to do with him.

But little by little the haze of grief began to lift from my eyes and life once more seemed interesting and worth living. I still grieved Fletcher's passing but now knew life would go on and me with it. My days were busy with daily chores and caring for the ill and injured but the nights were long and empty, and that was when I missed Fletcher most of all. Even though he was not one to talk, he was a good listener and companion and the love of my life but his time on this

Earth had ended and I decided it was time I accepted this and lived my life as best I could.

So when Jimmy Davis began to seek me out at church and drop by the house to see how I fared, I found myself looking forward to his visits because, unlike Fletcher, he was vociferous and kept my mind occupied instead of slipping away to times past with my deceased husband.

When Jimmy asked me to marry him two years after Fletch died, I accepted immediately. If I had been honest with myself, I would have admitted I didn't marry him for love, as I had Fletcher, but for companionship and security. I was lonely and tired of being alone and this was an answer to that particular problem. John was not happy about the marriage, as, like Fletcher, he didn't like Jimmy, but this was my life and my decision and I had made it and intended to stick with it.

Our marriage lasted for five years and all in all was a good one. We were well-suited to one another but I suspect Jimmy knew he lived in another man's shadow. He was not one to be bothered by this but, rather, accepted it. Perhaps he knew he would never be of the same caliber as Fletcher or simply didn't care. Whatever the reason, years flew by until I found myself a widow once more. Unlike Fletcher's passing, I fared better when Jimmy passed on of natural causes and faced life knowing it would not be long until I was with Fletcher again.

It was during this time that America's involvement in the Vietnam War brought discord and rebellion in America. Many, especially the young, opposed this war, marching on Washington, DC and in other cities, protesting our involvement. Young draftees fled to Canada and returning soldiers were met with hostility, some even being spit on by other Americans.

As with prior wars, many young men and women died fighting but many of those that didn't came home to a fate worse even than death, a condition referred to as Shell Shock in World War I, Battle or Combat Fatigue in World War II, then Stress Response Syndrome in the Korean and Viet Nam wars. Whatever name they gave it, it was never enough to convey the mindset of these tormented souls. I can't begin to imagine what it was like for those young people, how terrifying it must have been to repeatedly face the likelihood of their death during the time they were in those strange countries, far away from their families and loved ones, or to witness or cause another human being's death, and then to relive that torture over and over again once they were safe at home. It was as if my old friend Death, while not taking their lives, couldn't resist making them suffer every day of their life afterward.

I tended to a few returning soldiers, treating their wounds mentally and physically, and came to understand and admire those protesting a war that we had no sense being involved in. During this time of turmoil and revolt, it seemed to me that God had turned a blind eye to his people below and I began to wonder what the future forebode. One, to be honest, I did not wish to be part of.

As I grew older and more frail, my skin, once smooth and soft, now filled with wrinkles and covered with age spots, I prayed for an answer as to why God had allowed me to remain so long on this Earth, having outlived two husbands and most of my friends and family. I kept telling myself I would see Fletcher soon and it was that one thought that carried me through those next years, which proved to be hard financially and physically until I found myself in a nursing home in Asheville, being cared for by strangers, looking forward to visits from John and my remaining friends on the mountain.

Chapter Twenty-one

Winter 1970

She opens her mouth with wisdom, and the teaching of kindness is on her tongue. – Proverbs 31:26

I've been on this Earth for close to 90 years and the farthest I've traveled is less than 200 miles, to Knoxville, Tennessee to visit with Papa, and only once. As I've said, the city didn't suit me at all, and after that visit, I vowed I would never leave my beloved mountain again. And didn't until John drove me to the nursing home in Asheville. I reckon that would count as one of the saddest days of my life. I remember watching out the back window of his car until I could no longer see any trace of the place where I'd spent the happiest years of my life. I knew I wouldn't be back but consoled myself with the thought that I had more than enough happy memories that would live in my heart until I died.

And those memories did sustain me over the next couple of years as I adjusted to a different kind of life, one where there were no chores to be done, no garden to plant and harvest, no illnesses to treat and cure. I had two loves left to me, reading and writing, and plenty of time to indulge those. But the body wears down and the mind starts to dim and time, which for most of my life I looked upon as a good friend, has now become my enemy. Gone are dreams and yearnings and plans for the future and I am only left with the hope of leaving this old body behind so that I can be with those who have gone before me.

Last night, I dreamed I saw Fletcher standing at the foot of my bed, smiling at me. Oh, how I wanted to rise up from this bed and join him, to once more place my hands in his, kiss his lips, tell him I loved him, lean into him and feel his quiet strength and comforting embrace. He smiled at me then seemed to fade away and I woke with such joy, knowing that my time is close and he waits for me. I imagine, if I could look down upon my body, I would see my old friend Death swirling about me in a dark cloud, ready to claim me. But I am not afraid as I was the first time I encountered Him. I am only thankful.

Here, at the end of my time, I can't help but think what a glorious life I've led. I came to the mountain a young bride unsure of my own path other than to teach and will leave an old woman who has traveled many paths, that of wife, teacher, healer, gardener, and surrogate mother. A strong woman, I like to think, who hasn't been afraid to stand up for herself and others.

I've been blessed by God, who gave me my greatest gift, my husband Fletcher. A strong yet gentle man who walked his own path without fear or reservations. And who encouraged me to walk my own. A quiet man whose actions spoke the words that never left his lips. A man who loved deeply yet quietly.

And God blessed me again when He gave me John, the child I could never have. A young boy unsure of his place in life who became a handsome, intelligent man whose career reflected his artistic talent.

And the things I've seen! When I was born in 1881, the primary way of getting around was by horse or railroad or simply your own two feet. Now, men are flying airplanes through the skies and rockets to the moon. I've seen the invention of electricity, the telephone, radio, computers, television and movies. Hot and cold running water, flushing toilets, the touch of warmth or coldness with the flip of a switch or the spin of a dial, electric stoves and ovens, washers and dryers, irons even. I've seen men plant our country's flag on the moon and watched our country struggle over four different wars. I've witnessed evil come to power over the dead corpses of millions of Jews then fall and disappear, leaving behind devastation and heartbreak and the never-ending question, why?

I've seen the way women are perceived transform drastically, from once being looked upon as chattel to now having the freedom to live their own lives. If I were asked what I would have liked to have changed the most, it would be women's fight for independence. Many now hold jobs once only considered open to men and quite a few are heads of large corporations. Why, some even run their own countries. To be sure, I have seen a lot of changes but I wonder what other important accomplishments women will achieve after I am gone. Will one become president of our country one day? Will they too walk on the surface of the moon as I watched a man do or perhaps go even further and walk on one of the other planets, maybe Mars? Will the world ever recognize that women are as smart, or smarter, than men? I like to think they will in time and that women will someday be valued as much as men, a battle that continues today.

I've watched the Civil Rights Movement grow and become a force to be reckoned with. I think of our sweet George, murdered because his skin was the wrong color, and hope he is watching all this from Heaven. I pray that one day persons of all colors will be looked upon with equality and treated with respect but my greatest fear is that my great-grandmother Elisi was right in her view that humans must always have to have someone to torment.

I've helped babies into the world with tears of joy and happiness and watched them leave with tears of grief and rage. I've treated ailments and illnesses and even lived through a pandemic and dealt with a mysterious disease with no cure. I've lost friends and loved ones from an early time in my life and have battled with God over these losses but now find myself at peace with Him. After all, I'll be joining Him shortly.

Tonight, the words of the refrain to my favorite hymn, *Till the Storm Passes By*, keep running through my mind: "Till the storm passes over, till the thunder sounds no more, till the clouds roll forever from the sky, hold me fast, let me stand in the hollow of Thy hand, keep me safe till the storm passes by."

It is, I know, a sign that it's time. I am comforted by the words and know that I indeed stand in the hollow of God's hand and He will keep me safe in death as He always did in life. I'm not sad I'll be leaving this life soon. I look forward to seeing my loved ones again and all the others who have gone before me. I am comforted by the thought that it will probably be Elisi who greets me first, there to take my hand and guide me on the trail to the Darkening Land as I know she's done with so many of my family.

Yes, it will be soon now and I am ready. But I leave this life with only one regret …

If only I could go back to my mountain and plant my garden one more time.

A note to our readers:

Our Great-Aunt Bessie died on January 20, 1970 just five months short of her 90th birthday. We were at her funeral but don't remember much about it other than it was a sad trip over the mountains for our family. But in researching her life, we can say that she was a woman well-loved and respected by those who knew her, someone who is still talked about today and remembered with great love and affection, as is her husband Fletcher.

For those readers who are curious about the rest of the Daniels' family, Roy retired from the railroad after 50 years as a switchman and died in 1961 of prostate cancer. Jack died from cervical cancer in 1974 at the age of 74 and Loney from the same disease at 91 in 1976. Thee, known to us as Pap Daniels, died of natural causes at 86 years of age in 1980.

Books in the Appalachian Journey series:

Whistling Woman, Appalachian Journey Book 1

In the waning years of the 19th century, Bessie Daniels grows up in the small town of Hot Springs, North Carolina. Secure in the love of her father, resistant to her mother's desire that she be a proper Southern bell, Bessie is determined to forge her own way in life. Or, as her Cherokee great-grandmother, Elisi, puts it, to be a whistling woman.

Life, however, has a few surprises for her. First, there's Papa carrying home a dead man, which seems to invite Death for an extended visit in their home. Shortly before she graduates from Dorland Institute there's another death, this one closer to her heart. Proving yet another of Elisi's sayings, death comes in threes, It strikes yet again, taking someone Bessie has recently learned to appreciate and cherish, leaving her to struggle with a family that's threatening to come apart at the seams.

Even her beloved Papa appears to be turning into another person, someone Bessie disagrees with more often than not, and someone she isn't even sure she can continue to love, much less idolize as she had during her childhood.

And when Papa makes a decision that costs the life of a new friend, the course of Bessie's heart is changed forever.

Moonfixer, Appalachian Journey Book 2

In the dawning years of the 20th century, Bessie Daniels leaves her home town of Hot Springs and travels over the mountains with her husband Fletcher Elliott to live in the Broad River Section of North Carolina.

Bessie and Fletch stay with Fletcher's parents for the first five years of their married life with Bessie teaching in a one-room schoolhouse and Fletcher working at the lumber mill in Old Fort while they save to buy property of their own on Stone Mountain.

In 1906, they purchase 400 acres of the old Zachariah Solomon Plantation which includes a small house with a shack beside it, a branch of Cedar Creek, a row of dilapidated slave cabins...

And ghosts.

Thus begins Bessie's next phase of life where the gift of sight she inherited from her Cherokee ancestors grows stronger, her healing abilities are put to the test, and she encounters a vicious secret society that tries to force her and Fletcher to turn their backs on a family sharecropping and living in one of the cabins.

When Bessie and Fletch refuse to give in to their demands, the group strikes back, bringing pain and suffering to their once serene existence on Stone Mountain.

Bessie travels to the Broad River section of North Carolina with her husband, Fletcher, and assumes her first teaching position at Cedar Grove School while trying to meet the challenges of her new life among the quaint mountain people who call her Moonfixer because she is tall for a woman.

Beloved Woman, Appalachian Journey Book 3

In the second decade of the 20th century, major world events resonate even on secluded Stone Mountain where Bessie Elliott lives with her husband Fletcher. There's a great war, one that takes away many young men, including Bessie's kin, some never to return. Bessie's role of healer intensifies as she treats those with the Spanish flu and tries to keep it from spreading further on her mountain. She defends a young woman who's in the middle of a controversy that threatens to tear her community apart. And she finds herself involved in the suffragette movement as the women of North Carolina fight to gain their rights under the constitution.

Then when one of her family members makes an appalling decision, one that has the potential to damage a child, Bessie impulsively steps in to right the wrong.

Wise Woman, Appalachian Journey Book 4

In the mid 1920s, Bessie Elliott and her husband Fletcher take in their six-year-old nephew John. They are determined to give him a warm and secure home on Stone Mountain, a place where he will feel loved and know he is always welcome.

Having a child brings many changes to their daily life and even more for John, but it isn't long before he feels completely at home with his aunt and uncle. As he learns about the farm animals, the wildlife and plant life on the mountain, he grows into a young man Bessie and Fletch are proud to call their own.

But their life is not without turmoil. Bessie's healing skills are put to the test when she and Doc Widby deal with an unknown and mysterious illness, one they have no idea how to treat. While doing their best to heal their patient, they run up against a new doctor in Black Mountain who is involved with the Eugenics movement, a program Bessie fiercely opposes. And Bessie and Fletch, along with the rest of their neighbors, are torn apart by a foe threatening the natural beauty of Stone Mountain.

Acknowledgements

One last time, we'd like to extend our gratitude to the following people:

First and foremost, our dad John Tillery, for sharing his stories of life on the mountain with his Aunt Bessie and Uncle Fletch. For those and so much else, we are blessed to have you for a father and we love you very much.

Our Uncle Ken, for also sharing stories of his life on the mountain with his mother, stepfather Boyd Elliott, Aunt Bessie and Uncle Fletcher. We can't tell you how much we appreciate your generosity in sharing those memories.

And of course, our Great-aunt Bessie and Great-uncle Fletcher for their kindness and generosity in giving our dad a home at a time in his life when he needed love. They were a blessing to him and to us, also.

Our cousin Jackie Burgin Painter, for sharing the story of our relative Frank Henderson, the first man from Madison County to be put to death in North Carolina's electric chair. And for her help with other historical aspects of our books. Thanks, Jackie.

Our cover designer Kimberly Maxwell, for the beautiful covers of the last two books and the re-design of the first two. Kim, it's been a joy to work with you and we're so glad to have you in our corner.

Our husbands Steve French and Mike Hodges, who've stood behind us through the many long years it took to write this series. Once again, thanks for understanding our need for "alone time" and for the hard work at all the festivals and book signings. It goes without saying, but we'll say it anyway, we love you.

Greg Miller, the current owner of our grandmother's house and Camp Elliott, for allowing us to tour the camp as it is today and for telling us the story of the rabbit on the water wheel in front of the house. Also, the painting on the back of this book of Stone Mountain Baptist Church by our dad and given to Grandma many years ago that was left in her house when she died. Thanks for keeping it safe for us, Greg.

And of course, our readers, who've encouraged and supported us through each and every book. We're truly blessed to have you behind us. When all this started, we had planned on only writing one book, *Whistling Woman*, but your interest in learning more about our great-aunt and great-uncle persuaded us to write more. We are so grateful to all of you.

We've continued to use the same research books and online sites with each book but we do have a few print books that are new with this one:

"Chronicle of the Twentieth Century" Clifton Daniel, Editor in Chief

"Asleep, The Forgotten Epidemic That Remains One of Medicine's Greatest Mysteries" by Molly Caldwell Crosby

"Images of America Old Fort" by Kim Clark

And finally, a note to the many family members we've met online and off. The stories we've told in the books are the ones we grew up hearing from our dad and Uncle Ken, and in some cases from our grandmother and Aunt Bessie herself. We've tried to tell them as they were told to us but in some cases took the liberty to change certain elements to help the flow of the story and/or to enhance the plot.

About the authors

CC Tillery is the pseudonym for two sisters, both authors who came together to write the story of their great-aunt Bessie in the *Appalachian Journey* series. Tillery is their maiden name and the C's stand for their first initials.

One C is Cyndi Tillery Hodges, a multi-published author writing paranormal romance based on Cherokee legends under the pseudonym of Caitlyn Hunter. To find out more about her work, visit http://caitlynhunter.com.

The other C is Christy Tillery French, a multi-published, award-winning author whose books cross several genres. To find out more about her work, visit http://christytilleryfrench.webs.com.

For more information on the *Appalachian Journey* series, visit http://cctillery.com or on Facebook at http://www.facebook.com/appalachianjourney.

Questions or comments? We'd love to hear from you. E-mail us at cctillery@yahoo.com

Made in the USA
Middletown, DE
09 October 2017